Friedenszeit

David Roy

The moral right of David Roy to be identified as the author of this work has been asserted by him in accordance with the Copyright, Designs and Patents Act 1988. All trademarks are acknowledged. All rights reserved.

'It looks as if there is a black line which separates the sea from the sky,' she said, pointing at the horizon. 'If I was painting that, I would leave out the line. It wouldn't look right.'

'What would you do instead? How would you differentiate between the two?'

'Different colours. Different shades of blue or maybe use green for the sea. I would know when I'd got it right. The scene would still be authentic. It changes from day to day in any case.'

'Will you take up painting again?'

'Oh yes,' she said. 'Definitely. What about you? Are you going to write that book?'

'I've made a start. Fits and starts but I have some of it committed to paper and the rest is in my brain. Maybe I will have time now. More time anyway.'

'If they don't send you to the Pacific.'

'There has been talk,' I said, gravely. 'I'm hoping I'm at the bottom of any list. There are others who have just got going. Lots of young bucks who want to make a name for themselves before it all peters out.'

'You think that the RAF works that way?' she scoffed. 'That they give any consideration to those who have done their bit several times over?'

'You sound bitter,' I said.

I pulled her close and we continued to gaze out over the sea. The sun was out and the air was just warm enough. There was no breeze but she tucked her curls into the collar of her jacket as if anchoring them against a gusty wind.

'It's been a long six years,' she said. 'You were in it from start to finish. Let someone else take on the Japs.'

I knew that a force had already been assembled and was probably heading for Japan right now to assist the Americans on their assault on Kyushu, one of the Japanese Islands. So far my name hadn't appeared on any lists to be shipped out there but there were no guarantees. I'd actually considered staying on in the RAF, wondering what it would be like in peacetime and worried that jobs would be scarce in Civvy Street.

Behind us, I knew the Italian ice cream parlour was still shuttered, silent and dead.

'We will get an ice cream next time I come back. And we'll walk along the beach. In the evening we'll have chips and sit on the sea wall.'

'You always say that.'

'It's the sort of dream that has sustained me.'

I never discussed the times when I thought I was going to die, or the fear that had robbed me of sleep for all those years, or the – I struggle to know what to call them – stomach cramps, that had almost crippled me. There were times when my brain had almost frozen, when I just couldn't think about anything other than running and hiding from the war. I had always smiled, followed my orders and died inside a little more each day. I wondered what would be left of me if the fighting ever stopped; perhaps nothing more than a breathing corpse.

I turned at the sound of a car pulling up. It was an American staff car painted dull olive. An officer and his girlfriend stepped out.

'The ice cream place is shut,' he complained, loudly.

'Never mind, darling,' she said. She was English. Southern, pretty, not in uniform.

I turned back to Margaret.

'They'll all be going home soon, I expect.'

'I wonder if she'll go with him?'

'I don't know what his wife would have to say about that,' I joked. He wouldn't have been the first married soldier from Buffalo Bend, Arizona to seek female comfort in England.

Margaret didn't bother to argue his innocence. She understood the situation as well as I did. They made their way past us, arm in arm and there was something about her body language, the way she almost clung to him that suggested she knew their liaison was already doomed. It was as if she was trying to prevent his escape.

'It doesn't feel real.'

'It's an anti-climax, you mean?' she asked.

'I suppose so.'

'It's because you weren't with the boys when it happened,' she suggested.

'The boys? I hardly knew them.'

I'd been on leave when the Krauts finally surrendered. Margaret and I had been staying with her parents on their remote farm when we heard Winston's speech on the radio. I couldn't quite appreciate what I was hearing. Her father had left at some point and returned with a bottle of Scotch and five glasses. It was a sombre celebration. The fifth glass was symbolically laid out in memory of their eldest son, Margaret's brother who'd been lost at sea when his corvette was sunk escorting a convoy in the Med. Only a tiny amount of the precious spirit was added to his glass since he would never drink it.

When we married in 1943, I had become a surrogate son rather than a mere son-in-law and they had begun to worry about my safety as much as Margaret had. Probably not as much as *I* worried about it but that was a topic never discussed. These were times when stoicism and stiff upper lips counted for more than bruising honesty and compassion.

And now, although my leave had almost run its course, it would be a Germany at peace to which I would return. I was still dreading it.

Chapter One

'Take this,' said Phil, handing me a revolver.

'What?'

'In case we're ambushed,' he explained. He thrust the bulky revolver with its holster and belt at me. 'Go on. Take it.'

'Who's going to ambush us, Phil? The Indians?'

'Don't joke about it, Saul.' I took the proffered gun and set it in my lap as if in distaste. He started the Jeep's engine and put it in gear but didn't move off. I noticed a Thompson sub machine gun in the back of the vehicle. 'Werewolves,' he said, seriously.

I looked at the sky, an even blue, cloudless, a bright sun.

'There's no full moon. I think we'll be okay.'

'Not that type of werewolf. The werewolves are the German resistance. Left behind to fight on and so on.'

'You think they can be bothered?'

'They put up a hell of a fight, the old Jerries. I'm surprised you think they won't. They're fanatics.'

'Maybe, but they also follow orders, so if they've been told to surrender then that's what they will do.'

He pulled out into the traffic, content to let the matter drop. I'd spent the war – fought my part of it – high in the air and when I looked at the firearm in my lap I wondered what I would do if one of these German resistance fighters did actually put in an appearance. The revolver was easy enough to operate but that wasn't the point.

'What's the name of this town?'

'Don't know. *Bad* something.'

We were waved through by some MPs who manned an archway that led to the town centre. Wherever we were had benefitted from the war's end insofar as hostilities had obviously ceased before the town had come under any form of attack.

'This is one they won't have to rebuild,' I said as we trundled through behind a Bedford truck. Bored infantrymen in their over-sized berets sat in the back. Their ordeal over, maybe they still hadn't quite come to terms with the idea of peace, that they would never fire those rifles again or face death around every corner.

A German civilian, perhaps in his late fifties, stood outside his *Backerei*, seeming to assess the newcomers in terms of a possible source of income. Would we buy his bread rolls, just as the *Wehrmacht* had? He had yet to find out. People needed to eat, of course, even defeated ones.

'They look just like us,' said Phil as we slowed once again. I'm not sure quite what he expected. We came to a square with four Comet tanks parked up. The crews busied themselves making tea. It didn't look as if they were unduly worried about werewolves. They understood the lie of the land better than us. They'd fought on the ground. They knew utter defeat when they saw it and that is what they were surrounded by on all sides.

'This time last year they all loved Hitler. Now they have to look as if they love us instead, or at least tolerate us. These bastards are lucky to have houses and shops and drains that work.'

'They're talking about billeting the officers here, you know,' said Phil, tonelessly.

'In the midst of all the werewolves? Risky that,' I quipped. Phil made no response. A small party of dejected German soldiers stood under guard. They looked like regular troops but somehow diminished in defeat, their natural arrogance gone.

We continued to drive, exiting the other side of the town. I was surprised to see a gathering of Russian officers grouped round a map spread on the bonnet of a Russian-built Jeep.

'What are they doing here?' I asked.

'The Reds are everywhere,' explained Phil. 'No one knows where the borders are yet. That's what they say anyway. They'd over-run the whole place if they got the chance.'

'Do they speak?'

'If you wave, they wave back,' he said dismissively. There was something in his tone that suggested these few days of peace had given him some great advantage over me, that he was now the veteran pilot and I was the new boy. He spoke as if he had liberated this town by himself, while I was skulking in Britain like a war-dodging coward. I smiled.

I didn't put his 'waving at the Russians theory' to the test. We had passed them now.

'The airfield is interesting,' he said. 'It's like they put one of everything in the main hangar. One 109, one FW 190, an ME 262.'

He had piqued my interest actually. I'd seen the 262 once, flying high. It seemed like an enormous leap forwards over piston-engine aircraft as if the technology of Flash Gordon had suddenly appeared in our midst.

'In flying condition?'

'Eh?'

'Can they be flown?'

'Probably. They're sending some bods over to check them. I don't know why we can't do it. They probably don't want the Reds to get their hands on any German jets.'

'I would have thought it was too late.' I glanced over. Phil shrugged.

The road was pock-marked by bullet holes but still in good nick. We passed a church with the very tip of its spire shorn off. A burial party dug a fresh grave. They must have been busy during the war, a roaring trade done.

I was amazed that no signs of the Nazi regime existed. It was as if he – Hitler – had already been expunged from history and from the minds of his subjects. I don't know what I had expected to see of course. Flags? Something like that. They were ready to move on quickly. Rebuild. Good luck to them. I didn't even hate them anymore. Weariness had sapped my will to despise. Fear had supplanted anger. Sadness had blunted my need for vengeance. Peace would suit me well enough.

'What's the German word for 'peace',' I asked my driver.

'Do they have one?' he quipped. His comeback was rapid, funny. I chuckled.

'Good point. Not much call for it.'

'You're a Jew, aren't you?'

I was surprised by the question. My name – Saul Cohen – was something of a giveaway but the question of my religion, lapsed though it was, had never arisen.

'Yes.'

'You've heard all about the camps?'

'Obviously.'

'Well, what do you think?'

'I don't know. I mean…'

I fell silent, lost for words. We continued driving on the flat German plain. There was nothing to see. Well, there was, but nothing remarkable: trees, scattered farms, cows in fields, low hills. It was sterile, silent, with an air of abandonment.

'There's a camp near the airfield,' he said, trying to stimulate my interest. It nearly worked but I couldn't get worked up about being a voyeur to the Nazi atrocity I had done nothing to prevent. Perhaps in my own small way I had shortened the war through my actions but by how much? Ten seconds? Less than that. And had I been a better Jew, more devout, more honest about who I was, I would have been dragged to the camp by some idealistic compulsion.

We carried on. Refugees were streaming in from the East, escaping the Russians or perhaps just returning home. Phil knowledgably informed me that the men were mostly impressed workers from the subject nations: Belgians, Dutch, French. The only way they could find to return home was on foot.

We slowed as we came to a logjam of humanity. A group of Russians were pushing and shoving, shouting, bullying. Their victims were a similarly sized group of German soldiers, unarmed now, ragged, frightened, their Nazi hauteur stripped away in defeat.

'Just pull over, Phil.'

'Pull over? Why?'

'Just bloody do it.' I rarely found it necessary to pull rank on one of my pilots but I did so now and he immediately fell into a sulk. I remembered then that he was probably only twenty, just a boy. He did as he was told and I stood, gripping the windscreen of the Jeep as the slow surge of refugees edged past us, like a sluggish river.

One of the Russians, tall with a pock-marked face from some childhood illness, looked over and nudged his companions. They regarded me with peasant docility and in doing so let the Germans slip away. I heard one of the defeated soldiers say something like 'thank God', as he hurried past. I might have prevented an atrocity but perhaps the Russians were entitled to take their revenge. How could I arbitrate on such a matter?

The Russians, armed with rifles and sub machine guns looked, collectively, disappointed now that they had been robbed of their vengeful opportunity. They skulked away into the trees that lined the road until they merged with the darkness of the wood and were gone.

'Russkis everywhere,' said Phil. 'They're like sheep that have got separated from the rest of the flock. They need to round 'em up,' he said.

'They want their pound of flesh. You can't blame them.'

I continued when Phil made no reply.

'But the revenge has got to stop sometime.'

I could say this because the need for revenge was not a powerful force in my heart. That was probably the difference between having fought in the air and having fought on the ground. Rising up through the atmosphere to engage my enemies had taken me away from the reality of life's final bloody moments to some extent. I had rarely borne witness to the blood and gore of violent death.

Something happened to me then, some gentle prod from my conscience.

'This camp is near the airfield?'

'A mile or so,' said Phil.

'Maybe we *should* go. I need a reminder of why I fought this war.'

In less than ten minutes we had left the town far behind and were pulling up to the gates of the camp which were now guarded by British troops but I could almost sense the phantom presence of their Nazi predecessors as we came to a halt. I felt ridiculous and embarrassed as the sentry approached. I had no business here.

Upon seeing our badges of rank the sentry saluted and then asked why we had come.

'We're here to see the camp commandant,' I lied. He knew it was a lie and I felt even more preposterous and childish for being here.

He waved us through without further comment and didn't waste his breath on giving us directions to the commandant's office, so used was he to admitting rubberneckers to the camp.

We parked and I strapped on the pistol belt feeling ridiculous anew, like John Wayne preparing for a gunfight. *A man's gotta do what a man's gotta do.*

'We shouldn't have come here, Phil. It's a bloody stupid idea.'

'This is why you've been fighting, sir,' he replied, earnestly. The use of the word 'sir' jarred. 'Besides, we're here now.'

I took a deep breath and weighed up my options which didn't take long. I could leave immediately which would make us look stupid or I could stay and wander about this miserable place which would make us look callous.

'Come on then. I don't intend to stay long.'

We had parked next to a long, single-storey building made of wood which I took to be the guardroom. As we passed on foot, our shoes kicking up tiny storms of dry dust, I glanced inside just as the guard commander looked up from his desk.

I felt like an intruder.

'Let's make this quick,' I said as we hurried past. It was then that I noticed a smell, one familiar to me. Just as freshly cut grass releases an odour that stimulates memories of childhood summers, this brought me to the point, years before when I helped remove the charred body of a French pilot from the remains of his aircraft. Somehow that smell, that terrible smell, had stayed with me, lodged in my brain as some combination of chemicals and electricity and now it was lifted from its resting place and dumped on the front counter of my mind.

I couldn't remember why I had been involved. 1940. I was a sergeant pilot. The Frenchman had tried to make an emergency landing on our airstrip near the Belgian border but his Dewoitine fighter was too badly shot up…

'What's wrong, Saul?'

'I was thinking about something. That smell. Can you smell it?'

We carried on until we came to another hut.

I paused as Phil lit a cigarette.

'I didn't know you smoked,' I said.

'Just started. Good for the nerves. I'm surprised you don't smoke after all you've been through.'

'Maybe a pipe. People who smoke pipes always look calm.'

I noticed that we had picked up a mangy dog, some desperate mix of breeds, half-starving and quite malodorous.

'We've made a friend,' said Phil.

'Don't trust him. He's a bloody German.'

I said the words humourlessly. My stomach was gripped by a spasm of fear or anguish as if some great weight was pressing into me. I felt dizzy and clammy. I knelt before I fell and soon my senses, my equilibrium, returned. Phil knelt next to me.

'Are you alright, old boy? Taken a funny turn?'

'I'll be fine. Just a bit out of sorts.'

I stood again, things coming back to normal. Had the air been cleaner, I might have breathed deeply but I merely blinked away my fatigue, or whatever it was.

We stood for a few moments and I surveyed this ghastly place. Along one side of the barbed wire fence stood a series of wooden huts, single storey affairs. The very last of these was nothing more than a charred ruin on a concrete base. Next to that, some distance away, was a pond and along from that a strange pink hill stood, slightly more than head height. There were more huts on the other side of the camp, lining up alongside the fence and then several long pits dug into the earth. A fire burned, desultory strands of smoke trailing into the still air.

Phil and I were walking again, although I couldn't recall setting off. When I looked around me at everything which was going on – and there was plenty – I had the uncomfortable feeling that I was seeing through solid objects rather than viewing them in their natural state. I felt like a ghost in a still breathing body, an earth-bound phantom. Was I the ghost, or was I the living, breathing mortal in a ghost camp?

'Are you okay?'

'Yes Phil. I feel a little bit detached. Light headed, or something. Don't worry about me. Maybe we can get a coffee somewhere… not here obviously.'

A breeze tugged at a smoke spiral and bent it away from its vertical trail. Some chemical seemed to burn at my eyes. We kept walking but my semi-trance persisted. The silence was almost supernatural in its intensity but as I attempted to make some appreciation of this dearth of noise, my ears seemed to pick up sounds once again as though an unseen finger and thumb were turning the volume control in my brain. I guessed that I was emerging from the mental fog that had surrounded me, some tiny cloud worn like a cloak that I had shrugged off with difficulty.

Somewhere, a few birds sang and a dog barked. I heard voices and the rhythmic scrape of spades on hard-packed earth. Full consciousness seemed to return in waves and then, with a sudden lurch as if I was on a braking train, I was back in the present. German civilians and camp guards were taking corpses from the pile I had seen earlier – the pink hill – and throwing them into an immense lime pit. An earthmover sat at idle, its driver watching dispassionately. Four soldiers supervised the civilians, their

Sten guns gripped tightly, trigger fingers on trigger guards, a fixed look that transcended mere horror on their faces.

    They had stepped over a boundary which separated decency from its appalling alternative. But even to describe the scene as 'appalling' was to rob it of real meaning. To be appalled is too minor a thing, a feeling of the wrong magnitude and something from which a recovery is too easily made. The correct words for what I saw have never come to me. Perhaps they have never been invented.

Chapter Two

The burial party were mostly women and older men. The corpses had, in some cases, begun to decay. They were slippery with dew, clammy. The bearers struggled to get purchase on their burdens. Some of the women sobbed. Shock was written through them, but even then I suspected that they must have known what was going on previously. I continued to watch, in a daze really as they dumped the remains of human beings into the lime pit. My mind wouldn't quite let me make any connections between these empty, starved and naked bodies and real people. Had they once climbed trees, read books, chatted to friends about their aspirations, sat round a table eating tea with their family? How was it possible that they went from that state to this? Where had their ideas gone, the heat in their bodies, their memories and emotions? And what about the God they had believed in?

The mangy dog was sitting looking on. He didn't seem to care.

Still, I watched, my mood more than mere shock until I was in some kind of stupor. This slow, unwieldy clearing up process ground on untidily. The corpses were not neat packages that could easily be carried. They weren't heavy after months of starvation but the arms and legs were difficult to grip, the heads lolled and when thrown the bodies accumulated at one side of the pit and not the other. Someone would have to get in and drag them across so that they were more evenly distributed. It was only fair that the job fell to the Germans.

I hated them at that moment. I hated all of them. There's no point pretending otherwise and although in the years to come that feeling might have diminished, it never went away.

'Let's get out of this hell hole,' I said.

***

The images stayed with me, of course. Perhaps we are programmed to remember such horror so as to recoil against any recourse to the means which brought it about. Maybe it is the brain's way of guarding against complacency. But if that was the case the mad corporal who must have seen so much death and mutilation in the Great War could not have created this new round of abomination and atrocity. I had no explanation for what I had seen beyond some crude understanding of the mechanics of death. Why anybody sought to destroy life in this way and on this scale was incomprehensible.

Phil drove and I sat in silence, having taken off the gun belt and returned it to my lap. The idea of further resistance from the Germans seemed even more preposterous now. They were a broken people and most of those who might once have fought on were dead anyway, their lives forfeit to the advancing Allies who had over-run their country. It was a satisfactory and fitting end to the greatest calamity to befall Europe and yet I was still troubled by what I saw, what they had managed to do even as defeat closed in on them from East and West.

I was fifteen when I joined the RAF in 1935. People talked about war – mainly the last one, but also about the prospect of a new one to come – and yet it had always seemed like an abstract idea. The discipline was tough and relentless in training but I had enjoyed it in the main and the idea that we would be fighting the Germans again in a few years just seemed fanciful. There were those who seemed to relish the idea but I was not one of them. To me, the RAF gave me money in my pocket, food to eat and a place to live. That was all I wanted from it. The RAF was my first warm home.

That was still the case when I had learnt to fly in 1938 and had then been posted to a Gladiator squadron as a sergeant pilot. Everyone loved the Gladiator for its turn of speed, its four guns, and its enclosed cockpit but there were even better aircraft on the way. The talk was always of war and what we would do to the Germans when it happened. We talked as if war could not be avoided and eventually that was indeed the case.

Yet, in my mind it would never happen. It was too stupid to countenance another disaster of that sort so soon after the last one. We couldn't possibly repeat the same mistakes, could we? Especially when the memory of the Great War was so fresh in the minds of those who had lived through it in one capacity or another.

I slipped back to the present as we approached the gates of 'our' camp.

An RAF sentry checked our ID and saluted.

'Home sweet home,' concluded Phil. 'It's a fascinating place. Did you ever think you'd be operating from a Luftwaffe airfield?'

'I don't think I had any preconceptions… about anything. Now that we have won the war, people will forget that it might easily have turned out differently.'

'Well, thanks to men like you, that didn't happen,' said Phil, admiringly. I found this admiration embarrassing. Had he known of my terror and despair in those dark times he might have thought differently. I said nothing and we continued to drive until we reached a brick building which was hurriedly being transformed into the officer's mess.

Outside lay a pile of, what I suppose you would call Nazi bric-a-brac, including a portrait of the Fuhrer, a wooden Swastika painted gold and presumably hung on a wall, and flags and busts of prominent German heroes. In time – decades really – this stuff would be worth a fortune but for now it was just junk. I lifted Hitler's likeness from the pile and examined it in the light, trying to find some clue about how he brought about the deaths of millions. But, with his swept-over hair and toothbrush moustache he was ripe for parody. He was more like one of the Marx Brothers – Zeppo, Harpo, Groucho, Chico and Adolfo – or perhaps even the fourth 'Stooge', than a war leader.

I tried to picture him smiling or carrying out some tiny act of kindness but my mind just wasn't open to that sort of interpretation of the man.

Phil said, over my shoulder, 'he went to the toilet like the rest of us. Wiped his arse like the rest of us.'

'I reckon you're right. I was going to say that he looks so ordinary but that isn't really true. He looks very odd.'

'A few days ago, this was the domain of the Luftwaffe and now it's ours. How do you feel about that?'

I set Hitler's picture down before I spoke.

'I don't feel anything. This ought to mean more to me than it does. I can't really explain it. After nearly six years of war I am standing on the steps of a Luftwaffe officer's mess in the heart of Germany. I am the conquering hero.'

'You are. You deserve your moment, Saul,' he said, kindly. It felt as if he was giving me permission to be happy or relieved or that he was giving me permission to tap into *his* reserves of these things. I wanted to feel something more than this, something more profound. Instead, I felt empty. Perhaps the transition from war to peace had been too sudden but you couldn't just wind down a conflict; there had to be a precise moment in time when it stopped; war one second and peace the next.

I didn't feel as if I was in any danger but nor did I feel like a man whose next years on earth were assured.

'I need time to adjust.'

'You need a drink,' said Phil, emphatically. On this point he could not be moved…

I didn't really want to admit that he might be right. A glance at my watch told me that it was much too early in the day to be drinking alcohol and anyway, there had come a time when I had almost given up the demon drink. Excessive consumption of *anything* didn't really fit with flying but alcohol was the worst in that regard. There had been times during the Battle of Britain when recovering from a hangover had seemed as marvellous as having survived yet another sortie. Many times I had sworn off the booze but always I returned.

On one occasion – I was a flight sergeant, newly promoted and with the DFM on my tunic – I had almost been locked up by the Station Warrant Officer such was my state of intoxication. Only the intervention of my flight commander had prevented this since I was needed on operations the next day.

And what a day. What a hangover. Even then I had managed to bag a Heinkel 111, which got me off the hook rather.

'My round, Saul. A celebration. We've won the war, old man. Had you forgotten?'

As I followed him inside, I told myself that I just needed a little pick-me-up after my visit to the concentration camp. That might have been partially true but I felt some raw compulsion to improve my mood through strong drink. Was this the only way I could finally enjoy the victory? It didn't say much for me if so.

The mess was in good nick and a small band of erks were busy transforming it from a Luftwaffe mess into an RAF one. I'm sure they found it an ungratifying task, viewing the officers as part of the governing elite or some such. There were rumblings that the troops were going to vote for the Labour Party in the next election. I doubted if that was true, after Winston had led us to victory. We'd believed in him and our faith had been rewarded. Meanwhile they swept, painted and hammered.

This was my mess and these, by default, were my men, and yet I felt like an outsider. More than that, I felt like an imposter. I wasn't born to this. Had it not been for the war I would never have become an officer. Whereas I had left school at fifteen with just the rudiments of education in place, my squadron clerk was a Cambridge graduate. By a twist of fate he had taken my place in the social order and I had taken his. Eventually it would be reversed again, when things got back to normal. I almost hoped that was true. I believed that our social strata had developed by a process of evolution in which the leaders led and the followers followed. The war had thrust me into a role of which I was undeserving.

As we made our way to the bar a mess orderly appeared. The man was a corporal, probably fifty years of age and a veteran of the Great War doing his bit in the follow-up conflagration.

'Yes, sir. What can I get you?'

'Scotch please.'

'Make that two,' chirped up Phil. Once again he had adopted a proprietorial air, making me feel like his guest.

'Where are the others?'

'Still packing up. They'll be here in the next couple of days.'

We took our drinks and paid but remained at the bar. Behind us an RAF chippy repaired some broken tables and chairs. I recognised him but his name eluded me. Constantly cheerful, he was thrilled anew everyday that he'd been conscripted into the RAF instead of the Army. I didn't blame him; our regime was less dehumanising than that required by the Army. Your average erk rarely faced death.

'Rumour has it that we're going to get Meteors soon,' said Phil.

'I have not heard that rumour. You'd think that someone would tell the acting CO if something like that was on the cards.' I paused and breathed deeply. 'Actually, scrub that. They probably wouldn't. The RAF moves in mysterious ways, its wonders to perform.'

I didn't care one way or the other but it did strike me as peculiar that the RAF's last biplane fighter, the Gloster Gladiator, was still in service at the start of the war and that by the end, a new fighter, the first jet and also built by Gloster, was entering service. It was an enormous improvement in every respect. The Hurricanes, Spitfires, Typhoons and Tempests had had their day. In the space of just six years they had been built in their thousands, taken the war to the enemy *and* become obsolete.

I sipped my drink. I didn't even like the stuff but it seemed fitting.

'To peace,' announced Phil, holding his drink aloft in a belated toast.

'Yes. Peace.' Our glasses clinked. I took another sip and somehow my drink was gone. Perhaps they had been big sips…

'Another?'

'I don't think so Phil. I have things to do.'

'Really? Like what?'

'I don't know. Paperwork. Inspecting the billets. There is always something.'

'If you don't mind me pointing this out, you have no squadron, no aircraft and all the work is in hand. You haven't really had a chance to celebrate properly.'

'Celebrate?'

'The end of the war.'

'When did you join the squadron, Phil?'

'In 1944. March.'

I nodded. In the penultimate year of the war in Europe Phil had joined us and was now a veteran pilot with perhaps a hundred or more sorties under his belt. War produced veterans quickly. I tried to think who was still flying from my first squadron but I had lost track of who was alive, who was dead, who was flying a desk, who was a POW and who was training other pilots. I think my companion exploited my reverie to order another round of drinks. Without complaint or comment I sipped on the whisky... or was it whiskey?... noticing that it tasted much better now that my palate had adjusted.

I thought about Margaret and imagined her here next to me in some German bar, drinking shorts in the midst of a subdued gathering of locals whose defeat we had brought about. Soon enough we'd all have to get along: the victors and the vanquished.

This had been the biggest adventure of our lives and yet we probably hadn't appreciated it. It was the nearness of sudden death that had made each moment so important, so filled with emotion and yet that was what we yearned to leave behind. The war and the fact that I might suddenly lose my life had made me what I am and yet I was happy to let it all go. Would Margaret have been attracted to me if I'd been a cook or a driver? It shouldn't have mattered and yet it did. These were serious considerations.

'You intend to stay in, sir?'

'For a while. What is a Typhoon pilot going to do in Civvy Street? There'll be thousands of pilots let loose and only a few jobs. They won't need to many squadron leaders either, so I am expecting a demotion of sorts.'

'Really? That seems unfair.'

'I'm only an *acting* squadron leader. The tide was already turning when I got promoted. Someone was already thinking about what they would do with all these soldiers, sailors and airmen when the Germans packed in.'

'There's still Japan.'

'I think we'd know if we were being sent there. Someone would have said to us by now.'

'You have that much faith?'

I thought about this.

'No.'

I drank. Very quickly I had reached the comfortably detached state of early drinking. Life was good. This wasn't euphoria but it was something better, longer lasting, more durable, easier to maintain or to repeat on another day. I could have rationalised my way out of this sub-blissful condition had I forced myself to think about practical considerations such as the early hour and the responsibilities which followed me around like a gruesome shadow. It was me who led the squadron and me who did all the subsequent paperwork. It was me who was answerable to the wing commanders and group captains.

The buck stopped with me.

But I was able to dismiss all of that. To have a couple of drinks didn't seem like such a bad thing. It was excusable in the circumstances. After all I had been an operational fighter pilot on the first day of the war and on the last. I had become an ace – eventually – and been to the Palace to meet The King.

So why couldn't I have a day off?

I knew I had to pace myself.

'Same again?' asked Phil.

'My round.'

Another two drinks appeared.

'I have an admission to make,' I said. If Phil was hoping for some great revelation, he was to be disappointed. 'I can't really tell one whiskey from another. I'd love to be some kind of connoisseur but I am not. It all tastes the same to me.'

Phil laughed dutifully. If he wanted to make flight lieutenant before his discharge it made sense to laugh at the boss's jokes. That's just the way it was. Lots of my pilots considered me a friend but I did not often reciprocate. I had almost given up on friendship. It hadn't been worth the effort. Too many friends never came back. I swatted away these morbid thoughts.

By my third whiskey I had noticed that my good mood had plateaued rather. Each sip from my glass served to maintain my contentment rather than enrich it and I was still sober enough to know that if I kept drinking, happiness would easily turn to sadness, contentment to anguish, joy to despair. I was in the company of ghosts. They were always there but sometimes invisible, sometimes nothing more than a thought or a movement. Often, they crowded into my dreams but sometimes they came singly and just sat with me as I did with Phil.

'When we first got Hurricanes we could hardly believe how much better they were than the Gladiator. A hundred mph faster, twice as many guns. They were the only thing that could take on the German's 109s. None of the French kites were a match.'

'How many did you shoot down?' he asked.

'Just two. Two in France.'

'And after that?'

'Bagged one over the Channel and got another four in the Battle of Britain. Got the DFM, then posted to the Middle East as a pilot officer flying P40s. Ground attack stuff but I got a couple of Eyties and then back to Blighty as an instructor. From 1943 I was on Typhoons and the rest is history.' I looked down at my tunic to the ribbons beneath my pilot's brevet. DFM, DFC and DSO. Not bad for someone whose main battle had been with his own nerves. I couldn't reconcile my apparent heroism with the feelings I had borne during the conflict. Luckily, the fear of showing fear had been just enough to keep me going.

Another drink appeared. There was a danger that I might become maudlin if I drank it but I lifted it to my lips, eager to fend off any desperate grabs I might make for common sense. What the hell?

'I'm washed up now,' I said. Phil pulled a face. I hadn't really intended to be so honest. It was the drink. I was tumbling headlong towards a bout of weary introspection. I needed to stop drinking. 'Line 'em up, Phil,' I slurred. Since when have sense and drinking coincided?

'But I thought you said you planned to stay on,' he said. He indicated to the mess steward that our drinks needed to be replaced.

'But it's different in peacetime. I don't mind flying. It's when people are shooting at you that it gets a bit, er, unpleasant.' I was still sufficiently sober to embrace the use of understatement.

I was only twenty-five but that was old enough these days for me to draw from the great well of nostalgia my generation had created. I had lived long enough to remember the pre-war RAF, a small, professional force with more than its share of bullshit. How many of my fellow regular pilots had made it right through, I wondered? It was a sobering thought and another reminder that I had only become an ace, been commissioned and given command of a squadron because I had achieved one remarkable thing: I had survived. So many better men had died. I was a poor substitute for the proper officers.

From somewhere, another two drinks appeared. A radio was playing. It sounded like American music. I looked round and noticed that the mess was filling up. A couple of groundcrew officers sat quietly at a table. A USAAF pilot sat along from us at the bar. I hadn't noticed these men come in.

We were joined by an older officer, a captain in the Army. He said hello. The ribbons on his chest were from the last war.

'Who are these people, Phil?' I whispered.

'Just... I don't know. Blow-ins.'

'When do our kites arrive?' I wasn't sure if he'd already told me. In fact, I wasn't sure if he knew.

'In a few days. The ground staff should be along shortly.'

I took a deep breath and tried to assess my level of drunkenness. It was still early in the day.

'I'd better take it easy in case some brass turn up,' I slurred. 'Although why I should give a damn, I'm not sure. I mean I won their bloody war for them. Single-handed practically.'

I downed my drink, having decided that I needed to sleep for a couple of hours before tackling what was left of the day.

'Another?' asked Phil. The drinks appeared before he'd even finished talking.

'Last one,' I stated, with a show of determination. In reality I had passed some ill-defined tipping-point. I don't think I was really enjoying myself but my freewill had been subsumed by the powerful chemicals I had tipped own my throat with such abandon. I took another deep breath but it didn't help. It didn't restore my sobriety. Possibly it had the opposite effect but I was no longer in a position to judge.

The mess had filled up and I was tempted to ask each of my fellow drinkers to identify themselves. By clinging on to my last scrap of dignity and common sense I managed to avoid a drunken rant. I gripped my glass tightly.

'I need to lie down.'

'One more and then I'll show you your room.'

'Hmm. One more. Just the one.'

Chapter Three

The sun was streaming in through the curtains as I awoke to the sound of an aircraft landing. I swore, tried to find my watch without success and then lay still, ascertaining my whereabouts and state of health. Fragments of the previous day's events sort of dropped into place. I threw back the blankets, suddenly too hot, breathed deeply and then yawned and blinked.

My head hurt and my mouth was dry but it felt as if, overall, I might be able to rouse myself, wash, shave, eat breakfast and possibly face the day. I still wanted to recall a complete version of the previous twenty-four hours before I did anything else.

I had flown to Germany as a passenger in a Halifax. Phil had picked me up and we driven for some time, stopping off at a concentration camp on the way. Had my head not been packed with cotton wool I might have relived the horror of that experience once more but I was able to move on in my hazy recollection. Next, we had arrived at the airfield. Here. My airfield, I supposed.

Then we had gone to the mess for a quick celebratory drink. Just the one.

One had become two. Two had become three and after that only God knew.

***

Washed and shaved, I certainly felt more human. I could probably face the day ahead too with a modicum of resolve.

Phil was absent from breakfast but I managed a cup of coffee, from Luftwaffe supplies apparently, eggs and bacon. It all helped. Each step taken in my normal daily routine returned a little piece of what made me whole. Without thinking I glanced down at the medal ribbons on my tunic and tried to feel some appropriate emotion now that the war in Europe had finished and I was safe. But what, exactly, was I supposed to feel? These were the badges of courage which others craved and yet somehow, perhaps due to familiarity and hangover, they meant nothing at that moment.

The mess was almost empty. I doubted if anyone knew that I was the supposed commander of this fledgling RAF base. I just hoped that I'd made it to my billet last night without making a show of myself. How could I feel like an outsider in my own fiefdom? Had those few days spent at home with Margaret robbed me of my authority?

Breakfast done, and feeling a little bit better, I decided that it was time to explore. I was keen to see the abandoned German aircraft up close and to work out how one ran a fighter squadron when there no longer seemed to be an enemy to shoot down and no one to attack. It still didn't feel real to me, the peace that is. What was my reason for being? What would I do every day?

The sun beat down, and even this early it was clear that the heat would be oppressive. I was still a commander without a command but that odd state prompted me to greater efforts. The problem was, where were those efforts to be directed? What was I supposed to do? The rest of my pilots could arrive at any time, but then what?

Phil intercepted me as I crossed the pan towards the main hangar.

'I can show you to your office, if you like,' he said before adding, 'how's the head?' He looked spritelier than he deserved to be in the circumstances which made me wonder about his tolerance for strong drink. He was still young and yet he had the constitution of a much older man.

'It's fine. Yes, my office. That would be good.'

It was a short trip which took us past several Luftwaffe vehicles including a fire tender and ambulance.

'We could use those,' said Phil.

'I suppose so.' I was doubtful since we had our own vehicles but, perhaps he was right. It was certainly odd to come across so much usable equipment when previously the retreating Germans had been diligent, nay unsparing, in their pursuit of scorched earth. Generally, we had inherited little apart from hungry citizens, refugees, rubble and the twisted remains of war-making machines and yet, somehow, we must have caught them on the hop. This place was ready to use. I didn't doubt that in a few days, we'd be flying from here just as we had done from every other base we'd occupied.

'This is your office,' said Phil pointing to a low wooden building appended to the edge of the main hangar.

'Did you pick this for me?' I asked.

'It belonged to your predecessor; Oberst Becker, I believe.'

'A colonel. I'm honoured. Whatever happened to him, I wonder?'

Phil shrugged.

'The problem is that if a group captain wants to base himself here, then he'll want this office.'

'You got here first, Saul.'

Accepting his logic, it was my turn to shrug.

'Right. I'll get myself settled in and you can give me a tour later.' I cast my glance around my new home: the endless runway, the control tower, the hangars… and tried to make sense of my situation. I had never thought about how I might adjust to peace. In fact, for much of the time I hadn't expected to live long enough to see it. Yet here I was, in command of a *Luftwaffe* airfield, waiting for my own squadron to arrive. Phil had wandered off and I took a few steps towards my office, picking up the scent of coffee on the way.

The door opened silently, the smell of coffee was stronger and I realised that I was not alone.

'Good morning, *Herr Oberst*.'

I would say that she was just short of thirty, very pretty in that Germanic way and neatly dressed despite the recent privations suffered by her people. That's what she looked like, but who the hell was she?

'Good morning. It's Squadron Leader actually.'

She smiled and inclined her head as a way of acknowledging her error or perhaps to show that she had made a note of my status and that this new knowledge was secure.

'I am your secretary, Ingrid. Would you like coffee?'

I didn't really want coffee.

'Yes please. I didn't know I had a secretary.'

'Oh yes. It was all arranged,' she said. Her English was clipped, precise, economical as if she had pared each sentence down to its most basic form, devoid of ambiguity almost pure, with extraneous words clipped like thorns in a hedge. And yet she had told me nothing; who had arranged it? Why?

I had to take her at her word but the question remained – arranged by who? I supposed it would all become clear in time. For now it would be useful to have a secretary I supposed.

She was busy making hot drinks. I noticed that she had a plentiful supply of German coffee, powdered milk, sugar and so on. I had thought these things were rationed or impossible to get and yet that was not the case. How come she was so well provided for? These, like my breakfast, must have been *Luftwaffe* stocks, I reasoned. I still wondered who had sent her and what she would do when my own clerk arrived but, the war was over and we had to build relationships with the Germans at some point. They weren't the enemy any longer but that was a difficult concept for me to accept after six years of fighting.

Ingrid didn't ask if I wanted milk and sugar but I got both anyway. I took the proffered cup and thanked her before taking a seat at my desk. I wracked my brain for some small talk but what did you say to someone like her, so recently an enemy?

Did you get much bombing?

How many family members did you lose?

Waiting for any POWs to come home?

What do you think of the concentration camps? Pretty awful, eh?

By nature I kept myself to myself. I was comfortable with the other officers in the squadron but even then I wasn't an ebullient character in their presence; more of a steady hand, if anything. But now, to avoid an embarrassing silence, I felt that some type of conversation was required.

I sipped my coffee – it was okay, actually – and then glanced at my secretary half expecting to see a Nazi brooch pinned to her lapel.

'The coffee is good,' I said.

'The Luftwaffe got the best of what there was at the end of the war. People were hungry but not our pilots.' She shrugged sadly, although it was impossible to say if this was an expression of regret for the war's outcome or about the waste of life involved. Given time, I would figure it out but I just wasn't quite prepared to chat amiably with a person, who, even a couple of weeks ago had wished me dead. Had she actually wished me dead? Perhaps not. Perhaps she had wished for the war to end. Perhaps she had never supported Hitler. She wasn't likely to admit to ever having been a Nazi now.

I had to assume that not every German was a fanatical Nazi but it was hard to do so when, for so many years, it had suited me to think that they were. It made it easier to kill them… and I must have killed dozens of Germans. I looked at Ingrid as I thought this thought and she smiled. I forced a smile in return.

***

'That didn't take long,' I said. Phil was giving me a tour of my fiefdom and I pointed to a couple of erks busy with paintbrushes.

'If it moves, salute it. If it doesn't move, paint it.'

'Quite so. Imagine what would happen if that shed didn't get a new coat of paint; the world would drop off its axis at the very least. Standards must be maintained.' It seemed idiotic that the paint and brushes had been sent ahead of the aircraft but I couldn't be bothered to make the point, such was the heavy veil of lethargy which held me in its tight embrace. Only days had passed since I'd had a purpose in life. Now, I was treading water, or treading air perhaps. What troubled me most was the fact that I should have been enjoying it more.

'It's hard to adjust,' said Phil. Had he been reading my mind? 'I'm not complaining but it's almost an anti-climax. Now that the fighting has stopped, we just… do nothing? There's something missing.'

'Yes. Eventually the demob will take us away and we'll get new pilots, new aircraft and everything that we took for granted will be gone. People will go back to Civvy Street and to their humdrum existences. In a way we should never be asked to do anything again but who's going to pay us to sit around telling stories about the war? Soon people will forget. We won't even be heroes because everyone else is the same. A hero in a land of heroes is just a person.'

Phil didn't respond, which I took as agreement.

'This is the hangar,' he said, pointing.

We slid the door open and that gave us enough light to see the precious aircraft lined up as if for inspection.

'It's like an exhibition. A museum of German fighter aircraft.'

Two camouflaged 109s stood next to the entrance and behind them a Focke-Wulf 190, then a 110, then a Junkers 188 night fighter, a 262 jet and a tiny 163, this last looking like no other aircraft.

'Do we get to fly these?'

'I doubt it. Someone will come along and take them away for evaluation. Or maybe they'll go straight to a museum. They won't want to risk them in our hands.'

It was the 262 and the 163 which particularly grabbed my attention. They were quite unlike anything else, more like weird fish than aeroplanes.

'This is what fighters will look like from now on.' Time would prove my prophecy incorrect but I made it with great authority nevertheless.

I had to hand it to the Germans, they knew how to build fantastic warplanes. It made me wonder how they had managed to lose the war.

'What do you know about Ingrid?'

'Who?'

'Ingrid.'

'I don't know anyone with that name.'

'My secretary…'

Phil pulled a face which strongly suggested bewilderment.

'Oh. Er, I didn't know you had a secretary.'

'Well, unless I dreamt it, there was a woman sitting in my office this morning claiming to be my secretary. She says someone hired her but it obviously wasn't you.'

'And she's German, I take it.'

'That seems likely, Phillip.'

Phil left me alone and I naturally drifted down to the swept-wing fighters that the previous users had left behind. I had heard about these new machines of course but never encountered them at close hand in the air which was frankly a good thing. The Americans seemed to have had more dealings with them and some of their reports suggested that these aircraft were actually too fast to intercept the relatively slow B17s and B24s. That was a surprising outcome. Aeroplanes had become steadily faster as the war ground on. Speed had always been one's biggest advantage until now. I supposed it was the tactics which needed to change.

I climbed up onto the 262's wing and peered inside the cockpit, deciding that it wasn't too different to a prop plane in terms of controls. I wondered how it would compare with its British counterpart, the Meteor.

A sudden urge to fly this amazing aircraft took me then and I looked guiltily around the hangar, the crime of theft forming in my head. The canopy slid open with the expected German precision and I climbed inside, settling into the pilot's seat and surveying the instruments arrayed before me. It was an odd feeling to be so suddenly captivated with the idea of flying, for it had become a chore of late. More than a chore really. It was something I feared and had done for years now. A band of tension pulled tight across my chest and I forced myself to think of something else.

It did no good. Sweat seeped from my pores and I began to shake. I hoped that no one could see me for, in some way, I was coming apart at the seams. Was this what peace did after so many years of war? It was not what I had dreamed of. After a few minutes in which I sat still, controlling my breathing and trying to think calm thoughts, the situation eased. Just as well I hadn't been flying, I thought, for this near paralysis would have caused me to crash for sure.

Back in control, I scanned the unfamiliar German cockpit. From that cursory inspection it seemed likely that I would be able to fly this plane with just a little bit of instruction. The instruments were in German of course but I could figure out there purpose just by looking at them and the way in which they were marked.

Höhenmesser was altimeter. *Brennstoff* was fuel.

***

I returned to my office where the ever-solicitous Ingrid made me another coffee, seeming to judge that I had endured some sort of traumatic event but not inquiring about it.

'Would you like a cigarette, Squadron Leader?'

'No thank you, but please smoke if you like. I have been surrounded by smokers for years. I don't even notice it.'

I didn't recognise the brand but they didn't stink like cheap cigarettes and I began to wonder what other goodies my secretary had stashed away: chocolates, Champagne, a selection of gruesome *Bratwürste* made from animals which any civilised person would refuse to eat.

The coffee was good. It seemed to settle my nerves and a subtle feeling of wellbeing ran through me, pushing away whatever had happened earlier.

The peculiar thing was that neither of us had anything to do. The reams of paperwork which were the bane of my life had yet to arrive and be sorted into filing cabinets and drawers. The squadron was still far to the west. There was a telephone on my desk and I picked it up, surprised to hear the dialling tone.

Ingrid looked over and smiled.

'The phone system still works,' she said. Her tone was matter-of-fact, not triumphal. She wasn't bragging about how we had failed to close down this aspect of German life despite the years of bombing.

But there was something unsettling about her attitude as if she had no need for contrition, no need to explain, to apologise. Ingrid was quick to change sides, to ingratiate herself with the new regime, to put the past behind her and move on but it was just too easy somehow. I didn't hold her solely responsible for the war – that would have been ridiculous – but she had played her part even if that consisted of nothing more than a refusal to protest.

Who was she really? What did she know of the war? Who was she married to? What part had her family played?

'Are you fine? You seemed lost in your thoughts.'

'Yes. I drifted off. You speak good English,' I ventured.

'Thank you,' she said, but without any explanation as to why that might be so. She was an enigma.

'You worked for the previous commanding officer?'

'Yes.'

I nodded. If she was going to give anything away it clearly wasn't going to come in a landslide of words.

I looked at the phone on my desk and asked a question.

'Could I ring Britain on that telephone?'

Ingrid laughed.

'I don't know. I don't think anyone ever tried.'

'No. I suppose not.'

'You wanted to ring your girlfriend?'

'My wife. I probably shouldn't use an official phone anyway.'

That was it. I had laid the matter to rest. Besides, I didn't want to give too much away to Ingrid. She wasn't my enemy but she wasn't my friend either. A cup of coffee didn't change that. I couldn't quite shake the feeling that had we been introduced two weeks earlier she would have been an ardent Nazi, with a party badge and a picture of the Fuhrer in her purse. Germans claiming a dislike of all things National Socialist was quite a recent phenomenon as far as I could tell.

    Nevertheless, we had to start somewhere. It came back to the same old thing; the Germans couldn't be our enemies forever, although there seemed little justification for forgiving and forgetting in a country awash with war criminals. The camp I'd been to the previous day was evidence of that. I would be haunted by those images forever. I looked over at my secretary and wondered how someone so apparently sweet and charming could be associated with the monstrous people who had set up extermination camps.

    Oddly, the slippery-slap of damp, naked bodies landing one on top of another came to me then as I recalled the corpses being transferred to the lime pit without recourse to dignity, compassion or care.

    Had I not seen it with my own eyes I might have suspected that reports of such places was mere propaganda to make sure we hated our enemies in the approved fashion and to the approved degree. The truth was more terrible, more shocking than any propaganda. Had stories of the Nazi camps been created from nothing, I'm not sure who would have believed it.

When she spoke, in her perfect English, I was snapped from my reverie.

'These cabinets have the personnel records of the men who worked on the base I haven't got rid of them but they aren't much use now. You will have to replace them with your own papers, of course.'

Down to practical matters.

'I don't know what happens to these things,' I admitted.

'They are not incriminating. I could just burn them.'

Yet again, I had to remind myself that she had been my enemy until recently and I had no reason to trust her. But that being the case, if the documents *were* sensitive in nature, then why had she not destroyed them previously?

'We'll keep them until I hear what is supposed to happen to them,' I said with a shrug. 'What happened to the men who worked here?'

Just for a fragment of a fragment of a moment she seemed unsure of her answer but then she replied, 'they were taken prisoner by the British.'

'They didn't just scarper?'

'Scarper?'

'You know… run off. Desert.'

'Some of them.'

I let the matter drop. I was puzzled by her lack of detail in this matter. Maybe it was unimportant, or maybe this was her way of urging me to think about the future rather than the past. I imagined that a lot of Germans would be feeling that way now; their recent past was best forgotten, although I hoped it wouldn't be. My mind raced back to that camp and the images of heaped bodies, a pink tangled mess of flesh that had once been human.

The door opened and in came a group captain, whom I had never previously encountered. He looked like a regular, his uniform of good quality and a moustache bisecting his broad, ruddy face. I stood to attention.

'Broadhurst,' he said shaking my hand.

'Cohen.'

'Yes. I know all about you, Squadron Leader. Good show. Any coffee?'

Ingrid stood and set about making coffee as Broadhurst sat. He gave my secretary and appraising look before he turned back to me.

'A couple of things… By the way call me Harry. I was just a flight lieutenant when this whole thing started.'

'Saul,' I said. I wondered if Ingrid had connected my name to my religion. Saul Cohen. Did that combination set off anti-Jewish alarm bells in her head? The Germans had been conditioned to hate us without reservation. Had any of them escaped this curse?

'So, we are sending over some chaps to evaluate the aircraft in your hangar. If they can be flown, they'll be taking them away. I bet you wish you could take up one of those jets. Damned fine aircraft.'

Ingrid set a coffee cup down in front of him. He didn't thank her as if that was the best way of demonstrating his disdain. She set another cup in front of me, a slight smile on her lips as if anticipating the strain this would put on my bladder.

'The other thing is we need someone to oversee the town for a while. Sort of mayor. Just a couple of thousand people and probably not going to give you any trouble but we need someone in authority.'

'What about my squadron, sir?'

'Your 2ic can take over for a while, I'm sure. You're not going to be doing that much flying.'

'Okay, sir.'

'Just take a gun with you. Probably take someone along. Armed, you know? Just in case. The Huns are pretty cowed by now but you never know.'

'What am I supposed to…'

'Whatever is required really. You're Johnny on the spot. So whatever comes up, you deal with. Prisoners, Nazis, feeding the locals, keeping the Reds at bay.'

'The Russians?'

'They're everywhere. They seem to get a little bit lost now and again if you get my meaning. They need to understand that this is our zone. God only knows how this is all going to be resolved. You'll need to use your initiative and don't let them push you around. They want revenge more than they want to…' He considered his words for a moment. 'More than they want to herald a new dawn of peace, reconciliation and mutual… something…'

I smiled. I guessed he was right.

'Could I have a couple of soldiers from the camp?'

'Good idea. They'll be glad to get out of there. Lieutenant Pearson is the man in charge, Go and see him. Seems like a good chap.'

***

Pearson was a Scot with sallow skin and dark rings round his eyes. My guess was that he had risen through the ranks to get his commission.

'This place stinks,' he said as I took a seat in his office. 'The smell of death. Worse than anywhere I've known for obvious reasons.'

'I need a couple of soldiers if you can spare them. I'm going to be mayor of the town until someone better arrives.'

Pearson raised his eyebrows.

'Lucky you, sir. Mind you, I don't think they'll give you much trouble. I've only got a platoon but I can let you have an NCO and a couple of privates, if that's okay?'

'Yes. That would be fine, I think.'

'I'm waiting on some Royal Engineers to come with another bulldozer. It's the only way we can get these people buried. Bloody awful. We found more bodies in the woods. Hundreds, maybe thousands. Men, women, children. I never doubted that our cause was just but seeing this…'

'Not easy to forget.'

'I got a call through telling me to round up the townsfolk and show them what went on under their noses. Not sure I can manage it.'

'It's a good idea. That way they can't keep denying all knowledge of it.'

Pearson nodded.

'I suppose if anyone ever doubts why we were fighting…' He rubbed his eyes as though assailed by a fresh wave of fatigue. 'I'll get those men and send them over to you. Then I'll start rounding up the locals; see how shocked they actually are. You know, this time we need to destroy Germany so it can never become powerful again. Wipe it off the face of the map if possible. My old man was in the last lot – Coldstreams. He could hardly believe it when the Jerries did the same thing again. He wondered what they had done it for… The Great War, I mean. What had they fought for?'

I nodded my agreement but I knew it would never happen. We were too civilised to do to the Germans what they had attempted to do to everyone else. I thought it would be a mistake to restore the country but who cared what I thought? The veneer of respectability was so easy to fit back in place. As a case in point, I had a secretary who acted as if the war had never occurred and that millions of people had not died as a result of her leaders' cruel, deluded actions. I was sure that others were capable of demonstrating such nonchalance, perhaps the whole bleeding lot of them.

Already I had the feeling that the most unpleasant aspects of the conflict would be brushed away like dust. We had to live in the present, plan for the future and not dwell in the past. Personally, I felt as if the past was still the present, that I had not truly emerged from those awful events. Unbreakable connections had been forged in my brain.

Chapter Four

I slept well that night, possibly the best sleep I'd had for six years. It seemed as though my body and mind were adjusting to the reality that my life was secure for the time being, unlikely to be snatched away by enemy bullets, or consumed by flame. There was a point to making plans or maybe to just plan to have plans. Let's not rush things. The anti-climax, the transition from war to peace was becoming normal. I was safe.

    I arrived at the office after breakfast and found Ingrid seated in her place with a pile of documents on her desk. Rather, two piles. She was sorting them but I didn't ask what they were, why she was sorting them or what criteria marked them out for each pile. I didn't care.

    'Morning.'

    'Good morning, Squadron Leader,' she replied. The words could have sounded obsequious but they were business-like and respectful. And when I say 'respectful', I mean the sort of respect which has not been earned but rather that which is learned as though from a book on etiquette. I still had no real idea who she was, who had employed her or what I was supposed to do with her. The fact that she had allocated herself a task was good enough for the time being. Sorting these documents into two piles showed commitment and initiative. For now, the fact that she was doing so, and that her actions served no purpose that I could see, was unimportant.

Phil appeared shortly afterwards to inform me that the first of the unit's vehicles had arrived.

'And the aircraft?'

'Some are coming later today and the rest are having re-fit. I think obviously we're going to be stood down. They just need us to stay in Germany until they've figured out what to do with us.'

'I suppose so,' I said, suddenly weary and disinterested. My eyes were stinging as if I hadn't slept.

No sooner had Phil left my office than a sergeant from the infantry knocked, entered and saluted.

'Yes, Sergeant.'

'I'm collecting up Kraut civvies to take them round the camp, sir. Been told that some of 'em work here.'

'Oh. That's fine. Help yourself.'

There was an awkward silence and we all knew to what it related. I glanced at Ingrid, trying not to make it too obvious. She was staring intently at a document on her lap.

'What about this one, sir?' asked the sergeant.

'She's already been,' I lied. I don't even know why I did so. 'She went round with me two days ago. It was one of the conditions of working here.'

Lie upon lie. The NCO didn't seem to care one way or the other. He saluted again and left. The awkward silence remained, like a third person in the room. I didn't look at my secretary and she didn't look at me as far as I could tell, for such would have been an admission that something underhand had taken place, some acknowledgement that she'd lived a less than virtuous life during the war. I didn't know if that was the case but how could anyone spend a decade and more under Nazi rule and not become complicit in the evil perpetuated by it?

I heard the vehicle pull away and concentrated on reading a sheet of paper I had already read twice.

'I'm going to check on my new arrivals,' I said, standing.

'Yes, Squadron Leader,' she replied, obediently. How easily these Germans could switch allegiance, I thought, but her acquiescence was better than defiance of course; we had to cooperate.

I stood outside the office for a few minutes, enjoying the sun on my back and just listening to the bird song which filled the air. It seemed as though the transition from war to peace had heightened my appreciation of simple things, made me more aware of tiny pleasures. Perhaps my senses had been re-tuned, the painful static of war replaced by the serenity of the natural world. Sometimes just being alive was good enough.

The air was fresh and clear and I breathed deeply on this gaseous elixir before doing my rounds. In truth there was no requirement to check on my newly arrived airmen but I was a leader and expected to show an interest.

The trucks were parked up neatly and all about I saw airmen busy with the multitude of tasks required in the running of an airfield. They had done these things in southern England, then in France, then Belgium and now here in Germany. They had gone past the point where the NCOs needed to harry them; they simply got to work in most cases which made my life straightforward; I wasn't fussed on admin.

Now and again I'd had to deal with a defaulter but in the main my men had behaved themselves. Soon we'd go our separate ways and since few of them were regulars our paths would probably never cross. Even some of the regulars would probably leave. As for my conscripts, they had accepted military discipline with weary resignation rather than enthusiasm. I really didn't blame them.

As I made my way round this sprawling but sparsely populated empire, I was greeted with relative warmth and lacklustre salutes, which was fine. I made my way to the cookhouse where my cooks were getting to grips with unfamiliar German equipment. Already a smell of cooking oil hung in the air. The timpani rattle of pots and pans – dixies – was as familiar and comforting as a warm blanket.

'Morning, sir,' came the voice behind me.

I turned.

'Morning Flight. Does it look like a normal kitchen to you?' I joked.

'I'll tell you what, sir, they might have left in a hurry but the place was spotless. You'd have thought they'd wreck it before leaving.'

'They're a funny lot, the Germans. Not bothered about starting a war that killed millions but they don't want anyone to think they don't clean up properly.' I looked around at the room with its orderly rows of tables and chairs. 'The officers and senior NCOs can eat in here tonight. No point setting up messes when there are so few of us.'

'As you wish, sir. Makes it a bit easier. Some of the lads were asking about their demob…'

I held my hands up in mock surrender.

'God knows, Flight. It'll happen when it happens, I suppose. Remind them that we're still at war with the Japs.'

'Good point. I'll tell 'em that they'll get sent east if they complain. That'll shut 'em up.'

I laughed and left the senior NCO to get on with his work.

***

Later that day, after I had sent my secretary home, I tried to ring my house. I was taken aback when I ended up speaking to an operator and felt guilt as if I'd been caught breaking a rule. I had to explain who I was and who I wanted to speak to. Thirty seconds of clicking and interference followed before the operator came back on the line and told me she couldn't make the connection. I put the receiver down and began writing a letter.

It was full of the inane stuff that I thought served the purpose of reassuring my wife while we were parted. I had survived years of peril and not one word relating to that peril had been scratched out on paper, at least not in any letter I sent to Margaret. Now, with the arrival of peace I could have been more forthright but the truth was that the habit of documenting the banal and omitting the frightful was so ingrained that I didn't really know how else to put my thoughts down. And the danger was gone, of course. I had less to talk about than ever.

I laid my pen down for a moment, troubled. I had mentioned the move from Belgium, through Holland and then to Germany. I had talked about the new base. I had described my office and the weather… all the usual things, but I hadn't mentioned my secretary, Ingrid.

Why, I asked myself, as I sat there entirely at peace with the world, was that the case? There was nothing going on between us – we'd only just met for one thing – and I had no intention of consorting with the enemy other than in a professional sense. Yet, my reticence puzzled me. After a few moments deliberation I explained it away by saying that I didn't want to make Margaret jealous. That didn't make much sense. There was no need to mention Ingrid any more than there was a need to mention Corporal Clarke from MT or Flight Sergeant Williams, my mechanic. More than that, there was no chance of her being jealous; she knew me better than that.

With that in mind, I dismissed the whole notion.

***

Later that day the first aircraft flew in, each of my pilots executing a perfect landing, just as we had practiced again and again. One of my bugbears, and one which I cited relentlessly to my men, was losing and aircraft through poor landings and take-offs. Aerial combat was hard enough without throwing away men and equipment through carelessness.

I continued to watch as they taxied their fighters across to the main hangar, marvelling, not for the first time, at the sight of these enormous 2,000 horsepower beasts with their gaping mouths and wing-mounted cannon protruding like antennae. Compared to the biplanes I had first flown they were like something from a different planet and even these mighty aeroplanes were on the verge of obsolescence now that the new jets were coming into operation. A lot had happened in six years. I wondered if I too was obsolete but found myself quite unmoved at the prospect. Sometimes I struggled to feel any emotion at all, as if the war had drained me of that thing which raised us above the level of mere beasts.

I spoke to my pilots and we exchanged a few anecdotes relating to those momentous few days in which our enemies had hovered on the very edge of the cliff of defeat before finally toppling in. Flight Lieutenant Murphy, one of my most experienced men and an ace having shot down seven Italians over the desert, came to me when the little furore had ended.

'How are you, Saul?' he asked, solicitously.

I was used to batting away concerns about my wellbeing, rare as they were.

'I'm fine. Relieved or something.'

'You look worn out,' he advised.

'Maybe I am. The cumulative effect of six years of war and then it just crashes to a halt. I feel a bit lost without it.' I explained about my new role as mayor of the town and he smiled.

'The break will do you good.'

'I hope it is a break. You and Phil can run things in my absence, can't you?'

'Of course.'

'You can always come and get me if anything goes wrong. I'm going there shortly to assess my new responsibilities.'

'Good luck. Take a gun.'

'Werewolves?' I said, archly.

'Black marketeers, stray Russians and whoever else. The average German knows he's beat.'

I smiled at his use of language, which sounded faintly American to my ears.

Later, using a purloined German staff car, a strange boxy machine I had often shot up in the past, and accompanied by Ingrid, I made my way to the *Rathaus*. Ingrid seemed nervous but it had been a peculiar morning and we shared the secret of my inexplicable lie. For a second, as she took her seat next to me in the car, I wondered if I was… I don't know… harbouring a fugitive? For all I knew she was a convinced Nazi, or married to one or knew more about what the Nazis had been up to than she cared to recall. Not that we had broached the subject. It seemed impolite. I did notice that her clothes were smart and in good repair, and, although slim, she didn't seem emaciated as a result of the privations of war.

'Ready?'

'Yes.'

'I think I might need you to interpret,' I said as I pulled away towards the gate.

'Yes, of course, Squadron Leader.'

I wondered if we should drop the formality. Squadron Leader didn't exactly trip off the tongue and no one else used that epithet. Those below me called me sir and the rest called me Saul. But then I reasoned we weren't friends or equals, so why should we act as though we were? I was the victor and she the vanquished. The veneer of decency did nothing to alter that fact or to undo the Germans' crimes.

There was another problem. It shouldn't have been a problem – at least not for me – but it was there and it concerned my religion. I imagined that Ingrid had no idea that I was a Jew and I couldn't picture a situation in which she would have put herself at risk to assist me had there ever been cause. Just weeks previously, the Nazis had been murdering my people in their hundreds of thousands, probably millions. She must have known. In recent German mythology the Jew had been a hook-nosed banker, preying on the good people of Hitler's new empire. He had blamed the Jews for everything and by default his people had largely followed suit. I didn't look Jewish but I was.

The *Rathaus*, like the rest of the town, was largely intact. This sliver of territory had never been contested because the war had withered on its vine before the combatants had reached this point. Even so, there were reminders of the war. A Red Army tank sat in the town square, its crew lounging, caps on the backs of their heads, smoking but not drinking. They seemed to be challenging the locals by their presence, leaving them to contemplate the true meaning of defeat, to rue the day they voted Hitler into power, or the day they had dared to offend Stalin.

The Russians had suffered more than anyone else. Their revenge was all the sweeter and I didn't blame them for revelling in victory. I felt Ingrid stiffen beside me as we pulled up to the *Rathaus* steps.

'Stay close,' I said. 'They won't try anything.'

Naturally the Red Army troops, equipped with submachine guns and a tank wouldn't dare to question the authority of a single RAF officer with a side-arm. Who was I kidding?

Despite this worry, my spirits lifted as we entered the town hall and once inside with the door closed, I was able to attribute this to the birdsong, the warmth of the sun and the smell of wax polish. Ingrid seemed to relax at once, the stout well-fitting German doors becoming a barrier against the Russians outside. Not much of a barrier, or course, but it was all to do with perception.

'Here we are,' I said, idiotically. I watched her as she smoothed down the pockets on her jacket quite unnecessarily. I would come to recognise that gesture as one of nervousness. 'I suppose you've been here before?'

She looked uncertain.

'No. I don't think so.'

I nodded.

'I'm not sure what I'm supposed to do. I presume the town had a mayor previously. I wonder where he is now?'

She didn't seem to know the answer to that. She didn't seem to know much really and I began to wonder if I could completely trust her. Two weeks previously I would have scoffed at the idea of trusting a German – any German – and yet my defences had fallen quickly and easily.

We found the mayor's office on the ground floor and I opened the door, not quite sure what to expect. A picture of Hitler greeted me. Hung on the wall, behind the oak desk, the recently unfashionable Fuhrer gazed madly on the solitary conqueror. It sent a shiver up my spine and I said, 'I think we'll get rid of that.'

Without hesitation, she stepped forwards and snatched the offending portrait down, revealing a bright patch of wall underneath. I smiled at her resolute action but wondered if she was overdoing her display of dislike for the once great leader. Again, it shocked me that Germany's fortunes and direction had changed so radically in such a short space of time. She took the picture out of the room but returned a few seconds later. For all I knew she was going to take the picture home to put on the mantlepiece next to her existing copy. These Germans had a lot of changes to make, I thought. Their lives had been entwined with this man and their brains fixed on his theories and his cod military genius. They wouldn't become unbelievers overnight.

The mayor's office had an adjoining room which, upon inspection, was clearly intended as a typist's space. It was orderly and equipped with a typewriter and filing cabinets.

'This is your place,' I said. I assumed that she could type and do all the things that a secretary should do. It occurred to me then that I hadn't seen her actually do *anything* but that this could be attributed to the fact that I had not assigned her a single task, unless removing Hitler's image was classed as an instruction. She sat primly and looked at home, as if awaiting orders, but since I had none, I suggested we have a look around our new place of work. I had dozens of questions for her but I didn't ask one of them.

The *Rathaus* put me in mind of a hotel with a wood-panelled lobby, reception desk, framed pictures, carpeted stairs and a sort of restrained opulence. It was orderly rather than flash but quite comforting in some hard to define sense. A short corridor led to a series of offices, each once the domain of some departed local official. I thought that Ingrid might tell me a little bit about the function of each of the former users but she said nothing. When I realised that I didn't have any interest in what had gone on there, I let it go. Had my curiosity about National Socialist bureaucracy been marked on a sliding scale, I think a negative value would have been recorded. Nevertheless I was mildly – genuinely, mildly – interested in the fate of the absent functionaries.

'No one has come to work?' I suggested.

'It seems that way. I suppose they take holidays if no one is going to pay them.'

'I suppose so.'

None of the downstairs offices had a Hitler picture. Perhaps they had been reserved for appointees over a certain rank.

We didn't tarry.

'What's upstairs?' I asked but she shook her head and I remembered that she'd never been here.

Everything was spotless. Brasses were polished, the carpets had been thoroughly brushed and the bannisters gleamed. Catastrophic defeat was no reason for a drop in standards quite clearly. I might have admired the Germans had it been possible to overlook some of their other shortcomings regarding mass murder and so on. The thought that I was colluding with the enemy hit me then like light from a flash bulb. It was there and then gone. Of course these weren't my enemies any longer but nor were they friends. I wasn't ready for that. Was there a precise moment when that change – enemy to ally – occurred, or was it to be a gradual process? The problem as I saw it was the sheer scale of the Germans' crimes. Simply forgiving and forgetting seemed like far too much to ask of anyone.

As we took to the stairs, she stopped me in our tracks by saying, 'aren't you going to do something about the Russians?'

'What? All of them?' I joked but my humour fell totally flat.

'The ones outside.'

She seemed genuinely afraid and I realised just how terrified these people were of the Red Army. They had been conditioned to fear the Bolshevik Jews and their plotting and now, here they were parked both actually and metaphorically on the doorstep.

'I don't know what I can do,' I said, immediately registering the disappointment in her face. Why did I care what she thought of me? She was a German – the vanquished – she had no right of think any less of me. We'd won the bloody war, hadn't we? I turned and took another step up the stairs but she didn't follow and I was surprised anew when she spoke.

'But if you are the… *der Bürgermeister*,' she said indignantly. 'You must do something.'

Sadly, she was correct. Despite my annoyance at her unwarranted haughtiness, she was only telling me the truth in her uncompromising German manner. I sighed and closed my eyes in an effort to control my irritation.

'I have some troops under my command. I was waiting until they arrived before I…'

'You must say something now,' she insisted. Ingrid had quickly cast off the reticence of the recently defeated *hausfrau* and was being assertive. Or bossy and rude, if you prefer. I wanted to find some way in which to put her in her place and to restore what ought to have been the natural balance. It would have sounded churlish to remind her that her new employers had won and that she had lost.

'You speak the language? You speak Russian?' It was a challenge but her response was not what I expected.

'Yes. I will translate.'

I swore inwardly for she had taken away my last reasonable objection to the imminent confrontation. Strictly speaking of course, the Russians were still our allies, although I had heard rumblings that their benevolent attitude towards us was being drawn from a finite source and that they would one day revert to type i.e. *the true enemies of civilisation*. But there was something defiant in their attitude which suggested that these particular Red Army soldiers weren't quite ready to make a dignified withdrawal on my say-so.

I looked down at the wings above my breast pocket and the short row of medal ribbons beneath that, hoping that these were, in combination, enough to imbue me with the authority required for this task. I fixed a steely look on my face and made for the door.

'Okay then. Let's speak to them.'

I felt sick with anxiety and that was before I had even considered the huge flaw in my plan.

Chapter Five

They deliberately didn't look in my direction as I strode towards them and I took this, correctly, as a bad sign. It would have been different had it been one of their own officers closing in but I was fairly sure that they regarded me as somewhat second rate. I couldn't explain that I had been fighting the war when Russia had still been allied to Germany or that I had shot down many Axis fighters, blown up many trains and trucks. For these men, the war had been fought, at great cost, in the East and everything else was a sideshow. It didn't suit Uncle Joe to explain the niceties of the Allied efforts to his cannon fodder soldiers.

I had no idea how to begin. There was every chance of me sounding like a pompous idiot and away from the regiment to which they belonged with its senior NCOs and officers there was precious little incentive to react to my words with good humour and military correctness. Now that it came to it, I would have preferred Ingrid to be elsewhere, for although she would be my interpreter, she would also be a witness to my humiliation.

'Morning gents,' I began, cheerfully. 'Do you realise that you are in the British zone?' I looked at Ingrid expectantly and she began to translate with some hesitation.

'Utrennie dzhentlmeny. vy ponimaete, chto nakhodites vie britannic zone.'

The Russians exchanged looks of bovine incomprehension and one of them smiled nervously. As a reaction, this was less terrible than it might have been. By that I mean, they didn't burst out laughing or point their submachine guns at us.

None of them spoke but they managed to share a look of bewilderment through some act of silent communication.

'Did they understand you?' I asked. She said nothing but repeated her original statement with no greater effect. Humiliation. I felt a tiny shard of relief, for the humiliation was shared rather than mine alone.

They muttered amongst themselves but there was no sign of anger, aggression or, indeed, the need to move on. I cast my eyes over their tank, an imposing but crudely constructed beast that looked as though it had seen a fair bit of combat. The turret in particular was scarred with bullet marks.

'I think they are from some other Soviet republic. They don't speak Russian. I think.'

I cursed inwardly but was relieved when I saw a Jeep pull up with four British soldiers inside; my troops and Lieutenant Pearson.

He dismounted and saluted. Although he was giving away the fact that I was an officer we were no longer at war and therefore had no enemies who might wish to take a pot shot. Since our Russian friends were looking on, I guessed that the little exchange served to highlight my rank but the fact that the three soldiers carried rifles probably had a greater effect.

'A problem, sir?'

'Language difficulties. These chaps seem to have got lost,' I said, rolling my eyes in such a way that the Russians couldn't observe the gesture. He chuckled. 'My interpreter is speaking Russian to them but they're looking on blankly.' Pearson cast his eye over Ingrid. 'She's German but speaks the lingo,' I explained.

'The problem is that the Reds have many different languages. Not all Russians are really Russians, if you take my meaning. These men could be Kazakhs or anything.'

By now, his troops had also dismounted and stood looking ready for action; sort of poised but casual. They were unmistakably front-line soldiers with that sallow, haunted look that comes with proximity to, and familiarity with, death. I had seen it in my pilots and I supposed they had seen it in me. Oddly, their presence was enough to spur the tank soldiers into action, for the Russkis began to pack up and then returned to their vehicle, whatever mission they had given themselves seemingly completed. Pearson looked over at me and smiled knowingly. We stepped back as the tank's huge engine roared into life. It idled for a few moments, the street vibrating rhythmically under my feet, and then lurched away, grinding the ancient cobbles beneath its tracks. For a second, I imagined myself as a German soldier armed with a rifle watching as one of these monstrous T34s bore down on me. It would have been utterly terrifying.

It trundled off down the street, trailing swirling coils of black smoke and then turned left down a narrow entry, clipping the kerb as it did so. In twenty seconds the noise had subsided and normal conversation was possible.

'Just chancers,' said Pearson. 'Out for a little jaunt. Wanted to see what would happen. I'm surprised they could even be trained to operate a tank. Anyway, these are your men. Three of my best troops. I'm sending some rations over. We'll try and get the phone link working from the *Rathaus* to camp and see what happens. I don't honestly think the locals will give you any problems but they might keep you busy nevertheless.'

When I looked at him quizzically, he added, 'I mean, I'm not sure if the electric is working or the sewers. They're not up for a fight. In fact they'll be glad that you're here instead of the Russians. They're terrified of them.'

'So they should be. They scare me.'

He laughed again.

'Any problems, just let me know.'

When Pearson had gone, I was still standing there with Ingrid and my tiny army of three. I felt alone and confused. A tightening band of pressure constricted my chest and I felt a wave of dizziness run through me.

'Are you fine, Squadron Leader?' asked Ingrid peering solicitously into my face. I nodded and began to feel better. Strangely, what had affected me was the same thing that I experienced, not in combat, but in the thought of combat to come. It was blind, paralysing fear. Anticipation was harder to deal with than the reality. With anticipation anything could happen whereas reality was… real.

'Let's go inside,' I said.

We stopped in the lobby and I took a moment to appraise my three soldiers.

'I'm Squadron Leader Cohen and for the time being I am the mayor of this town. I don't exactly know what we're up against, if anything, but I suppose we have to be on the lookout for stray Russians who might accidentally claim the town for Mr Stalin. We must be polite but firm with them and in our dealings with the locals. You have to adjust to the fact that they are not the enemy now. There are things that will need to be sorted out so we have to ensure they have food, water and whatever else they need.'

I spoke with a confidence I did not feel. This food, for instance. Where was I going to get that if the town started to run short? The same with water. What did I do if the water supply went off? What about the people who normally worked in the *Rathaus*? Where were they? What if they turned up? What if they wanted to be paid? I had no idea about any of these things.

'So make yourselves comfortable and get a brew on or whatever. I'll give you a shout if and when I need you.'

They seemed happy enough with that arrangement – telling soldiers to get a brew on was never the wrong thing to say – and it was my guess that time spent away from their unit was an opportunity to relax and take it easy. That was fine with me.

Ingrid and I returned to the office.

'What would you like me to do?' she asked.

'I don't exactly know. I'm hoping that I get some instructions through soon but in the meantime get your office sorted out and…'

'Make coffee?'

'I suppose so. Are the shops open? Can we buy things?'

'I will check.'

'Do you know the people who work here normally?'

'No.'

Her answer was emphatic, flat and delivered in such a way that she clearly thought the matter was closed. I felt no option but to drop my enquiries right there like unwanted luggage. She should have been providing me with answers, solutions but instead she had made herself something of a closed book. I was dismayed not only by her attitude but by the fact that I was ill-equipped to do anything about it; I was a fighter pilot, not a diplomat or an administrator. But this job had been dropped in my lap and I had to do it right or look very foolish.

I wondered why I even cared. I was a decorated officer. I had survived combat over and over again, this latest episode in my career should have been easy. I listened as Ingrid bustled about in her office. Maybe the job I'd been given *was* easy. Maybe I was worrying about nothing. I certainly hoped so. I was still adjusting to peace of that there was no doubt.

By mid-morning I had sifted through the paperwork lodged in my desk and rid myself of anything that looked out of date or irrelevant. It felt odd to see the Swastika and the German eagle used in letterheads and on every official document. I presumed that something altogether more British was in the pipeline for newly appointed officials like me so that all traces of Hitler and his regime could abruptly be taken out of circulation. The process did make me curious about Ingrid and her views but, somehow, I couldn't think of an approach to make on the subject; it was a delicate matter and I was too polite to just demand answers from her. But for all I knew she was a devout Nazi who had adored the Fuhrer, worshipped at his altar and was now mourning his loss. These people had loved him after all. You couldn't just turn such adoration off like the flick of a light switch.

Ingrid made coffee with real milk and sugar. She had invited the three soldiers to the tiny kitchen opposite, where she provided them with hot drinks and little shortbread biscuits.

'Where do you get this stuff from?' I queried.

'Things are becoming normal,' she said. I doubted if this was true. More than that, I didn't see how it was possible in this ravaged country.

I made another tour of the *Rathaus*, this time alone, and for no other reason than boredom and the chance to think. The stairs comfortably took my weight as if carved from a solid piece of teak, each footstep without a warning creak and I put this down to the quality of the craftsmanship involved in building the place a century before. Every aspect of the *Rathaus* felt bomb-proof, although this, unlike many German buildings, had never been tested.

I toured the first floor and paused to look out of a bay window at my little kingdom, spotting a left behind Nazi flag hanging forlornly down the side of another official-looking building. I presumed that someone hadn't received the memo about the end of the war and I resolved to remove the offending and offensive item when I had completed my impromptu tour. I wondered if I should be flying a Union Flag. No doubt it would cause offence, but what did I care?

On the street below, a baker's van dropped supplies off at a tiny shop. A handful of people milled about. Young men of fighting age were absent from this scene. I supposed that the few survivors would start drifting back at some point although they could hardly expect a hero's welcome in the circumstances. It was hard to picture how Germany could ever recover. Did it even deserve to recover, I mused?

So far, my duties had not been onerous and I allowed myself to believe that my time as mayor might be enjoyable. It seemed likely that the town's inhabitants didn't even know that a mayor had been installed and therefore would not be calling in. Perhaps they were more concerned with the return of POWs and recently discharged troops. There was so much to think about that worries about the payment of bills or interruption to the electricity would be low on any list of priorities. I hoped that was the case anyway.

I turned away from the window and began walking along the corridor again, noting the cleanliness and orderliness of everything. Someone had watered the plants. I gave a short laugh. Even as Germany had crumbled some functionary had seen fit to fill a watering can and attend to the *Rathaus* flora! Standards had to be maintained.

A green-painted door held my interest for a second and then for a second longer when I tried to open it. The door wouldn't budge and this only made me curious. The latter – my curiosity – vied with guilt for a time until I realised that since this was my fiefdom I had every right to know what lay beyond. I crouched to get a better look at the lock and it was immediately clear that the door was obstructed rather than locked. When I pushed again, the door yielded a little but sprang back. A harder shove gave the same result.

Next, I pushed with some force and whatever lay beyond moved with great resistance. I had the door open enough to squeeze through but by this point the smell was really putting me off. It was the smell of decay. More than that it was the smell of death and I knew that the shapeless object at my feet, barely visible in the dusty gloom of this hidden part of the building, was a body. With no light switch apparent, I withdrew and took stock of my options, of which there were few. The stink made me feel quite sick. In the course of the war, I had killed often but never before had I come so close to the end result of those actions.

With the help of my three soldiers we forced the door and dragged the corpse out onto the corridor where we could see it better in the light. Ingrid remained downstairs but I had told her what was going on. I suppose I thought that she might be shocked or dismayed by what we were doing but for all I knew she'd seen much worse.

He was wearing a dark suit with a Nazi party lapel badge and he'd been dead for a few days. There was no sign of a bullet wound or any injury.

'Poison,' said one of the troops, Lance-corporal Cleary who sounded like he was from the North-East. 'Probably couldn't bear the fact that they'd lost.' He bent down and removed the little enamel badge from the dead man and then slipped it into his pocket. 'Worth somethin' someday,' he said. I found it hard to imagine when such an object could ever hold any value. Surely Fascism was gone for good now? I imagined that he had a stash of loot somewhere: buttons, badges, a helmet, a P38, a flamethrower…

Maybe not the latter.

'I'll get Ingrid to get an undertaker or something,' I said.

'You'll need to record his identity, sir,' said Cleary. 'Keep account of what had happened to each of these bastards. They're tryin' to get out of the country.' He was already retrieving the dead man's wallet from inside his jacket as he said this. He discarded a thin collection of worthless bank notes and took the identity card out.

'Frank Huber. The *Bürgermeister*. Couldn't go on without Hitler, poor thing. I'll pass this lot on to Lieutenant Pearson when I see him.'

Just for a second, I felt aggrieved that he was taking the card to his own officer rather than passing it on to me but that feeling passed quickly; I wanted as little responsibility as possible. The roar of aero engines was a distraction as the remainder of my squadron flew overhead on their way to the airfield. It was an impressive sight and one with which I was unfamiliar since I generally flew with them rather than watching them from the ground.

'Your lot, sir?' queried one of the privates. For a moment I was proud to say that these were indeed my aircraft.

'Yes.'

'We was always glad to see the Typhoons turn up, sir. 'Specially when there was Panzers about.'

I acknowledged the war-winning contribution of the Hawker Typhoon with a modest nod of my head.

Chapter Six

Next morning I visited my squadron and got the distinct impression that I really wasn't needed. Everyone was friendly enough but those few days when war had become peace had created a different kind of bond between the men which I, though my short absence, had missed.

'They want to know when they can go home, sir,' said Phil. 'I don't think they're on the verge of mutiny or anything but there's a definite feeling that the job is done and it's only fair that they get to leave the RAF.'

'I don't blame them. However, at least they've got jobs while they're out here. I don't know what the situation will be when they do get demobbed. Millions of men all going after jobs that someone else did in their absence…'

Phil nodded and we walked in silence past the row of Typhoons. There was something magnificent about them but they certainly weren't the most elegant of aeroplanes, not like the lithe Spitfire. I felt an unexpected pang of sorrow knowing that they would either be sold or scrapped and that their usefulness had come and gone so quickly.

'Those Jerry planes were taken away,' said Phil as we drew level with the largest hangar. He lit a cigarette. A breeze caught the smoke and pulled it across the vastness of the runway. The tiny cloud came apart and seemed to disappear like a ball of sheep's wool torn asunder.

'Not surprised. Very advanced machines. We'll be using all those elements in our own designs soon enough.

The men who designed and built these things must have expected to win the war.'

'How are things in town?'

'My town?' I joked. 'Master of all I survey. I don't really know what I'm supposed to do. I think I was just the only senior officer available at the time.'

'We're not far from the Russkis here,' commented Phil.

'I know. Had a bit of a run in with them the other day. A T34.'

He chuckled.

'Next time that happens give us a call and we can send over a couple of Typhoons. It would be good to let them know that we're still armed to the teeth.'

I smiled at his suggestion. Remarkably it hadn't even occurred to me to call on my squadron of fighter-bombers to reinforce my point. Was I too detached from them now?

'How is your friend Ingrid doing?'

'Fine. She spoke to the Russians but it made no difference.'

'She spoke Russian?'

'Yes.'

'Doesn't that seem odd?'

'I hadn't thought about it.'

'Who exactly is she?'

'Well… she's… I don't know but she has been appointed to be my secretary.'

Phil gave me a withering look and I found myself slightly irritated.

'By who?'

'I don't know. By someone. It's not as if she just decided to lay claim to a job. For one thing, someone must be paying her.'

He looked doubtful as he said, 'I suppose so.'

He had planted a seed of doubt in my head or maybe, more accurately he had assisted in the germination of an existing seed. The fact remained that she served a purpose. When the locals did eventually start coming in with a litany of complaints about food, water and electricity, there was no point having someone like me sitting there not comprehending a word they uttered.

'I think you're being over-cautious, Phil. She's not the enemy. And those so-called 'werewolves' you warned me about? They haven't turned up either.'

'You're still wearing that revolver.'

'I have nowhere else to put it, that's all,' I said with the mildest exasperation.

He smiled. He seemed happy enough. The sun shone, the birds sang and he was enjoying his cigarette as if it was the greatest of all simple pleasures. Not for the first time I was overcome with deep perplexity about the absence of war. Something had been removed, excised from my body or my soul, and a gap was left which I had no idea how to fill. So many individual moments of terror had merged tumour-like in my being. That tumour had become part of me, a malevolent reminder of mortality. Now it was gone but nothing had filled the void.

'I was thinking about what you said, you know, about staying on in the RAF.'

'Oh. You think you might?'

'It might be fun. The new jets coming into service, less danger.'

'More boredom…'

'I suppose so. But don't you think there were times when boredom seemed okay?'

'Yes. I dreamed of boredom. In 1940, especially, sitting in the sun waiting for the telephone to ring...'

My thoughts went back to that beautiful summer. It might have been idyllic had it not been for the battle which was fought high above us in the sky. My stomach knotted. Phil had been a boy when the events I described had been occurring. For him it had been exciting enough to draw him into the RAF, for me it was simply terrifying. It wasn't just the thought of death, it was the manner of that death that I struggled with. So we'd sat in the sun and waited. We chatted, dozed, listened to music. Then the scramble. We'd be out of breath by the time we slipped into our seats, strapping ourselves in, starting the engine, the prop becoming a blur, the chocks pulled away and that first lurch as we moved. Taking control of the aircraft at least gave me enough to think about, took my mind off death, being burned and all the attendant horrors of air combat.

The Hurricane was a lumbering thing on the ground but an agile beast in the air. It was a great machine, a joy to fly, tough and with eight guns but joy soon turned to horror when we met up with the Luftwaffe, which was after all, the point of us being there. I saw some terrible sights, of course I did, but the worst part was that period of time when we came back to the airfield and took stock of our losses. In some cases it took a minute or two for me to figure out who hadn't returned. Often, we lost new pilots whose face I could not picture.

There was the hope that they had landed at the wrong airfield and would return later, or that they had successfully baled out. On occasion they finished up as POWs.

But all too often they were simply dead.

One of the first to go was our squadron leader. Dead. Lost in the Channel. Never seen again. One of the flight lieutenants got promoted to take his place until he too was lost and so it went. I started out as a sergeant, finished as a warrant officer, then commissioned before going to the Middle East.

Dead men. So many dead men. Will anyone remember them? The war is over and everyone just wants to forget. Who can blame them?

'Are you okay?'

It's Phil's voice which drags me out of my reverie.

'Yes. I think so. I just need time to adjust. I don't fully appreciate that the war is over.'

'Really?'

'Well, I do but my body, or something inside of me doesn't quite get it yet.'

I looked over at him and it was clear that he had no idea what I meant. I wasn't trying to be enigmatic if that is how it seemed.

'The end of hostilities should have felt different. I spent the moment with Margaret but maybe I needed to be here with the squadron. I don't know really. It's the sense of anti-climax I can't quite accept. Six years of war and then nothing.'

'Some people will miss the war,' reasoned Phil.

I looked over at him for a second trying to gauge whether he was joking or not.

'Yes, but I'm not one of them, that's the thing. I've been terrified for much of the time. Did you know I have flown more sorties than almost any other pilot in the RAF? Each time, putting my life at risk. It… ground me down.'

'You always seemed to take it in your stride.'

'You have to. You have to look calm and untroubled for the sake of your pilots but the strain I felt inside… Even now, when I think about it, I have a sense of despair.'

Phil looked on, shocked at my words.

'I had no idea. It's over now. You can relax.'

We continued our tour and stopped to speak to one of our sergeant fitters, a man of fifty who'd won the DCM in the infantry in the first war. His bright blue eyes were somewhat at odds with his red cheeks; years of drinking.

'Sergeant Kinlin. How are things?' I asked. Kinlin straightened and saluted.

'Just fine, sir. I'm keepin' busy. I've heard a rumour that we're gettin' jets, sir.'

'I've heard the same thing but the truth is I have no idea. You fancy a course on how to fix them?'

'Not really, sir. My time's almost up.'

I wasn't sure if he was talking about retirement or death but I smiled and moved on. This little tour felt like me going through the motions of being a commanding officer, almost as though my purpose had been removed. Who benefitted from my presence here? Whose life was enriched by talking to me? I could have just not bothered and the world would still have turned.

By the time I had communed with my parishioners, an unexpected thirst had developed and it took me a few moments to realise that I was, in fact, yearning for alcohol. Something in my mood communicated itself to Phil but the message became garbled on its short journey.

'Cigarette?'

'Trying to stop, Phil.'

'These are American,' he reassured me. I smiled.

'Even so, I'm trying to give up.'

'A beer in the mess, then?'

'Does it seem to you that I must either smoke or drink?'

'Well, why not? The war's over.'

'The war's over' was the refrain set to replace, *'there's a war on'*. It was timely enough but it didn't feel like an excuse to just do *anything*. Despite my objection I found myself in the mess with Phil and had a couple of pints, which was twice the number I had intended to consume. After lunch I made my way back to the *Rathaus* only to find a Russian GAZ jeep parked up outside, with an apprehensive-looking driver at the wheel. He looked at me and straightened in his seat as I made my way inside.

Ingrid was fending off a Russian officer when I reached the reception desk, her voice raised, insistent, but to my ears, frightened; no German wanted to have dealings with the Russians. I could legitimately and uncharitably have waved their fears away as the expected consequence of their Russian excursion four years previously; they deserved everything they got. But somehow my view on the subject had softened a little, perhaps because the Russians worried me deeply.

'What's going on?' I asked, imperiously, in a voice I don't think I had ever used. The officer turned to me, glowering, his face written through with such contempt that I felt like reminding him of Britain's part in the war and how we'd been fighting the Nazis when Russia had been hiding behind a ridiculous non-aggression pact with Hitler. However, two things stopped me. Firstly and quite inexplicably, I didn't want to hurt Ingrid's feelings and secondly, I spoke no words of Russian. Not even one.

'The colonel here insists that the town is in the Soviet Zone.'

I suppose this is what I had been dreading. We did indeed temporarily abut the agreed border between zones but I was quite sure he was mistaken.

'Tell him that he is wrong… no, use the word *mistaken*, if you know it. Tell him that he must make his objection to me in writing – in English – and I will pass it on to Brigadier Rea. Be polite but…'

The Russian was speaking again with quiet menace.

'What did he s…'

'He says that we are to leave the town building… the town hall… and that his men will be moving in today.'

I wondered where my three soldiers where when I needed them.

'Tell him what I said and explain that we cannot move out.'

Ingrid did as I requested. Well, she said something and I *assume* it was what I requested. For his part the Russian officer reddened and looked as though he might explode. To hear this from a German was galling indeed, I supposed. He was the victor, Ingrid the vanquished. Had I not been there, heaven knows how he would have reacted.

Belatedly, my section of troops joined us, standing, armed, in the lobby, alerted by the sound of raised voices. I felt reassured by their presence although I had the uncomfortable feeling that my nemesis had the entire Red Army at his disposal should things not go his way. I was surprised at how quickly these gallant men were becoming enemies rather than allies. There was no sense of having fought together against a common foe. As if to emphasize the point, Ingrid drew closer to me as if I could protect her from three million vengeful Soviets.

He wasn't ready to quit. He said something else, his words suffused with menace, indignation and spite but their precise meaning temporarily lost of course until Ingrid translated.

'He says he has a map which shows where the Red Army should be,' explained Ingrid nervously. However, it was apparent that he didn't actually have a map at all. Not in his possession. The lack of such somewhat weakened his argument but that seemed to be an omission which did nothing to lessen his determination.

'He says he will come back with more soldiers.'

It sounded like an idle threat but I wasn't sure. The only thing I was sure about was that we were not going to give way and relinquish control of the town on his say so.

'Tell him he is mistaken but if he would like to visit the officers mess at our base, I will make sure he is entertained tonight and given a lift back to camp afterwards.'

She looked at me aghast.

'Are you sure?'

The Russian looked on bewildered as we spoke.

'Yes.'

'But he is a… savage.'

I might have bristled at her description of my distinguished ally but things had moved on quickly in recent days. Besides which, she had a point really. He might have been an officer but there was something in his demeanour that spoke of the peasantry.

'I am trying to defuse the situation…'

'Defuse?' she queried.

'Like a bomb. Make things better.'

My interpreter nodded doubtfully and repeated my words or a facsimile thereof in Russian.

The Russian officer grunted, unconvinced by my placatory words, my offer of hospitality. These people viewed the world differently of course, with suspicion and doubt inculcated in them by a paranoid leader. It made little sense that he would come here to threaten me and receive a cordial invitation to the mess in return. Why would anyone respond in that way?

He blurted out something else and then turned on his heel. Ingrid didn't bother to translate.

'Friendly chap,' quipped Cleary.

'Yes. Just make sure he's buggered off, Corporal, and then do a quick tour of the square to make sure there aren't any others hanging around.'

The NCO nodded and led his troops out.

I turned to Ingrid and congratulated her on her steadfast response.

'What option did I have?' she replied, dismissively.

She had a point but she'd dealt with the situation well nevertheless. She wasn't soft. Maybe that's what Nazi-ism had done for the German people.

***

I slept at the mess and drove to the *Rathaus* each morning, meeting my secretary/interpreter/assistant at her desk. She was, although I hated to admit it, indispensable. Without her I would have been utterly lost, like a man being thrown bricks as he drowns. The Germans who came to seek help were for the most part surprisingly docile and accepting of their lot and again I was secretly impressed by their resilience as they shifted their allegiances and treated their conquerors with stiff courtesy. If it was grudging courtesy I didn't notice; the subtleties of language and demeanour were lost on me. They were survivors – literally – and defeat had visited them for a second time in thirty years.

Ingrid translated and I had to trust that my words were being delivered faithfully. I began to pick up a few German words simply through repetition of hearing them but the language remained an enigma to me.

We were dealing with requests to locate loved ones who had yet to return from the fighting, requests for money, disputes over the ownership of houses and complaints about Russian interference in daily matters. I learned quickly but had it not been for Ingrid, nothing would have been dealt with properly.

The Russians continued to be a nuisance but overall the Germans in the British sector were protected and the Soviet compulsion to seek revenge was tempered by our presence. It did get to the point where I instructed Phil to take a flight of aircraft up to patrol the skies, taking care to skirt the border with the Russian zone and this he did, re-asserting our authority in a blatant reminder of British air power. I fully expected a reprimand for my unilateral sabre rattling but none came and the gesture seemed to work; complaints against the Red Army were noticeably reduced.

Through all of this I had some sympathy for the Russians of course. They had suffered terribly as a result of Nazi barbarity, their casualties running into the millions. That they were scarcely treated better by Stalin was of little importance in this context, since it was he who had rallied his people to defend the motherland. As the days wore on, I had to remind myself of the terrible crimes committed in the name of National Socialism. The wearied but respectful Germans who visited each day seemed to epitomise some sort of re-birth of civilisation as if they had been selected for this task. Biblical stoicism seemed to prevail… Collectively they might be a phoenix just beginning to rise from the ashes but I didn't really want to ascribe such noble imagery to these people and their lost cause. That was why I had to make myself recall the terrible cost of Nazi – German – actions, over the last six years. I didn't want them to get off so easily, to think that their crimes could be forgiven and forgotten. I needed more than an obsequious tip of the hat to make me consider universal forgiveness. At times anger battled with fatigue and I felt barely able to carry on.

This morning a middle-aged lady was asking for news of her husband and son, both of whom had been sent to fight in Russia. The husband had been in the Luftwaffe, the son in the army. As usual it was Ingrid who spoke and recorded the details as my anger simmered. The woman was slim but not emaciated, her clothes worn but not ragged. The unknown status of her loved ones may well have been a personal tragedy but *she* was alive and had food and a place to live. I wondered what she had thought about the concentration camp built practically on her doorstep. Did she still despise the Jews?

When she had gone, Ingrid turned to me and asked if I was okay.

'Did you know I'm a Jew?' I said, my words edged with unfathomable desperation. I studied her face as she absorbed this information, looking for signs of fear or disgust.

'I thought there was a chance that…'

'So what do you think of me? What do you think of having to work with a filthy Jew?'

I spat the words out and she looked on speechless, horrified.

And yet it was not the knowledge that seemed to create this horror so much as the manner in which it had been delivered. I wondered then if she actually cared what religion I subscribed to and if my ire had been misdirected. The matter lay unresolved. The next customer was now standing before us, literally cap in hand.

His problem, as relayed to me, was that his house needed repairs and he had no money to get them done. Ingrid, still wary, looked on as I considered the matter.

'Take his name and address and I will find out what can be done.'

She explained this to the man and he left his details in a small notebook after which there was a hiatus.

'Coffee, Squadron Leader?'

This was clearly her answer to every problem, possibly because the ingredients for a hot drink was all she possessed.

'Please. And call me Saul if you like.'

Knowing that I was Jewish – that's if she hadn't always known – I half expected her to recoil at the use of my first name. But, instead, she smiled and said my name just once as if practicing its sound.

Giving her permission to use my first name felt like a form of fraternisation and more than that, I felt weak having given it away so lightly when I was fully justified in despising Ingrid and her fellow Germans. Despising them for eternity, that is. Telling her my name was like an apology but what had she done to deserve it? We weren't equals, could never be friends, she'd been on the losing side and I'd been on the winning side. She was lucky to have a job. She was lucky, now that I thought about it, to have her life, a luxury not afforded to a great many in the greater German empire.

But it was done now. I couldn't retract permission to use my first name. She brought coffee and we sat in silence as sunlight streamed through the windows above the

Rathaus double doors. Our newly established familiarity felt like a betrayal. I was betraying my country and the people who'd died to defeat Germany, but there was something else and I was shocked when I realised what that something else was.

I was betraying Margaret.

The realisation troubled me. Had I done something wrong?

Over-reaction it may have been but I felt the blood drain from my face and that tight band of tension encircle my rib cage. The room swam before my eyes and I felt as if I was viewing everything through a sunlit mist that pulsated in time to my heartbeat. I had no right to this shared contentment, or rather she had no right to it. Those odd sensations described above passed quickly.

'Are you fine, Saul?' she asked, a certain controlled alarm evident in her voice.

The fact that she so easily used my name – the name of a Jew – grated a little but I nodded. After all it was me who, in a moment of weakness, had suggested dropping the formality of calling me by my rank.

'Yes. I'm fine. Sometimes I take a funny turn. Not ideal when you're a pilot.'

She smiled and nodded. I had the fleeting impression that she was eager to say something more and that night, as I tried to sleep, I would interrogate my brain for clues as to what this might have been. My favourite theory would be that she was going to ask why I had spared her the trip to the concentration camp. I was glad she didn't ask for I had no real answer. The truth was she had no more right to be spared that ordeal than any other German. It was increasingly clear that tens of thousands of Jews and undesirables had been executed – no one yet knew how many and possibly never would – and it was simply impossible that the civilian population knew nothing about it as most of them claimed.

I dealt with a few more locals that day but what had never been more than a trickle slowed and eventually stopped to become a drought.

'We should arrange for the mayor to be buried,' I said, recalling the dead man I had found upstairs. I supposed that the man, an ardent Nazi, deserved dignity in death. Maybe, apart from being a supporter of Hitler, he had been a good soul… Was there some kind of balance at work where one's good deeds could be measured against one's bad deeds? Had a Nazi ever tipped those scales in favour of virtue or did evil always outweigh the good? It wasn't a matter of cheating in an exam or telling a lie. The evil of Hitler's acolytes reached far beyond the mundane, the forgivable.

'Saul?'

Stirred from my reverie, I looked over at Ingrid as if seeing her for the first time.

'You looked lost.'

I nodded and drank my coffee, not wishing to share my reservations with her. She was neither a friend nor a confidante and there were still times when I struggled with the idea that she was not an enemy. I had my job to do and I wanted to do it properly but the idea that I might like or care about any of these people who came to me was abhorrent. It all came down to one singular fact – one which sounded a little childish when spoken – they, the Germans, had started the war. There was no getting away from it. Not only that but they had taken that war as an excuse to murder countless innocent people. And that's what it was. Murder. It couldn't be dressed up as anything else. Images of that pink hill in the camp jumped around in my mind as if illuminated by the flash bulbs of a dozen cameras.

I felt sweat break out from the pores on my face and on my back. My heart pounded and I felt weak as if I might be laid low by some tricky virus. I sensed Ingrid back off, as though she had just discovered that I was actually a bomb rather than a human being. Anger built inside me, lava in a volcano, ready to break out.

And then the anger was gone. I felt weakened by the experience and, not for the first time, wondered what was wrong with me. Had the war become an addiction and if so, what did I do about it other than start another one?

I looked at Ingrid and wondered if I had misjudged her. Perhaps she had been one of the Germans who had acquiesced merely from a lack of an alternative. There had been no practical way to resist Hitler I supposed. I sat heavily at my desk.

'Maybe you need a doctor?' she suggested.

'There's nothing wrong with me,' I said sharply and a faint shadow of hurt passed over her features and was gone like mist.

However, she might have been correct, although some stupid combination of pride and stubbornness prevented me from accepting her judgement. In practical terms, what precisely was I going to say to a doctor should I choose to visit one?

'Would you like a cigarette?' she said, the first time she had made this offer. A cigarette was precisely what I wanted.

'I'm trying to give up,' I replied, ungraciously. I found it easy to set aside my natural good manners when talking to Ingrid. After all, she was just a German and what counted for less right now? What was worse than being German now that the veneer of culture and civilisation had been scratched away to reveal what really lay in the soul of that nation? Did she deserve greater respect? Did she deserve compassion? I doubted it. I felt my anger rise as I considered these matters.

I didn't recognise the brand of cigarettes she had and wondered if they were special issue for the Nazi party or the SS.

Ingrid was attractive by any standards. Maybe not quite in the same league as Hedy Lamarr but close enough and quite un-German in appearance with dark hair and delicate features. She could have been… Jewish.

That was impossible of course but the realisation that she might have been was startling nevertheless. But just supposing she was, in fact Jewish, and had remained hidden in plain sight throughout Hitler's terrifying reign? I looked at her again and the question partially formed in my brain before evaporating like a summer puddle.

'I could make your tea tonight,' she said, suddenly.

'My tea? Er… why would you do that?'

'Well, just to…'

'No thank you. It wouldn't be right.'

She blushed but regained her composure quickly and I felt immediately and unaccountably guilty. I had to explain.

'We're not supposed to fraternise.'

'Aren't we already fraternising?'

'We work together. Quite different. Also, I'm married.'

She laughed, coyly.

'It wasn't a proposition. I was just being kind.'

'Well, thank you but it wouldn't be fair to eat your food when it is hard to find.'

'I have plenty,' she said and instantly seemed to regret her candour. I could have asked her how she had managed this feat when so many Germans were hungry if not starving but that was only one of many questions I had for her.

'Maybe another time. When things have settled.'

She nodded and busied herself with some pointless paperwork task.

After that, things were a little bit frosty.

Chapter Seven

'They are having Herr Huber's funeral today.'

I looked up from my desk where I had been writing a letter to Margaret. It was Ingrid who had spoken. I was unsure what my response should be. My office window was open, birds sang and the smell of newly cut grass was carried on a warm breeze. The world felt, temporarily, like a good place.

'Herr Huber? Who is Herr Hub…'

'The *Bürgermeister*. Your predecessor.'

'I see. I'd forgotten he was called that. If you want to go, that is fine. Was he a friend?'

'No. I meant that you should go. You should be respectful by attending.'

'I don't think so. He died clutching a portrait of Hitler. I can't really be seen to approve and I don't think we'd have been friends.'

She looked angry and for a few moments I questioned whether or not her anger was justified; was I being terribly disrespectful? However I swiftly concluded that it was not my place to attend the funeral of a stranger and prominent local Nazi, just as it was not her place to pass judgment on my decision.

I said, 'you look angry. The man was a Nazi. I am a Jew. We have yet to find out how many Jewish people the Nazis killed, so I do not feel inclined to wish the man well.'

I spoke firmly but kept my tone even. My choice of words was designed to suggest that, in my view, Ingrid had no connection to the Nazi Party or to the atrocities committed in its name. Of course I had no idea if this was the case. I was being diplomatic for the sake of good relations but this didn't extend to the deceased *Bürgermeister*, whose loyalty to Hitler was not in question.

'But if he was a friend of yours, you can have time off to go to the funeral so long as there is no suggestion that you are there as my representative.'

'He wasn't a friend,' she said, plainly.

'But you knew him? He was a prominent figure?'

Ingrid didn't answer.

'You *did* know him?'

'No.'

The matter seemed closed and yet curiously unresolved. Ingrid turned on her heel – presumably in disgust – and left me alone in my office. No coffee this morning.

***

'Quiet night?'

The soldiers of my tiny private army looked at me and confirmed that the night had, indeed, been quiet.

'They're good as gold, sir, the Jerries,' said Lance-corporal Cleary.

'They've had enough.'

'They deserved it,' he continued.

'Oh yes. Definitely.' I sighed.

'Brew, sir?'

'Coffee. Milk, eight sugars,' I confirmed. 'British soldiers… never far from a brew.'

'Keeps us goin'.'

For a moment it didn't matter that he was an NCO and I was an officer; we were united in our need for a hot drink. There was a bizarre, classless kinship involved which I couldn't really explain. It was perhaps a ritual which rendered class a temporarily discardable consideration. He made the coffee and sat.

'When did you join up, sir?'

'I was in the RAF before the war. A regular. You?'

'Conscripted. 1941. Dragged kicking and screaming.'

I laughed at his description. The manner in which you had been drawn into military service had long since ceased to matter. Conscripts, regulars, reservists, volunteers, had all stood shoulder to shoulder in a metaphorical sense at least. And it was true to say that some of the conscripts had served with greater distinction than their regular counterparts.

'You'll get to go home soon,' I assured him. Even as I uttered the words I couldn't quite picture this happening. I knew it would, but the sheer scale of the problem was huge; millions of men in uniform thrust back into a labour market that had managed without them for six years... how did they expect to do it, I wondered?

As if reading my mind he said, 'it'll be strange though, sir. People back home see it on the newsreels but they don't really know what it's been like. I feel like I shouldn't have to work ever again. There shouldn't be anything more required from me.'

I smiled sadly. I knew exactly how he felt because I felt the same way.

'Well, at least this should be a cushy number for a while.'

'So long as those Russkis don't come back,' he warned.

I nodded and we sipped coffee in friendly silence. I mused about the difference in our rank, our standing. In the years of war Cleary had risen to the lowly rank of lance-corporal but there was something about his calm assurance which strongly suggested that he could have progressed much further had he so chosen. And then there was me, who had risen far higher than was really warranted. I had just gone along with it but I hadn't done anything outstanding in the process. I hadn't inspired anyone. I had accepted promotion because it seemed... what as the word I sought? – unhelpful? ungrateful? – to refuse it.

'It's hard to see how the Jerries will re-build their country, sir. I mean bits of it are completely flattened.'

'It will take years.'

'And they'll be short of men to do the work too.'

'That's a good point. Maybe they'll hire British builders to do the job for them,' I said. 'It's all been pointless, hasn't it?' I mused. I didn't necessarily expect to draw my companion into a discussion about the course of the war but he responded at once and intelligently.

'We had to defeat the Nazis though, sir.'

'True. But we've blown their country to bits and then we'll have to build it back up. It's not exactly progress.'

'But better than letting them have their own way. They'd never have stopped.' He sipped his coffee. 'But now we've got to worry about the Russians. They can't be trusted.'

He was right of course, but for now they were our supposed allies.

***

If things had been a little frosty between me and my assistant, it didn't last long. Perhaps she had taken time to reflect on my decision to not attend Huber's funeral and come round to accepting my point of view. Or perhaps she just knew which side her bread was buttered on. There was always room for pragmatism, especially in this uncertain world.

This morning she smiled as I entered the office and began making my customary coffee.

'I have bought cakes for us,' she announced holding up a plain paper bag. 'The bakery is open again,' she explained.

So, this morning in addition to my coffee, I had a slice of cake which she had laid on a tiny porcelain plate, whilst she ate hers from the bag. Layers of choux pastry and cream with some kind of jam belied a confection that had all the flavour of cardboard and the texture to match. It was chewy to the point of near indigestibility but we gamely ate and drank with the appearance of two friends enjoying a well-earned break.

I wasn't even hungry.

Ingrid dabbed at her mouth with a handkerchief when she finished and I caught a glimpse of lip stick on the white linen as she returned it to her bag. It was only then I noticed the make-up that she wore and it gave me cause to wonder how she alone had circumvented the privations of war when most others had not. Ingrid, I realised, seemed to live up to pre-war standards. It wasn't wealth she was displaying but good breeding and… comfort. How did she manage it?

A small mountain of paperwork had formed on my desk. More of a hillock, really. It came from a variety of sources and the bulk of it was in German. Up to now I had employed a simple but inefficient system with which to deal with my bureaucratic burden; if it was written in English, I dealt with it at once and if it was written in German I either gave it to Ingrid or left it in the pile until such times as I had learned enough of the language by osmosis to read and digest.

As I said, it was inefficient. I spoke very few words of German. The victors lived in an English-speaking cocoon in which the need to learn the language of the natives was obviated by the mere fact that it was us who were in charge. If our former enemies wanted our assistance then they had to find a way to communicate with us. It was arrogance of a sort but generally we were contemptuous of the locals and enjoyed the fact that the so-called master race had been humbled and brought to heel. It had taken six years, something of a slog in anyone's books.

I pulled a face as I let my gaze ascend the pile of envelopes and letters. I supposed that each item was important to someone.

'Do you feel that you're being well-treated by us?' I asked Ingrid. I didn't really care how she answered; I only sought to delay my assault on the pile.

'Yes.'

She spoke quietly and without looking up somehow managing to make the word 'yes' sound like 'no'. Whatever her meaning, we had quickly stumbled into a conversational *cul-de-sac*. I kept going however. This discourse had been embarrassingly brief and I felt compelled to make it into something more.

'What do you think the future holds for Germany?'

This time a yes or no answer would not suffice. I had posed the biggest question of the day, one which must have played on the mind of every citizen. This was the beginning of a new era. The changes would have to be immense.

'I don't know. We must rebuild our cities and start to make things… Cars and…'

'Radios?' I suggested.

'We all have radios. That is how they told us what was going on and how to behave. I was thinking of things like refrigerators and others that the Americans have.'

'The Americans?'

'They are rich. Germany will need to become like America.'

'Not like Russia?'

She paled in a manner which denoted genuine horror.

'Not like Britain?'

She just shrugged.

'There is no use for tanks and Messerschmitts now.'

'What about all the Nazis? What should be done with them?'

For a fraction of a second, almost forgetting about everything which had gone before, I felt sorry for her. How was she supposed to answer that? How many true Nazis had there been in Germany? Was it one hundred? Was it ten thousand? A million? Ten million? Had any of them *not* been Nazis? Were there degrees of Nazi-ism; forced Nazis, sceptical Nazis, moderate, convinced, evangelical, fanatical? Where had Ingrid fitted on this spectrum of hatred?

'They should be… made to think differently,' she said without conviction.

'Re-educated?'

'If that's what you call it. We should deal with the papers on your desk,' she said, changing the subject. I nodded.

Ingrid came over and lifted a slice of documentation, returning to her own desk and dumping it there with an obvious show of disdain.

'Lots of bureaucrats in Germany. Papers for everything. Papers to work. Papers to prove you're not a Jew. Papers to prove you *are* a Jew. Papers to move. Papers to get coal or petrol.'

'It's the same everywhere,' I said, smiling. 'Well, not the Jewish thing. We'll have new paperwork soon, don't you worry.'

She worked quickly, decisively. I had no idea on what basis she was discarding one form or letter and keeping another for further action but she seemed to know what she was doing. Underlying this display of efficiency was the fact that I had no interest in how she performed this task. It all came back to one salient point: we were dealing with people who'd been defeated and who, in my opinion at the time, had no right to any help.

In a show of support I lifted a small section of the pile and leafed through it. These were mimeographed forms, replete with the symbols of Nazi Germany and the incredibly long words of the native language, words which would be phrases in English: *Schlüsselhalter für Benzinpumpen, Rathausschrieber, Entwässerungsingenieur.*

I could have asked Ingrid what they meant – she sat just a few feet away after all – and some of them made partial sense. *Benzin* was petrol. *Pumpen* had to mean pump. I thought that *schlüssel* was key. *Rathaus* was town hall.

But instead of making any effort whatsoever, I merely transferred these pieces of paper to a new pile which would eventually resemble the original pile but in reverse order and two feet to the right on my desk. I was overcome with bureaucratic inertia, riding on a tidal wave of apathy, tapping into hitherto undiscovered reserves of *ennui*. This wasn't really the sort of job for a man like me. I wanted to live with Margaret on some tiny island, writing novels and tending to a few farm animals, perhaps growing our own food.

I'd had enough of flying and of fighting but that didn't seem to mean that I was ready for the life of a desk warrior.

'What would happen if we just ignored all this paper, Ingrid?'

She looked over at me, her face gently creased in Teutonic confusion. I knew exactly what she was thinking, *why would anyone ask such a question?* However, the fact remained that I had won and she had lost. I could ask whatever questions I liked and she had no right to judge. German efficiency hadn't been enough to overcome British ingenuity, American might and Russian capacity for sacrifice. As a result, I asked the questions and she answered them.

I chuckled quietly as she formulated an answer in German which she would then translate into English.

'Why do you laugh?' she asked.

'British people laugh at things,' I said.

'Germans laugh also,' she said with such gravity that her words sounded like a lie. An image of an SS officer chortling to himself as he sent a mother and child to their deaths in a gas chamber flitted through my mind and my latent anger rose like bile.

'So, what would happen if we ignored these papers?'

She thought about that.

'They would either get sent to us again – but I doubt that would happen because everything has changed. Or perhaps nothing would happen. These are people who want to trace their missing family members or get their coal delivered. Or they want money or whatever.'

'If they are prisoners of war with the British, or, I suppose Americans, then we can probably trace them. If the Russians took them, I don't know,' I said.

'The Russians. They have hundreds of thousands of our soldiers. They are savages.'

Before I could stop myself, I said, 'but you did invade their country.'

It was enough to end the conversation with terrible abruptness. I had forgotten that the Germans thought they were doing the world a favour by invading Russia. Her face betrayed no emotion but she turned away slightly in her seat, making it clear that she didn't wish to engage in any form of communication. My guilt at bringing about this situation passed in the time it took to blink. I think she hated me at that moment but I didn't care.

A few minutes later my little army of three turned up and I instructed Cleary to conduct a patrol of the town just to make sure that the Russians hadn't begun moving back in.

'Don't shoot anyone unless you really have to,' I joked. Cleary chuckled and Ingrid frowned. I suppose in her defence I hadn't specified if the people he *wasn't to shoot* were German or Russian; maybe British humour, such as it was, didn't bear translation. I didn't care. The little band left without fuss, each one ready for battle… or maybe just a skirmish. At that moment I felt oddly contented. Perhaps it was the coffee, or the trace of warmth in the morning air, the sunlight or the feeling of having carried out my not too onerous duties for the day.

My desk and my wood-panelled office took on a homely air; understated luxury or token prestige. I was the mayor. The Boss. *Der Bürgermeister.* The best thing about it was that I was required to do very little and there was no danger involved. I felt free of stress in a way that hadn't been possible for years.

I surveyed my surroundings, picking out the spot on the wall where a picture of the Fuhrer had once hung and the ornate carving above the dado rail. Some kind of hunting scene was depicted: horses, hounds, foxes, bows and hedges. I was reminded of the Bayeux tapestry. To my untutored mind the carvings were actually quite crude as if the town hadn't been able to afford the services of the best craftsmen but still, it lent my surroundings some sort of discreet grandeur.

My predecessor had sat in this same chair at this same desk, master of all he surveyed, functionary of the powerful Nazi empire, a man to be feared, loathed and respected in some unfathomable combination. I felt as though I wielded greater power than him simply because I was the tip of some conquering spear. Smiling, I wiped a layer of dust from my telephone receiver.

'Why do you smile?' asked Ingrid, breaking into my reverie. Her tone was soft, her initial ire or discontent swept away perhaps.

'I was feeling happy.'

'Happy?'

Her tone suggested that my emotion did not fit the situation or was something unobtainable in these immediate post-war times. Did I need to explain the concept of happiness to her, or merely why such a feeling was possible?

'The sun is shining. The war is over.'

She nodded doubtfully, perhaps in faint recognition that the war's end hadn't gone according to the Nazi plan. They'd been told to expect something quite different, that they would be the masters of everything. Now they owned only what we permitted them to own.

I could have asked her more about herself and perhaps that is what I should have done but she'd been working for me for days now and I had accepted her presence, accepted her help and, I suppose, her friendship without querying who she really was. It had got to the point where it seemed impertinent to ask, too intrusive.

The problem was that I had not treated her with sufficient disdain and that had set the template for all our subsequent dealings. Had I been pre-warned that she was sitting in my office, I might have begun our association with a display of hauteur designed to establish the nature of our relationship which in no way included any level of friendship or equality. But as it was, she had practically ambushed me and my natural instinct was to be polite and accepting. It was too late to try to put her in her place and when I thought about it, I couldn't see any useful reason for doing so, especially when she was central to any negotiations I might have with the gallant but provocative Red Army.

'Would you rather drink tea?' she asked one day.

'I drink it sometimes but coffee is fine. Why do you ask?'

'The English like tea but I didn't have any so I made you coffee each time.'

'And now you have?'

She shook her head in incomprehension.

'I'm asking if you now have tea,' I explained.

'Ah. Yes.'

'It's fine. I have come to prefer coffee.'

'The soldiers would like tea?'

'Yes, but British soldiers always have the means for making tea. It's why we won the war,' I quipped. Ingrid looked unhappy at the reminder and I was pleased to discover that I still didn't care.

Chapter Eight

I had sent Cleary and his men out to find a union flag which could be flown from the *Rathaus*, having decided that this was a means of reinforcing the British claim to the town. They were gone some time and I began to worry that they might have strayed into Soviet territory and been taken prisoner; increasingly our allies were taking a hard line over minor slip-ups. It wasn't hard to picture my three soldiers locked up and under guard accused of spying for the imperialist British et cetera. I hope that wasn't the case for they were my primary defence against Russian intransigence and I really could not do without them.

      As I waited, the wind carrying spray from left to right across the town square, I thought about Margaret and home. I wouldn't ask for much, from the remaining portion of my life I had decided. Having survived the war I would be more than content with a little house, maybe a car, a job in an office – something I had no experience of – and marriage to Margaret. Children... maybe, although I hadn't thought that far ahead. My dreams were simple, repetitive, modest, even stunted in a way because I simply never got past the basic requirements in this inventory of civilian life as I pondered a future which bore no relation to my past. The notion that I might become bored or dissatisfied after the intensity of air combat never really took hold but instead fluttered like a moth in the peripheral vision of my mind's eye.

      Boredom was fine.

It stemmed, I assumed, from inactivity but I could use the time to do something that wasn't boring, although what that might be was never clear. With boredom came certainty or perhaps it would be more accurate to say that boredom stemmed from uncertainty. Whichever. It was fine.

The flag pole, bereft of a flag, rattled in the wind and the lanyard upon which I intended to fasten our flag hummed tautly like some arcane instrument capable of producing only one note. Below on the pavement a few people made their way to work, mainly women and older men and I tried to picture what jobs they did and wondered who paid them. Had they been British, I suspected they would have stayed at home in the circumstances, awaiting definite instructions to return and guarantees of payment, both of which were reasonable conditions. However, these were Germans, instilled with an innate sense of unquestioning service, an almost manic obedience. Even though the regime they had lived under was no more they still had an unshakeable belief in their duty, I supposed. It might have been admirable.

My job here was easy and safe. Ingrid, speaking the language, dealt with everything, often without consultation, which suited me fine since she probably understood what to do better than I ever could. Perhaps she even cared for these people. I most certainly did not.

I continued to watch the new day unfolding with a pleasant detachment, bordering on some form of muted elation. A young woman planted bulbs in a flower bed unaware that she was being watched. Another scrubbed the fountain, presumably in preparation for the time when its water supply would be returned. They worked diligently, using plenty of elbow grease. *Did the Germans have a word for that?* I smiled. *What was elbow grease exactly, I wondered? Where did you buy it? Did it come in a tin?*

The scent of bread reached me. Birds sang. The young women called to each other, exchanging a joke, laughing as if the world was a happy settled place. I heard my secretary typing, the staccato rhythm at odds with the general serenity of this time, this place. What was she typing? At whose request was she doing so? I posed these questions within the confines of my brain and found that I didn't care what the answers might be. Something – perhaps it was adrenaline – suddenly surged through me and my previous contentment gave way to elation. I was alive! Of course I was but it had taken this long for the news of my own personal survival to really make any emotional impact on my consciousness. Only now could I truly believe and appreciate the fact that my life would continue for the foreseeable future.

The idea of living in peace had been an abstract until now, unlocked perhaps by the scenes of normality unfolding in the square beneath my *Rathaus* window. Birdsong drowned out the discordant clacking of the typewriter and I felt no compunction to move or to break my own reverie. A tiny Citroen van pulled onto the square and its driver began unloading supplies at the bakery. The van was matt black as if designed for use at night and in secret, and, from this vantage point, appeared to be constructed from corrugated iron. It was angular, noisy, utterly un-Germanic. I wondered how it had ever been pressed into service so far from the country of its manufacture.

The driver and the baker chatted on the street for a few moments. Both were older men – sixties at a guess and neither seemed to have suffered unduly from a lack of sustenance; they both enjoyed a comfortable girth. They laughed as if the war had never happened and I hated them, bitter resentment like a puncture wound from a stiletto, there and gone. The little van – a tin shed on wheels – drove off sounding like a child's mechanical toy and it was then that I spotted Ingrid darting down the street and into a side alley.

***

'So, where do you think she was going?' asked Phil. He raised his glass to his lips and drank deeply, his eyes fixed on mine.

'I have no idea. She was being very...' I'd had three drinks by now and my brain was just slightly fuddled. 'I can't think of the word, I need.'

'Furtive,' said Phil, proudly.

'Yes. That's exactly what she was being.' The strange scene opened up once again in my mind, replaying so that I could pass on the details to my subordinate. 'There was something in her actions which suggested – I don't know – secrecy or something. It's the fact that she had sneaked out without telling me... had used my absence to run off down the street.'

'And you didn't ask her where she'd been?'

'No.'

'I would have,' said Phil, assertively. 'Definitely would have.'

'Yes, but perhaps it's not my business.'

He made a noise like 'pshaaw' which indicated disbelief or disdain.

'Saul, you're the boss,' he reminded me. He took another drink. I took another drink. Perhaps the consumption of alcohol would bring clarity. You never knew.

'Maybe I am but maybe it was none of my business.'

'She works for you. If it was Sergeant Prior sloping off, you'd ask him where he was going.'

Prior was the squadron clerk. Prior would never 'slope off'.

I related this fact to Phil and he gave a shrug of acceptance. For a moment I lost track of whether or not comparing Prior's behaviour with that of Ingrid had strengthened my case or weakened it. The alcohol was eroding my powers of perception and deduction. I needed more practice. At that point, as if reading my thoughts, Tommy Wilson thumped a fresh pint of beer in front of me.

Tommy was a pilot officer. Fresh faced, he would nevertheless have become an ace had there been enough Germans to shoot down by the time he'd got into the war.

'There you go, sir. You won the war!'

'By myself?'

'Near enough. Can you recommend me for a DFC?'

'Because you bought me a pint?'

He nodded eagerly. I gauged that he was on his fifth or sixth pint by this point.

'I'll check the regulations tomorrow and see what the criteria are,' I joked. 'It might be two pints but let me check first.' Tommy raised his glass in mock salute and lurched off.

'Where was I?'

'You were defending that German whore who works for you,' said Phil casually.

I raised my eyebrows at this description. It seemed harsh and inaccurate. Whatever flaws she had, and there were doubtless many, did not warrant such a damning opinion. I opened my mouth to disagree, to defend her but then clamped it shut again. I barely cared enough. Who was I to judge really? Why take a positive view of a German, after all? Alcohol was suppressing my natural humanity or setting free my antipathy... either way, the result was the same.

Phil spoke again, having warmed to his subject, his tongue loosened by the beer which I suspected was stronger than the stuff we were used to.

'You can't trust her. Whore.'

'Whore?'

'Sorry, *Nazi* whore.'

'I don't get the impression that she was...'

'A Nazi?' he snapped. 'I hope you're not falling for all that bloody tosh about them not being Nazis. Very convenient to claim that you never supported Hitler now that he's gone.'

'I suppose some of them didn't, Phil. It would have been impossible to stand up against the Nazis. What would have happened if it had all taken place in Britain?'

'No Englishman would follow a scoundrel like that,' he said with a sort of slurred defiance.

I smiled. He was wrong but it suited him to believe such a thing. He was every bit as indoctrinated as a Nazi.

'Think about it, Saul. What do you actually know about her?'

'Nothing but what difference does it make? The war is over. They have to rebuild their country. Look at what happened last time.'

Phil scoffed and for a moment I had the impression of stepping outside my body and watching our exchange like a phantom hovering above our table. In that tiny period of time I wondered exactly why I was defending Ingrid when Phil's views roughly matched my own.

Around us, the mess was filling up and from some unknown source a bottle of clear alcohol had appeared. I examined the label.

'Vodka?' I said.

'Polish stuff. Eric found it. He is kindly re-distributing it. Booty. The spoils of war.'

Eric was another of my pilots, a cheery Scot.

'Right. Okay.' Through my fogged brain I noticed that we had no glasses to drink our newly acquired spirit from. I made no comment.

'She could be a spy or a saboteur.'

'Dear God, what would be the point of being either of those things? They've lost already. There is no one to spy for. What could she find out? What good would it do anyone?'

'You're more trusting than I am,' said Phil. 'We need to keep on top of these bastards, never let them rise again.'

'It's not going to be like that.' I had the feeling that this conversation was merely a replay of an earlier conversation. If so, I couldn't remember who it was with.

Maybe it was just my subordinate's bellicose manner that was familiar rather than the precise content of the discourse. 'Having flattened the place we're going to help them re-build it,' I said with casual authority, although I couldn't remember who had informed me of this intention, if anyone. I fully expected Phil to argue against my assertion but instead he blew air from his lips, shook his head and slumped in his seat as if suddenly punctured.

'I might have drunk too much.'

I laughed and said, 'probably. I think I have too.'

With that established, Phil stood.

'I'll get a couple of glasses for this vodka,' he said, his previous assertion regarding over-indulgence seemingly swept away like dust on a sideboard. I didn't challenge him although somewhere at the back of my brain, somewhere almost hidden, I heard a muffled voice pleading with me to stop this chemical assault on my nervous system. In his absence I cast my glance around the room, looking for familiar faces and finding almost none. I was assailed by guilt, then elation, then confusion in quick succession. When my companion returned, he practically slammed the two glasses onto our table as a sign of intent I supposed, and then sloshed a healthy measure of spirit in to each of them. We unwisely dispatched these and Phil refilled our glasses.

Despite my befuddled state, I fully understood what was happening to me and what the likely consequences would be but, showing a lack of both leadership and common sense, I followed the younger man's lead, toppling, metaphorically at least, towards oblivion. Why shouldn't I do so, I reasoned? I'd won the war... with some help. I'd taken to the air countless times, flown into danger... My justifications came easily as if practised, learned by rote.

The mess was noisy, a dozen conversations merging incomprehensibly into a drifting, almost pulsating aural cloud. Music played but I couldn't recall there being a record player being there. Smoke fumes displaced the breathable air and at once I felt the desire to leave that place and stumble off into the cool summer evening for a period of temporary oblivion...

'What?' said Phil over the din.

'Er, temporary oblivion, I think.'

'Is there such a thing? Can oblivion be temporary?'

How had this esoteric conversation started? I had no idea.

Phil supped and looked at me with the eyes of serious drunk.

'Remember I said about her being... I don't know... a spy or something. And you said there was no point in her being one because...'

I smiled as I watched Phil try to put his thoughts in some sort of logical order.

'Well, what about these Nazis? These Gestapo and SS bastards? Where are they?'

'They're rounding them up,' I replied. I hoped it was true.

'And then what?'

'They'll put them on trial I suppose and then... sentence them. Hang 'em. Hang the bastards,' I said, belligerently.

Phil arched an eyebrow and straightened in his chair as if he was about to utter his own profound thoughts on the matter. He confounded me by remaining silent. I wondered if he was gathering his thoughts for another attempt at explaining his theory. Either way, I used the time to picture Ingrid and decided that whatever else she might be, she wasn't some sort of post-Nazi secret agent.

'Hmm,' he said eventually. 'All of this stuff can't just stop. One day they're all Nazis screaming for blood, doing their Heil Hitlers and stomping around and the next it just stops... Not possible Saul. You can't turn it off like a tap. You said yourself you don't know anything about her. Where is her husband? Where is she from? What was she doing during the war? You don't even know where she lives.'

All of which was true. Maybe I was too busy thinking ahead to a period of protracted peace or maybe I had taken a shine to her. I shrugged away my drunken guilt and said, 'Okay, I'll ask her.' I forced myself to dispel any unworthy thoughts that I might actually like Ingrid and that I gave her too much credit as a result. She was attractive and clearly intelligent but that didn't mean she hadn't been a devout Nazi with a picture of Hitler on the wall, a husband and three brothers in the SS and a father who ran one of the camps in which so many Jews had lost their lives. Maybe Phil saw through my naivete.

I tried to change the subject onto something less... controversial.

'I sent Cleary and his men out to find a Union Jack.'

'Who?'

'Cleary. He's one of my soldiers. My army of three.'

'You versus the Red Army?'

'Yes. Salt of the Earth type. Conscription was good for the armed forces, you know. Lots of good men, with good brains who'd never have joined up otherwise.'

'And a few poor ones too. Some who'd have been turned away had it not been for the war. Do you remember Kelly?'

I did remember him but I had got past the point of simply mocking a man with some sort of malfunctioning brain. Kelly was one of life's unfortunates.

'He should never have been called up. He had his place in society but it wasn't with the RAF.'

'You weren't that sympathetic when he crashed a truck into the Anson.'

I cringed at the memory. The air commodore had paid us a visit in his personal Avro Anson just before D-Day. Kelly had shorn off a wingtip with his Bedford truck. Thankfully I wasn't commanding the squadron at the time.

'Well, I have had time to order my thoughts since then. The fault lay with whoever let him drive the truck.' I sighed and blinked before looking around the room at the assembled... guests? Were they guests? Where had they come from? They were air force types in the main, knocking back the booze as if doing so somehow consolidated victory. Three French pilots, their uniforms of such dark blue they might have been naval officers, huddled together, talking quietly in the midst of the raucous British and Americans. At least one of the Yanks sported NCO insignia on his jacket and shouldn't therefore have been here. But I was past caring; I'd been an NCO myself once.

'What are you thinking?'

'Thinking? Oh nothing. I think,' I said with an inebriated chuckle. 'I need to stop drinking.'

'You need to get your second wind, you mean.'

'I don't know if I have such a thing.'

'We've won the war, man!'

'Yes, I know but I think we've already celebrated that, haven't we? What am I celebrating now?'

'Does it matter?'

'Propriety,' I said, although that single word did not fall easily from my tongue.

'Well, in that case, we're celebrating peace.'

'Fair enough.'

'Do you ever wonder what would have happened if we'd lost?' asked my bleary-eyed companion. His kept his gaze fixed on me as he drank heavily, hoping perhaps to secure my answer.

I lied.

'No. It didn't happen anyway.' In fact I'd thought about it often, especially in the early days.

'But it could have done. They could have destroyed us at Dunkirk and then invaded. We'd have been... fucked.' That last word he uttered with surprising distaste as if he was surrounded by prim clergymen.

'Thank God for the Channel then.'

'What if they got across?'

'They didn't. They couldn't have done it and even if they got to our shores, we'd never have let them take control. We have the Royal Navy.' I rubbed my eyes. 'The RAF was just the final nail in the coffin. We put the matter beyond doubt.'

Phil opened his mouth to speak but no words came and I seized upon this intermission to state that I was going to bed.

Chapter Nine

The sun shone, making me squint. My brain pulsated against the thin skull in which it was seemingly imprisoned and I rued my decision to drink the previous night. I had no idea where Phil was and didn't care. More than that I wished to encounter no one today if it was possible. Ingrid had not come to work as if she knew that I was in bad shape and wishing to make it through the day undisturbed. But that couldn't have been the case. How could she have known that?

    I groaned as I stood, pushing the chair against the wall of my office with a dull noise that made me wince. I made the short journey to my window and watched as the town came alive: businesses opening, a bus, a baker's van, two women hurrying down the street. It was hard to believe that this bustle was occurring so soon after the end of a war which had left much of Europe in ruins. Steam rose from puddles formed around the fountain and I was reminded of smoke.

    My thoughts went on a journey all of their own, a jumble of things concerning the war, aircraft, my childhood and odds and ends which couldn't easily be classified. I paused them as if lifting the needle from a gramophone record and briefly mused that if this was a *train of thought*, then each disparate strand represented a stop on my journey. Thinking this way benefitted me naught; really, I was just trying to occupy my time until the hangover dissipated. Guilt and shame vied for emotional dominance and merely swiping them away as the inevitable result of alcohol did nothing to lessen their impact.

    I sat heavily once more, the chair protesting woodenly as it took my weight, then rubbed my temples, eyes shut, mind... as free from thought as I could make it, although the very act of not thinking required me to think. How long I stayed like that I couldn't say. Noises from the street seemed to flow over my seated form, vibrations that did little to disturb my peace. I felt a burst of elation at having survived the war and then spent some contemplative moments wondering why this established fact had come back to me then. My head continued to pound, but with my eyes shut and with nothing to disturb me, it became a bearable kind of pain, almost mere discomfort. I found myself praying that my day would continue in this fashion, experiencing a stab of fear when it seemed unlikely.

    When I glanced at my watch with one bleary eye it was 0845 and when I glanced again it was 0851. Six minutes. If I did that ten times, an hour would pass and if I did that, say, eighty times, I would be justified in returning to my room back on the base. I didn't even want to make these crude mental calculations but once I'd started my brain just worked its way through the process without any help from me. It seemed like a laborious way to spend the day.

    The headache slowly began to migrate from my brain to my right eye, taking up station there, still throbbing, still aching. A wave of nausea broke over me and then, thankfully disappeared, leaving a few moments of what might have been hunger.

My stomach rumbled, angrily.

Still no Ingrid.

I felt relief at her continued absence for I really didn't want her to see me semi-indisposed. It wasn't embarrassment that I would have experienced had she turned up, rather something akin to shame. I couldn't rid myself of the belief that most Germans still looked down upon their new conquerors, quite unable to believe that defeat had been inflicted upon them by inferior nations. A hangover could only have reinforced this disbelief. At the time my self-loathing managed to obscure the fact that, unlike my assistant, I had actually made it into work.

It was 0935 when my little party of soldiers – my army – reported in for the day. If Cleary detected signs of my hungover condition, he was respectful enough and wise enough not to allude to it. Indeed, he might have been similarly troubled.

'Everything okay, sir?' he asked.

'A bit under the weather, that's all,' I explained. He nodded and so I continued, 'just patrol the town and report back to me at lunch time.' If he felt like he was being given the brush off then he was correct but he didn't care and I didn't care that he didn't care. Before he left, he seemed to look in the direction of Ingrid's office but he made no comment about her absence. Alone again, I decided to make myself a cup of tea using ingredients from a ration box which had been left in the *Rathaus* by one of Cleary's men. I was the only inhabitant of the little staff kitchen as I boiled a kettle on one of two gas rings.

I sat as I waited, my mind a jumble. The previous night's over-indulgence had produced in me an air of unreality such that, at times, I felt myself existing outside of my physical body, almost becoming my own sentinel in the process, watching over myself, taking stock. This feeling became so profound that it became a comfort to me, protecting me from the realities of life, creating a distance between my physical self and my self-induced illness, providing a barrier which separated contentment and duty. My guilt was pushed aside like an unpleasant secret; I knew it was still there but for now it couldn't touch me.

For some time I sat in this virtual trance, able to regulate the pain behind my eye in a way which I have never managed since. My contentment only deepened until it became a state of grace, almost spiritual in its intensity... and I was not a spiritual man – far from it – and yet...

I didn't move. My heart beat gently in my chest, its rhythm subdued by this peace which had unexpectedly settled upon me. The sounds of the street, diluted by closed doors and windows, reached my ears, as did the geriatric creaks and groans of the old building, but neither of these sets of invisible vibrations disturbed my reverie. Background noise and nothing more, the world still turned and its countless small actions ran their course. Nothing really changed.

I was just ticking over, a car at rest, a sleeping dog, a tree closed up for the winter. My brain registered almost nothing: no smells, few sounds, I felt nothing, the sour taste of alcohol smothered, my senses on standby. How long could I stay like this? Now would be the time to say that someone burst into my office with a matter of great import that required my instant, unwavering attention but oddly, that didn't happen. The still, quiet peace remained intact like a blanket of snow insulating me from the pointless tasks that had been dumped upon me in this pointless town after the end of this pointless war.

I could have slept but I knew that mere sleep would be less soothing than this borrowed time. In truth I had nothing better to do and this was the ideal opportunity to not do it. It's hard to convey in words how absurdly happy I felt then, ensconced in a world of inactivity, safe from the need to take action, to lead, to administer, to even move. I was as important as a leaf on a tree, as a beetle, my actions or lack of such had the same impact as a butterfly resting on a rose. I felt no sense of loss, of responsibility, the need for action, no date with destiny. I was just taking up space in a partial vacuum and doing so with such complete stillness that nothing, no event big or small, could possibly be influenced by my continued existence.

I had become less than the sum of my parts. I had no function. I had nothing and wanted for nothing. I wanted to bend the laws of physics just enough to take this 'nothing' and bottle it for future use.

I suppose I had found happiness.

***

After a time, I gradually re-emerged from my near-trance, coming back to a greater level of consciousness, with my train of thought stopping off at a station named 'contemplation'. That was okay.

I looked at my watch.

11.32

Had I slept? I didn't think so. The pain in my right eye had gone but I was a little stiff from lack of movement. What had changed since I had last thought about life? Probably nothing, I reasoned, for all the big things that could ever happen to me *had* happened unless I got sent out East to fight the Japs. Things would be humdrum from now on and that was fine. Sitting at this desk was humdrum. Going back to my room on the base would be humdrum. Humdrumness was the future for me.

***

Cleary and his merry band returned at 1230 and began making sandwiches and cups of tea. I was invited to join them and did so without any hesitation.

'This is good tea, gents,' I said, sipping my brew.

'Well, if you can't make a good cup of char by the time you leave the Army then there's no hope for you,' said Cleary. He omitted the word, 'sir' from his sentence and yet I knew there was no disrespect intended. Cleary was just a decent man dragged into the army to fight a war for which he was not to blame, trying to get through the experience and out the other side intact. There were millions like him.

'What are you planning for after your demob?' I asked the soldiers.

'Anything that doesn't involve getting shot at, sir,' said one. There were nods of agreement as if he spoke for them all, after which we lapsed into companionable silence.

'Anything of note on your patrol?' I asked eventually, although they would have reported it already had it there been.

'Nothing much, sir. A big queue at the bakery and an argument at the butcher's. Two women fighting over a joint of meat, I think.'

'Not a pretty sight,' confirmed Cleary. 'Very spirited, you might say.'

I laughed at his description.

'So, no saboteurs or black marketeers?'

'Well, actually we did see a couple of Yanks trying to sell stuff out of the back of a truck but they packed up sharpish when they saw us. I don't think the Jerries have any money to buy things anyway,' said one of the men.

'And you haven't seen my secretary?'

'She's not come in, sir?'

'Not this morning.'

'That's a bit odd. I mean, give 'em their due, the old Jerries are pretty reliable for things like that. Good workers. A friend of my dad's has a farm and he had four Italian POWs working for him. Said they were right lazy bleeders. Anyway, they were released and he got a German POW in their place. Just the one, mind. Anyhow, this friend of my dad's said that the single German did more work than all four Eyties put together.'

I had no idea if his story was true but from personal experience, I feared the Italians in combat much less than the Germans; I sensed that their heart wasn't in it.

'You should report her, sir. She'd report you...'

'I don't even know who to report her to,' I explained. 'I could report her to myself I suppose.'

My little army dutifully laughed at the notion I had put forth, but they each knew that nothing was impossible, no act too bizarre when wearing the King's uniform.

'Just be sure you fill in the correct form if you are going to report her, sir... you know how these things go.'

Cleary was right. Later when I was alone again, I thought about the fact that Ingrid had come to me unannounced, unrequested, not quite unwanted because she had subsequently proved her worth. But it did make me think. Who did she work for and where was she now?

***

It comes to something when you finish work early and no one either notices or cares. It suited me well enough. I drove the Volkswagen back to the base, acknowledging the sentry's salute and intending to head straight for my billet. Much as I liked him, I did not want to be intercepted by Phil and dragged off to the mess for drinks. Right now it felt as if my thirst had been permanently quenched – quenched for all time, you might say – and that my nervous system was only just recovering from the previous night's alcoholic assault. Tiny rodents of hunger gnawed at my stomach but even that couldn't dissuade me from completing my simple mission which was to go to bed and sleep until the following day.

 Dark grey clouds had formed an unbroken canopy overhead and as I pulled to a halt I either heard thunder or the noise of some vast, metal cylinder being rolled across a hangar floor. I couldn't picture any cylinders of that description in our possession and it suited me fine to think of thunder; going to sleep, warm and safe in the midst of some epic storm pleased me greatly.

 The block was deserted as I would have expected returning so early. My footsteps echoed in the hall and I thought about putting a 'Do Not Disturb' sign on my door. I was the boss after all. If I didn't want to be disturbed, who was to argue with that? In the end, and just as the storm really picked up momentum, I decided against the note. As I climbed into the cool cotton embrace of my bed I thought about Ingrid and then sleep took me.

Chapter Ten

I felt oddly invigorated when I awoke the following morning as if some illness had been cured or a burden lifted from my shoulders. In fact what I was experiencing was merely the lack of a hangover and yet I was filled with energy, purpose, determination and hope as a result, the only problem being a lack of outlet for these new emotional helpers. My job – mayor – required occasional tact and the ability to make easy decisions but it did not require determination. It gave me little sense of purpose. I didn't need hope – or more accurately my hopes were aimed in other directions. Energy? Being the mayor didn't use up much energy. In other words I was equipped for something much more demanding than sitting at my desk hoping to be left alone.

When I considered my position over breakfast: bacon, eggs, toast and a cup of tea, I was able to pinpoint the reason why my current role was making so few demands of me: Ingrid. I briefly debated the manner in which I would deal with her absence of the previous day – briefly because I quickly came to the realisation that she'd inadvertently done me a favour. I'd been in no state to deal with her unvoiced admonishment or her disapproving looks. Even in defeat the Germans were able to show disapproval for things not done in the German way. I felt, what I can only accurately describe as a 'pang' of loathing, there and gone, like the pain of standing on a tack or the prick of a blood test.

I just didn't know what to make of someone like Ingrid, other than to say that I needed her. I was fortunate that no great issues had been raised yesterday because she was the one who dealt with them, merely seeking my approval for repairs and only occasionally asking for my advice. With Ingrid present, the language barrier was removed and it never occurred to me that I had no idea what she was saying on my behalf. She could have been ordering a mass uprising for all I knew, or commiserating on the death of the Fuhrer.

But that was unlikely, wasn't it? I had no idea.

The short drive to work was easy, even pleasant. The morning air was warm and the remaining puddles from last night's storm were drying up like islands of steam. Somewhere the grass was being cut. Birds sang. The road was devoid of other traffic. It was, in fact, idyllic, so much so that, irrationally, I suspected a trap. Why else would such simple perfection be visited upon me in this land of unspeakable evil? How could the sun bring itself to shine upon Germany?

But that's just how it was. If it didn't seem to make sense, then so be it; I was merely moving across the earth's surface like everyone else, with no special concessions. That I was doing so here was just an accident, a collection of circumstances thrown together at random.

As I reached the outskirts of the town, the tall houses undamaged, I began to think of Ingrid, hoping that she had collected something tasty from the bakery, boiled the kettle, sorted out the neglected paperwork... I knew then that I was not going to challenge her about her absence, if only because I didn't care one way or the other. Oddly, when I drove past the bakery, the owner, arranging his modest window display, waved and I waved back as if we were old friends and I had grown up here. I chuckled at the thought. That was fate. I'd grown up in Britain not Germany. I'd had no say in the matter.

In my state of muted elation, I was going to say something to Ingrid about finally being accepted. *'When the baker waves on your way to work, you know you're part of the community,'* something like that.

But when I got to the *Rathaus*, there was no sign of her. The room was cold, there was no smell of freshly brewed coffee, no hint of her perfume.

***

I fairly slumped at my desk, good humour snatched away in an instant. She was either late, or more likely, absent for a second day. Whatever, I was certainly going to speak to her about it now. One day I could overlook but two days I could not. Those were fleeting thoughts and as I organised my tiny pile of paperwork and loaded my pen with ink which would dry up through lack of use, I realised that I was early for work and had merely beaten Ingrid to it today. There was no reason to think that she had abandoned her post. That's what I told myself.

Once again, I made tea and listened as Cleary and his troops came into the *Rathaus*. They chatted buoyantly and accepted my offer of tea, even though they had probably taken some with their breakfast.

'This is why we won the war, sir,' claimed one of the men, holding his mug aloft.

'Tea?'

'Yes sir. We drink it and the Germans don't. Twice we've beaten them.'

I wasn't sure if it was purely down to tea.

'You don't think the Americans and the Russians had something to do with it?'

'They helped,' he conceded, grudgingly. 'Mainly tea, though. Kept us going. You must have drank it, during the Battle of Britain, sir. Was you in the Battle of Britain?'

'Yes. And we drank lots of tea,' I assured him.

'Tea and our sense of humour, that's what won us the war,' said the youngest of the soldiers. 'And Vera Lynn.'

'Rita Hayworth,' suggested Cleary.

'She's a Yank.'

'So? What's wrong with that?'

'What about ITMA?' I suggested and was pleased when the others agreed vigorously.

'Tommy Handley's funny.'

'Has that woman turned in today, sir?' asked Cleary.

'Not yet.'

'Do you think she's done a bunk?'

'Possibly. I wasn't even expecting her in the first place... I mean when I first got to my airfield. She was just sitting there, waiting. No idea who sent her or where she came from.'

'Handy that she spoke Russian, though,' said the NCO.

'Yes.'

A short silence ensued, the first time there had been any awkwardness between me and my Army... colleagues.

'You think that was suspicious?'

'A bit,' said Cleary. The others looked on in silent agreement. It seemed then that this was something they had talked about before. Of course, I'd had my own doubts about her but she'd been far too useful to me to let these cloud my lazy acceptance of her presence. And it was lazy. If you were to divvy up who did what in the running of the town it was ninety percent down to Ingrid's efforts. If anything I was a figurehead, nothing more than a symbol of British rule.

'She could be a Russian spy, sir,' said the youngest of the soldiers earnestly. I guessed that his level of education was higher than the others, maybe a grammar school boy.

'Because she speaks Russian?'

He pulled a face and shrugged.

'Okay, supposing she was, what could she learn from being here?'

'But it is strange that she just turned up like that, sir, isn't it? You don't even know where she lives or how she's paid. You don't know what she did during the war or who she was married to. And now she's gone without so much as a by-your-leave.'

'I still can't see how working here was of any use to her if she's a spy or whatever.'

I hoped that I wasn't sounding defensive now. I mean, did they think I had been too accepting of her? Had they been talking about it, about me? It gave me pause to think about my own motivation. Supposing Ingrid had been less attractive? Supposing she hadn't spoken such good English or been so friendly? What then? Would I have taken her on so unquestioningly?

I rubbed my eyes and groaned.

I was about to speak when a sheet of paper, some sort of requisition, blew off the table and floated gently to the floor. This disturbance in the air was caused by only one thing – the *Rathaus* door being opened. The sound of her heels on the tiled floor was unmistakeable but I took my time checking out the identity of our visitor, not wanting to seem too excitable.

'Ingrid,' I said and she turned at once.

'I'm so sorry. My father was ill and I had to get the train to see to him...'

I cut her off saying, 'it's fine. It's just I didn't know where you were. You should have telephoned.'

'I have no telephone,' she said quietly as if divulging a shameful secret. My suspicions evaporated.

The troops left at that point for a patrol of the town as had become routine. None of them spoke and my secretary took her seat as if nothing had happened, shuffling papers and getting back to work.

During the course of the day we dealt with a few matters: permits, enquiries about POWs, requests for assistance with repairs and so on.

I was surprised by one lady of indeterminate age, who came to us, seemingly protesting, such was the racket she made. As usual I understood not one word of what was being said but Ingrid took notes and made encouraging sounds. Her patience only aggravated the situation however: the woman's volume increased, her arm waving became more violent, her tone more curt, more imploring, her face redder. I sat there, a spectator essentially, although much of what she said was directed at me. Her anger was shot through with dismay verging on panic or fear.

'What's she saying?' I ventured but Ingrid waved my inquiry away as if I was a mere irritant. I sat there dumbly after that, assessing the woman, her well-worn clothes, her shoes which looked as if they belonged to a man, the deep lines in her face, the grey pallor of her skin, suffused with patches of angry redness. For a moment I wondered if she was a survivor from the camp but there was too much meat on her bones for that to be the case.

I craved a cup of coffee but I sat there and listened, my perplexity deepening with each terrible word spoken. After a few minutes, she left and we sat in a sort of vacuum of silence adjusting to life without this screaming banshee in our presence. I cast my eye at Ingrid who seemed to be assembling her thoughts, preparing her explanation of events but she was dismissive when she finally spoke.

'It was nothing.'

'Nothing? Really? It seemed like something to me.'

'A storm in a cup.'

It didn't sound like it to me and I said so, more or less forcing her to tell me what the woman had said. I sensed great reluctance on Ingrid's part and it made me suspicious, rightly so as it transpired.

'She has told me that the person in the next flat is from the... from the SS.'

'She is clearly anxious about this...'

'It is nothing. She is mad, probably.'

'Even so, SS are supposed to be taken in.'

'It is not worth it.'

'Well, I'm afraid that's not your decision to make.'

'There are thousands of such people. How will you arrest them all?'

I was on the point of explaining that we would arrest whoever we wanted to arrest and that it was none of her business, and that we'd won the bloody war, and that the SS represented the greatest evil and deserved no leniency. But instead I suffered from some sort of minor moral collapse as if my reserves of indignation had suddenly run dry like the fuel tank of a German car.

'I'll have the address and pass it on to the security police.'

With reluctance she handed over the note she'd made. I thanked her and picked up the telephone.

'I wouldn't mind a coffee,' I said, hoping to get her out of the way. Sullenly, she scraped her chair back and stood, and when she was gone, I rang the security police, speaking to a Sergeant Ralphs who took the address and promised to investigate. The matter was closed so why did I feel as if I had betrayed Ingrid? There were plenty of arguments to be made which explained why no betrayal had taken place but I suddenly found myself overtaken by *ennui* – an afternoon slump which visited me often. I blew air from my cheeks and accepted my hot drink from a returning but rather taciturn secretary.

'I'm ready for this,' I said. She smiled, coldly. I wondered if now was the time to broach some of the questions I had: how did you get this job? where do you live? who pays you? There were others lined up in my brain like tins on a shelf and probably more that would occur to be as we went along but my courage failed me. Probing her for details of her personal life wasn't the right way to go about a thawing our frosty relations. Again, the question – put to myself – could have been, 'why did I even care?' Ingrid served a function, that was all.

That's what I told myself. Admittedly she was very attractive, intelligent, calm, hard-working but she was here to do a job and nothing more.

The day wore on and the frost thawed somewhat. I gave her money to get lunch from the bakery and she returned with brightly coloured cakes that had almost no taste whatsoever. In better times, perhaps German bakers had the means to impart flavour in their wares but I couldn't say one way or the other and feigned enjoyment.

'Very nice,' I said and she gave me a look which told me that she saw the lie immediately the words fell from my mouth. But what was I supposed to say?

Cleary and his men returned around 1500 hours.

'Any chance we could knock off early, sir?'

'I don't see why not. An important appointment?'

'ENSA, sir,' said one of the men. Ingrid looked up.

'Ensa?'

'Every night something awful,' explained the NCO but his quip was somehow lost in translation and she returned to her work. I smiled at him. British humour...

'Yes of course, Corporal Cleary, you get off. Laugh at a joke for me,' I said, fatefully.

None of them got to the show.

***

I would estimate his height at six-six and with the addition of an enormous peaked cap he was taking on the appearance of a seven-foot circus giant. His body was correctly proportioned for someone so tall, except in the matter of his cloud-brushing head which was probably designed for five-ten or so. An ancient revolver sat on his hip in a leather holster and when he removed his hat it was clear that a bullet had almost ventilated his skull at some point, just missing and leaving a long groove in his shaven cranium. He was joined by three other soldiers of mixed appearance, two of whom were of Asiatic origin.

I heard Cleary mutter something as his men drew close, protectively. I was startled when the tall Russian – by this time I'd worked out that he was an officer – spoke in English.

'Hello,' he boomed. Seemingly his knowledge of our language was exhausted at this point and when I responded with a 'hello' of my own he smiled and began jabbering in Russian. I could smell alcohol and in my mind it had to be vodka because that is what Russians drank. This impression was confirmed when he produced clear, unlabelled bottle and a collection of tiny glasses. With these in his huge spidery hands he lunged towards my desk and laid them down triumphantly in the manner of someone bearing great and welcome gifts.

He spoke again and his soldiers, each armed with a sub machine gun, laughed as they closed in on the bottle.

'What did he say?' I asked Ingrid.

'You are to drink with them for the victory in the Great Patriotic War.' Her words were run-through with bile; these were the last people she wanted to encounter at the end of the week. My question, and by default her answer, were already redundant by now since my 'host' was now trying to thrust a glass of vodka into my hand. Disguising my reluctance I took the drink and quietly uttered a single word – cheers – as they toasted victory. It wasn't all that new a victory but nevertheless they were very pleased.

Impatiently he gabbled something else. I turned to my interpreter.

'He wants to know if you have got more glasses. He wants us all to drink.'

'Christ,' I muttered, fearing alcoholic oblivion but keen not to upset my new friends who had probably parked a tank outside. 'Corporal could you go to the kitchen and find some...'

'Yes sir.'

I wondered if the ENSA show had been forgotten about. Were they staying behind out of loyalty or from the promise of free booze?

The vodka burned my throat but I tried not to wince or show any signs of discomfort. When Cleary returned with a glass and four China cups, vodka was splashed liberally, much of it over my desk. It didn't seem to matter. I imagined them having a crate of the stuff in their T34. Another toast was made in Russian and this time Ingrid raised her glass, muttering '*prost*' under her breath. She was self-conscious, which made perfect sense in the circumstances because our new pals couldn't have failed to realise that Ingrid was a German civilian.

As these unexpected events began to unfold, my mind raced emptily, and that isn't an oxymoron. Unconnected thoughts, unmemorable, jumbled and useless swirled around my brain, tangling, untangling, colliding, disintegrating, merging, demerging. Some were flung from this mental vortex into the void and others kept their station whilst remaining virtually incomprehensible. It was clear that some type of event was playing out but that was the extent of my clarity. The clues were lined up: the vodka, the Russian officer, the Red Army peasant soldiers, the weapons. But what did it mean? This felt like a hostile celebration, a hollow friendship, utterly meaningless and yet laden with intent. They had come with the gift of vodka but I knew they wanted something in return.

This second helping of the Russians' alcohol didn't burn like the first. I caught Cleary's eye and was reassured that my suspicions were matched by his own. For the first time I noticed the glazed eyes of my allies; they'd been imbibing long before they stopped off with us. What had their intention been? They certainly hadn't expected to find a British officer and some soldiers present, so had we not been here, what would they have done? What would have happened to Ingrid? They felt like the enemy. Ingrid felt like a friend. How quickly things changed.

'Ask them what I can help them with,' I said to my secretary. She stammered a few words and then we waited for the response. The officer spoke, sounding put out but in a jokey way.

'He says he just wants to celebrate.'

He spoke again, this time less friendly in manner.

'But he wants me to leave.'

'You don't have to,' I said quickly, leaping to her defence.

'It is time to go to my home anyway.'

'I'll have you escorted there. One of the soldiers can go with you.'

Ingrid looked alarmed at this suggestion but recovered quickly.

'I am fine. Thank you. You are worried that they will do something but... it will be fine.'

I tried to persuade her otherwise but I could see that her mind was made up and that the Russian officer was getting rather tired of waiting. Waiting for what? I hadn't asked him to come here. He sipped vodka from a tiny glass and watched me carefully as if I might make a break for it.

The situation was nonsensical of course. They – the Red Army – were in my domain and yet acting as if the reverse were true. Ingrid dutifully packed a few belongings into her hand bag, straightened the papers on her desk and left, wishing me well.

A few seconds later I heard the main door to the building slam shut and I was reminded that my work – such as it was – was complete for the weekend. I was expecting a letter from Margaret and intended to meet my officers for a drink or two in the mess tonight but it was obvious that the Reds had other ideas. I was stunned when the officer spoke again.

'Now that Nazi bitch has gone, we can talk properly,' he said.

He laughed coarsely when my mouth dropped open. My glass was refilled. I heard but didn't see the same hospitable act being carried out for my troops. It occurred to me that we'd all be squiffy pretty soon but my mind was racing and my potential state of drunkenness was not the biggest issue with which it was dealing.

'You speak English...' I said dumbly, stating the bloody obvious.

'Ha. Yes. It is not accident that I am here.'

His words although heavily accented, sounded more refined now that he spoke in my mother tongue, although that may have been my shallow perception of the situation, gratitude that I wasn't in a linguistic battle I could never win. He held up the bottle, offering another drink. I shook my head to decline and waved him away affably. He filled my glass anyway. His eyes were glassy but he seemed to be in full possession of his faculties, his blood suffused with vodka, not just today but every day.

'So you have come here for a reason?' I ventured.

'Yes, yes but first have a drink.'

'I don't think...'

'Drink to victory. Much blood spilled. We have won. We are the great allies. Stalin, Churchill, Roosevelt.'

'Roosevelt is dead,' I pointed out.

'Yes, yes. Drink.'

His was a gentle form of coercion, but it was coercion nonetheless. He was used to getting his own way.

'I am Colonel Novikov. My mission is to cooperate with you on particular matter. It concerns the Nazis.' He downed his glass of vodka like liquid punctuation.

'Cooperate? We're happy to co...'

'Yes, yes. I know. This concerns the nearby camp.'

'The concentration camp?'

He nodded, drank a little too quickly and with watering eyes said, 'yes, yes.' By now the colonel's troops were mingling with mine. They had moved outside the office and I could hear the clink of glass on glass as vodka was liberally sloshed into whatever drinking vessels had been found. From the corner of my eye I saw Cleary examining a Soviet sub machine gun with great interest. His rifle was nowhere to be seen. I sipped my vodka and my head span. These were the early stages of alcoholic euphoria. I either needed to stop at once or keep going. The first course of action would probably be a diplomatic disaster and the second would put me a great disadvantage since it was clear that Colonel Novikov's system ran on vodka. His heart pumped the stuff through arteries and veins. It stopped him from freezing solid in the Russian winters.

'Do you listen?'

'Yes, of course. I'm intrigued.'

'I didn't hear your name,' he said tilting his back as if examining me through invisible *pince nez*.

'I didn't tell you my... I'm Squadron Leader Cohen of the Royal Air Force.' I held out my hand to shake but he shook his head.

'Jew?'

'Well, yes.'

'It doesn't matter. We will drink to seal the deal.'

'What deal?'

'Yes, yes.' He refilled my glass and we toasted our new enterprise about which I knew almost nothing. The vodka didn't burn my throat now. I was becoming accustomed to it. Outside I heard laughter and realised that my troops were in the process – well advanced by the sound of it – of getting drunk.

Naturally Novikov didn't answer my question but rather posed one of his own.

'You fly Spitfire? Fantastic aeroplane.'

'Typhoon, actually,' I corrected, gently.

He looked at me as though I was lying. *Why not a Spitfire?* he seemed to be asking.

'Do you know what sort of thing happened in camp?' he asked, perching on the edge of a desk.

'The Nazis kept the Jews locked up and, well, they certainly killed some of them. I visited that camp myself and saw what they had done.'

'But do you know what else they did?' He continued before I could respond, holding up his non-drinking hand to shut down anything I might say. 'Experiments.'

'Oh. What sort of...'

'On Jews. Medical experiments. They didn't care if these people lived or died. They tested different medicines... er, drugs... on them, injected them with viruses and bacteria. They subjected them to cold and to heat and to pressing of the air.'

'Pressing of the air?'

'Yes. I cannot think of the word. What you have had when you fly high.'

'Oh, pressure,' I said.

'Yes, yes. All sorts of things and then they have recorded results and used it to improve their aeroplanes and medicines and weapons. They shot people with different bullets and examined the injuries, timed how long before people died. They transfused blood from animals to see if it worked on injured men.'

The camp had been ghastlier than I'd known. The sheer degree of depravity he was revealing came as a new shock.

'It's terrible,' I said, my words inadequate.

'Yes, yes. But we must... drink up...' He poured another measure of vodka which I foolishly drank. 'We must use the things they found out. The data. We must make sure that it is not waste.'

'I'm not sure that I agree.'

'These people, these Jews, died and we must ensure that their sacrifice is not waste.'

'It's immoral.'

'It's immoral to throw away knowledge that could save living in future.'

For a moment I thought he might have a point but that had to be the drink talking conspiratorially in my brain.

'No, I think it must be destroyed.'

He straightened as if he was about to stand. He pointed at my chest.

'You think the British will destroy this informations? You think Americans will destroy?'

I had no idea.

'Of course they will,' I said.

Novikov pulled a face and smothered a belch. Vodka fumes assailed my nose. In the hallway, the British and Russian allies seemed to be getting along well judging by the laughter. I couldn't imagine what they found to laugh about considering the language barrier.

He splashed vodka into my glass as I casually inspected his medal ribbons, wondering what each was for. It occurred to me then that if the 'informations' were going to be used or destroyed, it would have been done by now and that he was much too late to get his hands on them. When he next spoke it seemed he had read my mind.

'They don't even know where it is kept,' he said.

'Where what is kept?'

'The data,' he replied. His eyes glistened glassily as if he was truly excited by this revelation. It was as if he was trying to enthuse me, gather me up as an ally in this venture.

'Why don't you just go to the camp and ask to see it... or ask for copies to be made.'

He scoffed at this but I continued with my appeal to reason.

'I'm the wrong person to ask, you know. I have nothing to do with the camp. I'm the mayor. Temporary mayor, that's all.'

It was with a great sigh – almost seismic – that he took his next drink. Just in the time we'd been chatting, he consumed enough alcohol to anaesthetize an elephant and yet he continued to function as a rational, considered human being. Novikov looked around the office, appraising it. I thought he was building up to some unwarranted compliment about how clean it was or how neatly arranged the various journals and files on the shelf. Instead he smothered another belch, his one visible concession to drunkenness. He nodded appreciatively. I didn't know what he was appreciating.

'We should cooperate,' he said at last. 'The Russians and the English.'

'We have cooperated,' I replied. 'Since Germany attacked you, we supplied you with tanks and Spitfires and Hurricanes. We sent convoy after convoy to Russia, bringing weapons, which we could barely afford to give away.'

He seemed to think about this, then nodded decisively. He topped up my glass, his way of showing agreement and appreciation, perhaps re-kindling the friendship between our nations that was otherwise on the wane. Novikov could have made the point that, without Russia, the conflict might have turned out differently but he let this opportunity slip either from neglect or a desire to maintain the semi-drunken state of harmony we had attained. I drank my vodka and smacked my lips.

It was time to bring things to a conclusion. I looked at the thin dregs of vodka in my glass and imagined the tremendous hangover I would have if I continued to drink, but Novikov took this to mean that I required a top-up.

I groaned as the clear liquid filled my glass.

'I really need to go, Colonel. You've been terribly... hospitable and I hope we can continue to cooperate but...'

'I haven't even told you why I am here,' he protested.

'It's to do with...'

'Yes, yes. It's because you hold...' he waggled his wrist and frowned. 'You hold key!' he said triumphantly. 'You hold key. You don't realise but it's true.'

Chapter Eleven

I actually had very little to drink after that but I still woke on Saturday morning with a raging thirst, pounding head and a deadweight of guilt on my shoulders. I made it to breakfast, where I was one of the few officers in attendance and had my fill of bacon, eggs and some brown bread that was scarcely edible. Two cups of coffee later, a look at a week-old copy of The Daily Mail and a short period of contemplation and I felt as if I could manage to get through the day.

The sun shone, the birds sang and someone cut the grass, releasing that most beautiful scent into the air. As my headache receded, I decided that life was good. But I was very tired. Tonight I would avoid the mess and have an early night with a cup of Horlicks. The thought of these simple pleasures merely reinforced my contentment and I was able to brush away the doubts that Novikov had dumped in my head like a pile of autumn leaves.

I wandered slowly back to my room, acknowledging the salutes of two airmen who patrolled the perimeter fence, armed with 303s. Novikov's words remained in my consciousness but their intended shock effect had dissipated rather, to the point, in fact, where I no longer believed him. It wasn't just the case that it suited me not to believe him but his statement now seemed incredible. Incredible not just because of what he said but also because I couldn't really see what he was hoping to achieve.

One thing was clear to me however. Novikov hadn't just 'stopped by'; his sudden appearance was calculated. There was an aim. But it didn't make sense.

Later that day I bumped into Phil and we spent a pleasant hour strolling around the airfield, which was quiet and calm on a peacetime Saturday.

'I didn't see you in the mess last night, Saul.'

'That's because I didn't go, Phil.'

It was beginning to sound like a conversation between Laurel and Hardy, over-emphasis on the use of names.

'And why was that, Saul?'

We stopped by a pastel green-painted hangar and Phil lit a cigarette, sheltered from the warm breeze that swept across the concrete expanse of the airfield. He listened intently as I described my encounter with the Russian colonel, explaining about his assertion that the camp had been an experimental facility of the basest kind. I mentioned that the entire exchange was soused in alcohol.

'They like their vodka,' he said.

'It seems to be an accompaniment to any business dealings.'

'So why did he come to you? What did he want?'

I sighed and blew air from my cheeks for I was still in a quandary about what action I should take.

'He wanted the records of the experiments,' I said.

Phil dragged on his cigarette contemplatively. In the distance I watched a Bedford truck pulling out of the camp gates.

'Well, the obvious question is why did he come to you? Why not go to the camp itself?'

'For one thing he probably knows they wouldn't just hand them over. For another he isn't sure if they actually know they have them. And for another he thinks that I am the person with the power to get my hands on them on his behalf. It's Ingrid. He called her the key. She knows all about it. She is trying to smuggle the scientists and doctors out of the camp. I'm talking about the people who carried out the experiments.

'According to Novikov they are nearby but they want to get hold of their records before they do a flit.'

'Crikey. You need to tell someone. Go to the camp. We can get a Jeep and go there today.'

'But there's a problem with doing that,' I said.

'Really?'

'He says that the Americans are also looking for it.'

Phil shrugged and said, 'let them have it then. No skin off our noses.'

'There's something else, Phil.'

'What?'

'I don't exactly know what.'

Phil just laughed and shook his head in gentle scorn.

'In that case just keep out of it. You've come this far. Just let our allies fight it out between themselves. We're not paid enough to worry about it.'

It was good advice. I hoped I'd be able to take it.

***

When I returned to my room, I found a letter had been slipped beneath my door. As expected, it was from Margaret, and also as expected it contained details of her life in England, the peace, the worries for the future, the ongoing war with Japan. One of her cousins, a captain in the Royal Engineers, had returned from Italy, having been mentioned in dispatches. The family were rightly proud of him.

In other news, her father, a veteran of the Great War, had handed back his Home Guard uniform, even though they'd been stood down the previous year. It was the end of an era. Having met Margaret's father I could testify to the fact that he would have been a redoubtable fighter had the Germans dared to set foot on British soil. He didn't exactly frighten me but I never wanted to put his good humour to the test shall we say.

The letter was shot through with reassuring tedium and inconsequence; that was how we had communicated throughout the war in good times and bad. My letters to her barely contained any reference to the trials of battle I had faced, did not acknowledge the fear, mention the thin line that lay between heroism and cowardice, and the number of times I had only just managed to land on the right side of that divide. Had she not known better she might easily have concluded that I was having an easy time of it and not really contributing to the war effort.

And now, in peace, our missives continued in the same vein, hardly daring to talk about events of the last six years. The point of our letters was mutual reassurance rather than the passing of accurate and important information. Letters were morale boosters for the most part and nothing more, although I'd had to write a few letters to parents letting them know that their son had died bravely, hadn't suffered and so on. They weren't easy to write but much harder to receive.

When I had finished reading, I slumped on my bed and stared at the ceiling, my mind almost blank. I had 'thinker's block', like writer's block but without the requirement to add anything to paper. I was in a quandary, or I thought I was right up to the moment when I decided to forget all about the vodka-swilling Novikov and his party of troops. At once, I felt better and my mind emptied itself of thought again. Minutes later I was asleep.

***

I didn't remember my dreams only that I had them. I awoke feeling oppressed as if a great many matters had slipped through my hands and my enemies were waiting to make these omissions public. It was dark now. Moonlight illuminated my sparsely furnished room, picking out tiny details and casting muted shadows. An owl hooted to complete the clichéd scene.

I undressed and climbed beneath the blankets. The cold white sheets offered no initial warmth and I curled up as I did when young in that freezing house of my parents. A tiny avalanche of memories tumbled across the cinema screen of my mind: ice on the inside of my bedroom window, my dad blundering about as he got ready for work in the factory where they made very basic furniture, the sound of my little sister crying, the smell of cheap cuts of meat being fried, my mum bringing in frozen washing from the line. This last recollection made me smile: sheets frozen like billowing sails, my dad's work shirts stiffened in such a way as to suggest occupancy.

Inch my inch, I straightened my body as the bed warmed and, eventually, I lay flat on my back, staring once again at the ceiling and trying to clear my mind and make sense of recent events. It had worked the last time, but now, when I tried to dismiss Novikov's visit and his words from my thoughts, they lingered like corner boys. I had no idea what, if anything, I was supposed to do. Simply pretending that nothing had happened didn't seem quite as perfect a solution. Maybe, I supposed, my worries were heightened by lasting feeling of doom, draped across my shoulders by those difficult dreams.

Deciding that all of these problems could be addressed on Monday, I drifted off to sleep for a second time.

***

I attended church parade in one of the hangars the next day, not because I still believed in God or heaven or really took comfort from my Jewish faith but because I was expected to offer moral leadership to my men. A chaplain, given the rank of wing commander, led the service throwing in a few generic prayers, delivering a quick sermon and initiating some desultory hymn singing. I could tell from his turn-out that he was a duration only serviceman, his uniform worn like a suit, his demeanour that of a kindly mentor more than an officer. I didn't care and, in fact, I warmed to him slightly when he brought the service to a swift conclusion citing a need to repeat the process in another camp later that morning. He – and therefore God – was spread too thinly. God had been spread too thinly throughout the conflict in my view and let's not forget that some of his extensive flock operated under the banner of National Socialism. It made you wonder what God was playing at. To say that he moved in mysterious ways didn't quite cut the mustard.

My officers put in a good showing and I chatted with them when the service had ended.

'I heard we're going home soon,' said P/O Huggins. Huggins was twenty but looked five years younger. Nevertheless he'd flown about fifty sorties and shot down a Jerry reconnaissance plane, which had been a notable event at that late stage in the war when the Luftwaffe had almost disappeared from the skies.

'You heard this from whom?'

Huggins looked sheepish when he replied, 'the grapevine, sir.'

'Well, let me know if you get any more gen since it is clear that no one is going to tell me anything.'

He chuckled. The idea of being kept in ignorance was a common theme. My officers understood that, as a lowly squadron leader, I was not generally speaking, *in the know*.

I was intrigued at how readily they had adapted to peace after the extreme pressures of war, the boredom, the moments of terror, the shock of losing friends. This was like the pre-war RAF, not really fully believing that a war could start. They were still boys and yet not naive. Each of them had fought bitter aerial battles, flown their Typhoon fighters into a cauldron of flak, watched as cannon shell and bomb had torn the enemy asunder. Each was a killer and that fact alone would colour the remainder of their lives.

'How are things in the town, sir?' This question came from John Sweet, an Australian pilot, operational in the RAF since 1941, one of my true veterans.

'They have running water, electricity, food... life's essentials. They're lucky. Luckier than the people whose countries they over-ran.'

John hated the Germans – all of them – which I had always thought odd given that he was from a land far removed from Germany itself. His hatred, like that of the Poles, had served him well as he'd dispatched at least six of them to their graves in aerial combat. He was the original cool cucumber, never known to flap and always with a wry smile on his face.

'Bastards,' he said.

'Bastards indeed. But they will have to be our friends soon.'

'You've been to the camp, Saul? You've seen what they did? They'll never be my friends. And you a Jew, how can you even think like that? Those bastards tried to wipe your people out.'

'Everyone hates the Jews, John.'

'Some people but not enough to do that. They think it is hundreds of thousands killed. Maybe millions. The Krauts can't ever be our friends. They need to keep them in their place this time, make sure that they are just slaves from now on. Or even better just put them in the camps they built.'

I sighed. I didn't necessarily disagree but I knew it would never happen like that. Once the furore had died down and memories faded there would be moves to rebuild the country we had flattened. No one wanted to repeat the mistakes which had given Hitler the hateful ammunition he'd used to create this mess.

'Do most people feel this way, think like you?'

'Yes. Well, they should.'

***

Later that day, slightly bored, I took the little boxy Volkswagen car to the concentration camp. I had a vague notion about digging around and seeing if Novikov's theories held water. I wasn't all that bothered one way or another but it was something to do.

A Canadian sentry waved me through without bothering to check my ID or salute and I parked up next to a low wooden building not far from the main gates. The sun was warm on my face and the ground beneath my feet had dried and cracked. Grass was sparse. The camp felt... dead, which was appropriate of course. Tentatively I sniffed the air but there was nothing. What had I expected?

I began to stroll, taking a course maybe ten metres within the perimeter fence. I tried to look casual and once I was confident that no one cared about my presence I *felt* casual too, maybe relaxed. Despite my surroundings I experienced a surge of hope, the source of which I couldn't place. Maybe my subconscious had taken delivery of enough reminders of the war's end and that had given me something like a belief in the future. This camp – this terrible place – no longer functioned and its inmates had been moved on to centres where their health could be improved and where they could be prepared for a return to normal life if that was even possible given everything they'd been through. I couldn't picture how this process would work any more than I could really picture the torment they had suffered. I recalled John's assertion that the German's should be crushed forever and wondered if he might be correct.

I paused and looked out over a barren field edged by trees, a sliver of which was visible between the gable walls of two wooden huts. I tried to think of myself as a Jew, as one of those people who could have been taken by force to a place like this, there to die, had it not been for an accident of birth. Essentially, it was the English Channel which had kept me safe, although I had crossed it in the air more times than I could count. That I was a Jew was undeniable and I had neither wish nor need to deny it but I was badly lapsed... really a non-believer. It would have made no difference to the Germans of course.

No matter how hard I tried to think about my race and my ancestry, my thoughts just tumbled around in my head like marbles on a tray, colliding, changing course, never forming into a cohesive mass. It felt as if something – the opposite of a bond – separated me from the Jews who had suffered and died in camps like this. Their deaths were a fact. I had seen the bodies. I had smelt the smell of their decay. The images would never depart. And yet they seemed different to me, a different kind of Jew.

I'd been warned often enough about the dangers I faced should I be brought down over enemy-held territory but even that wasn't enough to close the gap between the reality of the European Jews and the life I led. As a fighter pilot I had alternated between intense danger and relative comfort. These Jews had only known terror, torment and, ultimately, death.

Still, I persisted in my desire to understand, to feel... It was my duty to truly comprehend the nature of the fight I had undertaken, to know that it had been worth it, that something had been achieved. Was it too much to hope for a better world, one in which peace was the norm and war gradually, with the passing of the years, became an aberration like something you read about in the scriptures? As I tried to rationalise and organise my mind, an image of Ingrid kept appearing. I didn't want to think about her now. I wasn't even sure why I was thinking about her at all.

I was lost in the maze of my mind and yet aware of this fact even as my eyes glazed over and the crisp vista to my front blurred and dissolved. A voice disturbed my reverie and plucked me from the forest of my mental wanderings.

'Are you okay? You seem a little lost,' he said with a chuckle. My new companion was a major from the Royal Military Police and he looked on with a mix of concern and curiosity on his face.

'Er, yes. I was just...' No words came to complete the sentence for at that moment I couldn't actually explain why I was there, why I was staring, why I had questions the answers to which seemed impossible to construct. It occurred to me in a flash of inspiration that I needed a blackboard and chalk to lay out the various aspects of this complex conundrum and to make connections.

'It's a hell of a place,' the major continued. 'I've seen a few and this isn't the worst but even so...'

'Is it your job to round up SS men?'

'It wasn't initially but when we realised the extent of the problem it became my duty, or part of it. Not solely mine of course. Seems like there are hundreds of such places. They might have killed millions of Jews. We simply don't know yet.'

I sighed but even as I did so I was assailed with a new sense of the unreality of my situation. In the brief silence that followed I tried to picture this place as it once was, a sort of camp but more than just a prison. Rather this was somewhere in which hope had ceased to exist and death was to be welcomed in the absence of anything better.

'They did experiments here,' I said finally. 'On the inmates.'

He seemed surprised and said, 'what sort of experiments?'

'Medical experiments... finding out how long people could survive in different conditions, which bullets killed best... that sort of thing. Inhuman.'

I turned to face my unsought companion, hoping to discern a look of recognition or a lack of such. I wondered if he already knew.

'It doesn't surprise me, unfortunately. I almost wish it did. I suppose we can take comfort from the fact that we fought a just war. That can't always be said.' He lit a cigarette and offered me one which I declined. 'I just hope this doesn't get covered up.'

Surprised by the comment, I asked him what he meant.

'Just that. Some people think that the Reds are going to be the new enemy and that means we will have to cosy up to the Krauts. It's a bloody joke really but we were never really natural bedfellows of the Russians, were we?' He shook his head and drew on his cigarette. 'So we can't very easily make friends with the Germans *and* pull them up about these camps. Do you see what I mean?'

'Maybe. They've got to do something though. The Russians aren't going to sit back and let them get away with their crimes.'

'They're no better,' he said.

'True but for now we're all still friends – just about. Did you know about the experiments? I mean, before I told you? Had you heard anything?'

'Not in connection with this place, no. There are other camps were things were done. I don't think we know the true scale of it yet.'

'So you didn't come here specifically because of that?'

'No.'

I nodded. I hadn't shared everything that the Russian had told me. When I tried to figure out the reason for my reticence, an image of Ingrid came into my mind. I wasn't sure what she had to do with the camp, if anything, and I was loath to divulge her name lest there be some truth to the Colonel's accusations.

'Quiet, isn't it?'

'Very,' I agreed, my eyes still fixed on that oblong vista between the two huts.

'I was told that the ashes of the camp victims had changed the chemistry of the soil and killed off the insects that lived in it. In turn that meant that the birds had left the area because there was no food for them. I don't know if that's true. Sounds a bit fanciful if you ask me.'

'It is quiet though. No birdsong. I suppose it might be true. Probably the least of the crimes committed round here.'

My thoughts flitted back to my home and the fact that Britain had not had this level of torment visited upon it. For a second I wanted to be back there with the English Channel between me and my enemies, new and old. Most of all I wanted to be with Margaret.

'If they did carry out experiments here, then whereabouts?' I asked glancing around me, my reverie dispensed with.

'No idea. Feel free to poke around.'

'Have there been any Americans here, you know, looking around?'

'Not seen any myself. Not their area of course. They should really stick to their own zone but I doubt if anyone would challenge them if they did turn up.'

'I've had a few run-ins with the Russians.'

'Yes, they're prone to *straying*,' he replied, raising an eyebrow.

I bade him farewell and tore my unseeing gaze away from the blurred shapes in front of me. I wasn't qualified to tackle this situation – dare I call it 'a mystery' – but still I wanted to find the truth for myself and then decide what to do with it. On the other side of the camp I spied a party of German civilians being given their tour of the place. I hoped that the loathing and scorn they'd once shown for the Jews could now be turned inwards. Bitterness and anger suddenly welled within me, rising like bile. At that precise moment the only punishment I could think of for these people was to put them into the camp, starve them, beat them, experiment upon them and eventually kill them and yet none of that would happen. Essentially there was no justice. They had created the monster but they would never really be adequately punished for doing so.

As I stood there, seething inwardly, I unintentionally summoned up an image of Ingrid and for the first time I hated her. I should have hated her all along. With a sigh of resignation I straightened my cap and began a slow stroll, wondering if I would come upon some sign of the experiments I had been told about. There was nothing that looked like an operating theatre – I'd assumed there would have to be one – and every building was the same single storey wooden structure that had housed the camp's inmates. It was unrelentingly grim despite the sunshine.

An operating theatre. What else could it be? Perhaps I reasoned that it would be just an ordinary hut from the outside. I quickly counted the number of these squat brown buildings: six orderly rows of... fifteen, and a couple of larger buildings to one side, one of which was now the guardroom and another which looked like an HQ.

Far removed from the main camp stood another building, this time made of brick and with two tall chimneys, one at either end. I had assumed that this had been an existing factory, here long before the rest of the place had been created but now I wondered if this was a crematorium and also an experimental facility. For a second I pictured dismembered corpses being hurled into a vast fire place, a metal door being swung shut and pressed workers – possibly inmates themselves – wiping their hands on filthy trousers as they took a break from their terrible task. As ever I found it hard to comprehend that life in Europe had ever taken this turn. It felt like something I could never possibly accept.

It was becoming clear with each passing day and each new revelation that the Germans had tried to wipe out the Jewish people from Europe. I didn't know how far they had gone in this process but they had built some kind of ghastly industry around their desire for extermination of the Jews. I didn't bother to distinguish between the Germans and the Nazis either. As far as I was concerned they were one and the same, especially when faced with the reality of their activities as I was now. Someday, I knew that someone would be preaching about forgiveness and reconciliation but those words had no meaning for me at that moment and certainly couldn't displace or dilute my anger.

I frowned. There was nothing further I could do. I thought about that building with the two chimneys but my resolve had deserted me. Someone must already have checked inside by now, so in theory it would be easier to find that person and ask them what they'd found than walk down there and try to gain admittance. I was beset by doubt and disinterest. I was suddenly worn out.

Chapter Twelve

That night I struggled to sleep. By 0200 I was awake thinking and feeling that I had not slept at all. Yet, when I lay there in that impenetrable darkness and desolate silence, it became clear that my thoughts had, in fact, been dreams, certainly some fanciful blend of fact and fantasy. I tried to clear my mind, hoping to let unconsciousness flood in and take me away for another five-and-a-half hours but each transitory void I cleared in my brain filled immediately with unsought visions, voices, even the words of a song.

'I've got a gal in Kalamazoo.'

I mean really. I didn't even like the bloody song and had no interest in visiting Kalamazoo. As soon as I cleared it from my mind it came back, not the whole song, just that line. Was it the first line? I didn't care either way. Eventually I was able to consider my other thoughts, visions, whatever with Kalamazoo playing in the background as if on a record player in the mess. I didn't want any of it. I wanted to sleep. All of this happened as I drifted from wakefulness to disturbed sleep and back. I had a dozen tiny dreams, some of which I could remember and some of which I could not, although they left behind a residue of dread and foreboding which did nothing to induce proper rest.

Margaret featured in my dreams as did our final walk on the beach and the American officer with his English girlfriend who'd been unable to purchase an ice cream. I pictured Margaret in a cottage, painting at an easel, a fire in the grate and a dog curled up on a rug. That little scene remained vague, almost misty as though I was viewing my wife and future life through a net curtain. I felt compelled to put myself in the picture, sitting nearby, smoking a pipe and tapping away at a typewriter as my latest literary gem came to life in ink and paper and yet my attempts at bringing this about were confounded again and again. I was locked out of my own dream. I knocked at the window through which I looked but no sound came and Margaret did not look round, engrossed with her canvas. The dog continued to snooze. This scene of contentment became a source of distress as I knocked and knocked. Now my knuckles hurt from the effort but admittance was refused. I thought about finding the door and simply letting myself in, this was after all my house in my dream but my feet remained fixed to the same spot. I began to panic, to call out, to twist from side to side with increasing violence, to break free of my invisible restraints. Something was gripping my shoulders in an unbreakable embrace. I tried to turn my head but it too was firmly fixed ahead and now my eyes would not turn…

    I called out and in so doing woke myself.

    I sat up and spent a moment or two figuring out where I was, for in the absolute darkness there were no clues. Oddly, it was the ticking of my alarm clock which provided the stimulus I needed to place myself in my room in the new officer's mess. I reached out for the little metal cabinet which lay next to my bed and felt the ungainly shape of the revolver in its webbing holster. Did I really need it now, I wondered?

It was a warm night, muggy. I climbed out of bed and stood in the darkness hoping to foster the need for deep sleep. Essentially, having survived the war, my troubles were over and yet I found myself plagued by doubts and fears that really should have been banished by now. Was it the case that I needed some form of background stress to enable me to function? Perhaps my body's chemistry had undergone some transformation in the course of the war, something that kept me going despite fear and fatigue and that this transformation was permanent or at least very difficult to displace.

Still standing – it would have looked very strange to an observer – I considered my options for the day ahead, reasoning that I could tell my officers that I'd be at my *Rathaus* office and telling Ingrid, I'd be staying on base. This double deception would enable me to take my little Volkswagen staff car out into the countryside and find a place, possibly next to a river, where I could lie in the sun and rest. If sleep took me, then so be it.

I felt better at once. The realisation that my presence was not vital to anyone was a blessed relief rather than an admission of uselessness. I reminded myself that the war was over. I could only benefit from the cessation of hostilities by constantly reminding myself of this fact. Peace brought with it a selection of things I no longer had to do, risks I no longer had to take, decisions I no longer had to make. If I was to enjoy this new status then it seemed as if this necessitated the taking of a regular inventory of responsibilities shrugged off and discarded. I didn't have anything extra. I didn't possess something new that I could pick up and examine.

The war was over. Something had been taken away. I needed to turn a negative into a positive by actively taking stock of the benefits that peace would bring. If not, then every day would feel like a stand down rather than another day of peace in which to be complacent, lax, lazy.

It was a relief to have finally made these connections in my brain for the end of the war had been an anti-climax, and after six years I needed something more than that. Looking back to 1940 I had been unable to contemplate this new era. Back then, I had suspected that we could still lose, or certainly not win and in the latter case the fighting would continue forever and I would eventually die. I was determined to enjoy the peace now.

Feeling much better, I climbed back into bed and pulled the blankets up round my neck just as the bloody Glenn Miller Orchestra started up again.

'I got a gal in Kalamazoo.'

***

My alarm sounded at 0730 and I knew that sleep had taken me into its warm embrace at some point, if not for long enough to feel the benefits. I lay still and instantly discarded my nascent plot to take my little car to the river and spend a day alone. It wasn't that the idea had lost its appeal so much as that it felt like almost as much effort as just going to my office. I could stay in bed of course. I outranked everyone else so who was there to order me to get up? But even in peace I felt a compulsion to go through the motions of duty. After all, a mere lack of necessity was no reason for inaction. Not in the RAF. There were things that needed to be done and if that was not the case then something would be invented to stimulate some form of toil.

Labour was its own reward.

Who'd said that? The Bible? William Shakespeare? Saul Cohen?

At breakfast I joined a short queue of officers. We chatted about inconsequential matters such as the football league, cricket, rationing and de-mob.

When I had drawn parallel to the hotplate I asked one of the cooks if the pigs which had donated their bacon to us had died of malnutrition.

'I'm not sure, sir,' he said, seriously.

'It was just a joke,' I explained.

'Okay, sir.'

Since the world of comedy was plainly closed to me, I decided on the spot to stay on in the peacetime RAF.

I sat with a couple of my officers.

'What's on the agenda for today, chaps?'

It was Flight Lieutenant Saunders, a South African, who responded.

'Well, sir, I plan on mooching around, staring at the sky, smoking in the morning. After lunch I'm going to go around the squadron and kick the tyres on the aircraft. Probably drink tea after that. And more smoking. Come back here for tea and then have some drinks tonight.'

'Sounds good, Alan. Productive.'

'I want the RAF to get full value from me before I go home. What about you, sir?'

'Well, as you know I am the *Bürgermeister* so I have lots of civic duties to perform.'

'Such as?'

I blew air from cheeks. 'Well, you know… paperwork and that sort of thing. Signing things, drinking coffee. Liaising with the Russians. Inspecting the… drains. Weddings too.'

'Really, sir? Inspecting the drains?'

'Probably not. I was just struggling to think what my job is exactly.'

Saunders laughed. He'd been at university before the war. He was much cleverer than me and would make a name for himself at something. With a sigh I remembered my visit from the tall Russian colonel and the potential repercussions of his words. As if reading my mind Saunders asked:

'Are the Russians a problem?'

'Put it this way, if we cleared out of Germany right now they would have no hesitation in taking our place. They keep turning up unexpectedly and because we are close to their area, they seem to think we've got our boundaries wrong. It's all nonsense of course.'

'Some people say they're as bad as the Jerries.'

'They might be worse but we're all still pals for now.'

'By the way, we had a couple of P47s drop by yesterday.'

'Really?'

'Huge things.'

'Yes, indeed. What did they want?'

'I don't really know, sir. I think they just came for a bit of a look around. A lieutenant-colonel and a major. We took 'em around the place, lunch in the mess and then they buggered off again.'

'Strange.' As an afterthought I asked, 'were they looking for information?'

'Information? I don't think so. It was very informal.'

'And they didn't ask for me?'

'No, sir.'

'Did they ask to speak to your CO?'

'Now that you mention it, they didn't.'

'It would have been good manners to have asked for an introduction. There's a certain etiquette to be followed when you land on someone else's airfield.'

Saunders pulled a face.

But I was in no mood for a conspiracy. There was nothing to say that a couple of USAAF types couldn't turn up now that the fighting had ended. Maybe I would reciprocate one day, although as soon as I thought about it, it sounded like too much effort.

The sun was in my eyes as I drove to the town, past the usual shops and offices, the usual civilians preparing for another day of commerce and bureaucracy. It didn't seem as if things were back to normal – although I had no experience of normality in this location – but peace had definitely settled on the populace. The air smelt fresh and clean and I imagined rather than heard, birds singing.

Ingrid stood as I entered – not out of respect but rather because she was about to make her way out to the bakery.

'Good morning, Squadron Leader. I was just on my way to buy bread. Can I get you a cake?'

'Erm, yes, that would be nice. I will give you some money,' I said reaching into my pocket. She waved my offer away.

My army of three entered while she was absent.

'Not turned up, sir?'

'Gone to the bakery,' I informed him. 'I should have ordered for you three.'

'It's fine, sir. Those Jerry buns don't taste of anything. By the way did you get your flag, sir. I noticed it's not flying.'

'No. You got a Union Jack?'

'Couple of days ago. Left it on your desk, sir.'

I frowned. 'This desk?'

'Yes, sir. Brand new and still wrapped in paper,' confirmed the NCO.

'Okay. Well done. Ingrid must have moved it,' I said, puzzled. I heard one of the soldiers suggesting that she had chucked the flag in the bin. He may well have been correct.

I didn't disagree nor did I confirm his opinion on the cakes minutes later when I sat drinking decent coffee with terrible pastry in the company of my mysterious clerk. She seemed to be in a good mood.

'When the sun shines, the earth looks much better,' she said. 'It even smells better, I think.'

I smiled, resisting the urge to make some comment about the smell of the experimental camp nearby. I say, 'resisted' but in truth I was in the full grip of morning *ennui*. I was sure the Germans had a long word for this condition but sufferers probably couldn't bring themselves to use it or in my case, ask what it was.

'You look tired, Squadron Leader.'

'Saul, remember?'

'Saul. Are you tired?'

'I didn't sleep well.'

'You need some schnapps in your bedtime drink,' she said. I presumed it was a joke but you could never tell.

'Maybe,' I said wearily taking a bite of the layered cake she'd brought me. Brown and cream, it promised much but delivered little except and an excess of mastication.

'Or iron.'

'Pardon?'

'You might feel tired if you don't have iron in your food. Or enough iron in it. My husband used to…'

She didn't finish her sentence and the unuttered words hung in the air like some flighty spirit stunned into immobility. Perhaps I should have asked her to finish what she was saying but my usual reticence held me back. Partly it was good manners and partly it was the wish to avoid causing offence. Anyone else would, in my place, have felt no compunction in demanding that she complete her sentence but I did not. It was weakness. A lack of leadership. Mainly it was my disabling *ennui*.

'Did you see a flag on my desk?' I asked her.

'What sort of flag?'

'You, know a Union Flag, a British Flag.'

'No. I'm sorry.'

***

That afternoon, I excused myself and drove over to the camp where the experiments had supposedly taken place. The sentry let me in, saluting smartly like a regular, and I parked up behind the guardroom.

There seemed to be virtually no one around and much of the burial work had been completed if appearances were anything to go by. I set off for the two-chimney building, casually wondering if it had been possible to identify any of the people they'd buried. I'd heard mention of Nazi photographic records of prisoners but had it been possible to match these with the new occupants of the mass graves? It seemed unlikely given the terrible state of the bodies I'd seen. Even thinking back to that event shocked me and I was pleased because the last thing I wanted was for a sight like that to become normal or acceptable to me or anyone else. Whoever coined the phrase, 'man's inhumanity to man' could scarcely have envisaged anything so debased, so bereft of humanity as the Germans' treatment of their prisoners.

I passed the wooden blocks, silent now, and kept walking until the building I sought came into view. I was much closer when I realised for the first time that it lay *outside* the boundary fence. Assuming there was a gate, I kept going until I was just yards from the perimeter wire. I looked left and I looked right, then took a couple of paces back and did the same but there was no sign of an entrance/exit gate of any type. It was later, when I was heading back to my own camp, that it occurred to me that I could have simply cut the wire and gone through, for the camp was no longer a holding point for prisoners. But since I didn't have any wire cutters the point was academic.

I continued to stand, wondering how many inmates had done the same during their years of captivity – that is if any of them survived for a period of years, of course. The sun shone down on me as I tried to order my thoughts. I kept my gaze fixed ahead and took in the details of the building, trying to divine some purpose for it and wondering if, since it was outside the camp boundaries, it actually had any connection to it at all. It was the two chimneys that had first caught my attention. One was right at the front above the main double doors. The building's façade was perhaps forty feet in height with the chimney adding another eighty or a hundred feet. For an estimate, the building, factory, whatever, was two hundred feet long. The second chimney appeared to be sited similarly to the first one but above the back wall.

I noticed that all the windows were well above head height but there were many of them, each held in metal frames. The roof seemed to have glass sections too but I couldn't see these clearly from my vantage point.

So, it was a factory of some kind but perhaps unconnected to the camp. It was a five-minute walk back to my transport and once there I started it up and drove back out of the gates, taking a right turn and trying to pick up a road which would lead me to the factory. In the first instance I came to a dead end surrounded by tall hedges on three sides. It was only with difficulty that I managed to turn the car and drive back out.

'There has to be a bloody road,' I muttered, the logic being that whatever had been produced there had surely to be transported by lorry. No road meant no lorries.

I needed a map but maps were in short supply now that hostilities had ceased. It seemed as though the urge to know where you were or where you were going had evaporated rather. Perhaps no one was going anywhere. So, in the absence of a map I used a process of trial and error to find the road I needed and when I found it, I drove straight to the building, arriving at the back where tall metal doors stood locked and impenetrable to me.

I wasted no time there and found a path which took me to the smaller doors I had seen from the camp. I parked, looked through the wire at the camp and noticed that it still looked empty but not quite abandoned. Now, on the cusp of sating my curiosity I felt suddenly like an intruder. More than that I felt a twinge of fear, a sort of tiny electric shock in my scalp, perhaps a warning to take care. For the first time I wished I brought someone with me. I tapped the revolver as if doing so my keep me safe but in reality I was just reassuring myself that it was still in my possession. I stopped short of drawing it from the holster.

The double doors, predictably enough, were locked. They were made from stout wood – I assumed it was oak – and the fitments were of thick metal painted black. There was a single handle and a large keyhole and brief inspection told me that the fitments couldn't be removed from the outside which was probably fairly standard in terms of security. There was no way in without the key but I tried the handle anyway just in case.

'Bugger,' I said. On either side of the door two large windows could be found but as I mentioned these were above head height. I looked over my vehicle and wondered if, by repositioning it, the required altitude might be attained.

It was worth a try.

Chapter Thirteen

'So what did you see?' asked Phil. I had decided to share my concerns with him, although I scarcely knew what they were myself.

'Me.'

'What?'

'Me. I saw me… my reflection.'

'Oh, I see.'

'It was dark inside and light outside so the window was like a mirror.'

'Then you really need to get inside.'

'I suppose so. Not sure if I can be bothered. That Russian chap hasn't actually been back and it's probably just an ordinary factory. I mean, if it was connected to the camp in any way it would be inside the fence, wouldn't it? I think I've just let my imagination run away with me a bit. No one ever said anything about the factory. I've just put two and two together and come up with five.'

'Perhaps but it isn't beyond the capabilities of the RAF to gain admittance to a single building is it?'

'We certainly flattened a few. What do you suggest? Rockets?'

Phil chuckled.

'I was thinking that the armourer probably had some useful tools to help us get the job done. I presume that we're no longer allowed to attack German targets now that the fighting has stopped.'

'Damned red tape.'

'In the interim why don't you just ask your assistant, Helga, what it is.'

'Ingrid.'

'Yes, him.'

I laughed at his unexpected quip. 'According to the Russian chap who came to visit, she is something to do with it.'

'It all sounds like twaddle to me, Saul. Do you really think the Krauts conducted experiments like that? It's inhuman.'

I looked at him askance and replied, 'yes, I do and I'm surprised that you don't believe it.'

'Well, just remember that we're all going to be friends soon enough and no one will want you stirring up the ashes.'

'I'm sure that's a mixed metaphor but I know what you mean. That's a long way off, though.'

'Is it? I doubt that very much. Things will change quickly.'

Perhaps he was right.

'Where's Kalamazoo?'

He looked at me in surprise.

'Like the song? That Kalamazoo?'

'Yes.'

'I think it's just a made-up place like Shangri-La or Timbuktu.'

'There's no such place as Timbuktu?'

'I don't think so. Sounds made-up. Rudyard Kipling or something.'

***

I explained to Ingrid that I wouldn't be in until the afternoon.

'Any problems with the Russians and Corporal Cleary can sort it out,' I explained. She looked doubtful but Phil and I set off for the camp armed with a huge crow bar from the stores. It was the sort of thing used to prise aircrew from the wreckage of a crashed plane but I have to admit, I'd never seen it before.

'We'll be breaking the law,' said Phil as we surged through the countryside. He had to shout about the noise of the air-cooled engine in our tinny transport. I gave him an old-fashioned look.

'I think we'll be okay. Who's going to arrest us? We're the bosses round here – at least for the meantime.'

He said nothing in return which was either agreement or a lack of will to battle with the little Volkswagen's engine cacophony. In fact he was rather prescient in voicing his doubts, for our arrival at the factory coincided with the arrival of another group.

'Hold on. Who's this?' he said, urgently. I pulled up short and switched the engine off in a belated nod towards stealth. Just visible from our current position next to the longest section of factory wall was the tailgate of a US Army truck. 'The Yanks? What are they doing here? Worse than the bloody Russkis.'

Phil had brought a Sten gun with him. God knows where he'd got it from or why he thought it might be necessary.

'Do you know how to use that thing?' I asked him, nodding at the ugly weapon.

'There's not much to it,' he said, which wasn't quite the answer to my question.

'Let's complete our little journey on foot but don't shoot any Americans unless you really have to.'

'Crow bar?'

'Leave it for now. Don't forget that this place is in our zone so they have no right to be here no matter what they might say.' I tapped the holster of my Webley and said, 'let's go.' I certainly felt a degree of trepidation and I had to remind myself that whoever we were about to confront were the intruders and not us. Phil and I had every right to be here. We'd no objection to the Americans coming over, of course, but there was definitely something underhand going on.

Our feet crunched on the gravel and so we took a couple of paces to our right where the grass would mask the sound of our approach. I took the lead. There had to be some innocent explanation for this odd situation and yet no logic suggested a real need for the US Army coming to this place about which, when I thought of it, they should have had no knowledge.

We took our time. No such degree of stealth should have been required but six years of war had made us wary I suppose. When I turned to look at Phil he smiled, seemingly enjoying this outing, which was a break from whatever routine had become established at the airfield in my absence. My heart rate had increased and yet rationally this was not comparable to aerial combat. Rather, this was, on paper at least, a meeting between two sets of allies.

I had never laid claim to a sixth sense and yet something was telling me to be extremely careful here. There was a distinct undercurrent of menace, but later, when I had time to recount these events and examine the precise nature of the forthcoming encounter, it became clear that this menace was a product of my own imagination. I was tense, ready for confrontation and I imagined that Phil was the same but we kept our pace steady and soon drew level with the factory doors.

It would be fair to say that the GI assigned to guard the truck experienced quite a shock as Phil and I appeared round the corner. His mouth dropped open and for a few moments he was struck dumb. At no point did he point his carbine in our direction. For him I supposed there was some type of crude juxtaposition at work; it was one thing to be confronted by an enemy intruder, quite another to face a *friendly* intruder. The former lent itself to a particular course of action involving quick thinking and aggression but with the latter the correct response was somewhat harder to define.

'Sir?' he called out but not to Phil and me, although he kept us in his line of sight throughout. In this case 'sir' was one of the men trying to prise open the factory doors. They both straightened at once. One was a junior officer, the other a sergeant of some description. They were united in a state of total guilty bewilderment, blank-faced like school truants cornered by the local bobby. The NCO mouthed some sort of silent oath but the officer just frowned until his frown became a look of intense anger.

'Who are you?' he shouted, pointing at his British allies.

I introduced us before adding, 'I also happen to be the town's temporary mayor.'

His mouth flapped open and shut a few times as if he was gathering air in his lungs for his next outburst.

'So you say. How do I know you're the mayor?' His anger was now shaded with doubt but he wasn't yet ready to drop the bluster just yet. In his position I would have done the same thing.

'Well, I can't actually prove it but I outrank you and you are in the British zone and trying to break into a civilian building. I think you're the one who should be explaining yourself.' Throughout this exchange the junior soldier – just a private or maybe a PFC – kept his gaze on us, astonished that his officer was being subjected to this line of questioning. The NCO continually shifted his gaze between us and his boss as the dialogue rolled on.

'How do you know this is the British Zone?'

'I just do. If you've got a map I can show you. What exactly are you doing here? You're a long way from American lines.'

'We're liaising.'

'Liaising with whom?' I asked.

'You.'

'Me?'

'Well, the British Army.'

'I haven't been informed of this,' I said, omitting the pertinent detail that I was rarely informed about anything. He didn't need to know.

'You're not in the army,' he replied.

'No, but I am the senior officer here for the meantime and I'd like to know who gave you permission to come here and what you are trying to do.' I paused for effect. 'You were obviously trying to break in but I'd like to know why. What is inside?'

There was an element of hypocrisy in my show of restrained, frustrated outrage since I had caught these men in the very act I had planned to carry out myself. Being British in the British Zone I had more right to break in than they did… that's certainly how I justified it.

'Who said we were breaking in?'

'What were you doing if not that? What's your name and where is your authorisation?'

'My authorisation comes from General Lee,' replied the officer puffing up his chest like a pigeon. He was average height and tanned. His blue chin indicated that he was perhaps one day away from his last encounter with a razor, something which would not have been tolerated in the British Army or RAF and definitely not where an officer was concerned.

'I don't know who that is and you still haven't told me your name or proven to me that you have authorisation to be here or to enter that building.'

He held his head up, chin forwards in a bullish manner as if daring me to tackle him further. He had a Colt pistol on a webbing belt and the NCO had a little M3 sub machine gun. Taking into account the rifleman nearest the truck we were rather out-gunned but that should not, in the circumstances, have been a consideration. These were our allies after all. We'd had greater cooperation from the Russians whom we looked on as a rather savage bunch compared to the very westernised Americans. Something was definitely off-kilter here.

'I suggest you vacate the area. Please feel free to return with the appropriate paperwork and we can perhaps make an arrangement. I'm usually at the *Rathaus*.'

'The Rat House? What's that?'

'The town hall. In the square. By all means come back tomorrow...'

'Listen pal,' began the officer, disrespectfully. Was he really an officer, I wondered? 'What's the problem here. I mean, we won the war didn't we? Who cares if I take a look inside a Kraut building? Who's cares about it? Who is going to stop me?'

My heart was beating a little faster now but I was sufficiently annoyed by this uncouth Yank that any fear I might have felt was subsumed. I'd been in tighter scrapes than this.

'As I said, come back tomorrow with the appropriate paperwork and we can discuss, er... access. But until then...'

'This is just a pain in the ass,' he said.

'What is inside that's so important?' asked Phil, speaking for the first time.

The officer shook his head and said bitterly, 'let's go fellas.'

It was a large truck and all three fitted comfortably in the cab. The engine started with a rumble and they drove away.

'We'd better hang on to make sure they don't come back,' I said to Phil.

'I thought *we* were going to break in?'

'Er, yes, we are but just let them get away first.'

'We're *allowed* to break in.'

'I'm not sure that's strictly true.'

'More right than them. Do you think that chap was really an officer? Didn't seem terribly refined to me.'

'Maybe American officers aren't refined. He did need a shave though.'

We gave it a few minutes. Phil lit a cigarette as I brought my purloined staff car round to the front.

'You should have asked them where Kalamazoo was,' said my companion as I reached into the back of the car for the crow bar.

Chapter Fourteen

I was reluctant to go to the mess that night because I had lapsed into some sort of unexpected pattern in which a combination of fatigue and relief led me to drink more alcohol than was wise. The bar was now stocked with Russian vodka, German beer, American whisky, which made me believe that a strange set of manufacturing priorities existed even in these calamitous times. But for all my doubts it was in the mess bar that Phil and I convened to run through our findings.

'What are you having?'

'I'll have a vodka and if there is anything to put in it to make it less deadly, I'll have that too.'

'Very debonair,' he joked.

'I don't think so. The vodka drinkers I have met thus far have been one step removed from barbarians.'

He returned with two rather large glasses of the clear liquid and a rare can of Coca-Cola.

'Pushing the boat out there, Phil. Does this symbolise a hope for the future, the two great allies with opposing ideologies taking steps to find common ground for a new, shared, peaceful future in which mankind lives in harmony and comfort, free from war and disease?'

'Yes. And it was free. I think they're trying make us addicted to it so that they eventually corner the market.'

'Doubt it but since it was free… Now to business. Is this a de-brief would you say?'

Before we began I took stock of my fellow imbibers, who for the most part were squadron officers with a selection of brown jobs from the Royal Engineers and two Canadians of the RCAF whom I'd met briefly on one previous occasion. They were the crew of a Mosquito, pilot and navigator, and had spent the latter part of the war seeking out and destroying German aircraft at night.

The record player provided the music, thankfully not 'I've Got a Gal in Kalamazoo' and men chatted quietly reliving old battles or discussing peacetime plans. I got a sense of optimism from my fellow officers, a prevailing view that things would turn out well and the future held surprises – good ones – things that we deserved and had earned. This cheery view was in no way inhibited by the consumption of strong drink…

'You know that they see you as 'the old man', don't you? You, who have been in it since the start, the ace, the leader.'

'All of those things by default. I simply survived and for want of a better person being available these things fell into my lap.'

'Too modest.'

'Not modest enough. There were better men than me who had less luck.'

He shrugged. It wasn't false modesty on my part. I couldn't take the credit for mere good fortune.

'So, remind me. What did you hope to find in that factory?' he asked. I took a sip of my drink before answering. It tasted good I have to say. Ideal for a warm summer's evening. It made me think of peacetime on the veranda of an exotic hotel, palm trees swaying in a warm breeze, the sea lapping lazily on the shore.

'Hope is the wrong word. 'Expect' would be more apt. I *expected* to find something related to these medical experiments I'd been told about.'

'And bearing in mind you found nothing of the sort, what do you think the Americans were expecting to find there?'

'The same. I can't see any logical reason why they would go so far out of their way. They didn't just stumble across the factory. They had to know it was there.'

'But you said yourself they seemed more like criminals than genuine troops. That officer for instance didn't seem like an officer at all if you ask me. They were more like racketeers.'

'Racketeers?'

'You know, black market that sort of thing. Now if they had been expecting to find barrels of booze or cigarettes, something like that, then it would make more sense. So, if that was the case then how come they thought the factory contained booze or whatever and we thought it contained medical equipment? It doesn't make sense. Unless…' He raised his eyebrows and held up one finger speculatively.

'Unless?'

'They were sent by someone else. Someone who just needed a couple of hoods and a truck driver with few morals.'

'Hoods? You've been watching too many gangster films.'

'Gangsters are real. Are you saying that gangsters didn't end up in the US Army? There are bound to be plenty in our army.'

'There are a couple in our *squadron*, Phil. Corporal Meadows for one. If he isn't an East End gangster then I'll eat my hat. Looks like he'd slit your throat as soon as look at you. Probably should have been a commando.'

The truth was we'd found nothing. Admittedly there were spaces where machinery of some kind had been bolted to the floor and there remained some kind of internal crane or hoist overhead that presumably couldn't be taken away due to its size. But the factory had otherwise been stripped bare. It was dusty and grimy, and there was no indication whatsoever that it had been a medical research facility of even the most basic kind. Not that I was an expert but I would have expected to find white tiles and maybe a sluice of some kind, things that could be kept relatively sanitary with disinfectant and clean cloths. But there was nothing like that at all. It was just an empty factory.

'I said before that I just put two and two together. I think I was right.'

'So where did these experiments take place?'

'It may not have been true. You know how the old rumour mill works. The Nazis certainly got up to some terrible things but perhaps not round here.'

'Don't forget, Saul, that those Yanks *were* looking for something. And you were told by your Russian chum that the Americans were sticking their noses in.'

'Not those Americans though.'

'So, a coincidence?'

I shrugged. I had no idea.

'Yes. For all we know they were just doing the rounds, looking for whatever they could find: booty, weapons, souvenirs, booze.'

'So, it's back to the drawing board?'

'I don't think so. The whole thing was a dead end, a bit of hearsay. The Russians haven't been back. There's no evidence to back up his claims. Besides why not just take the evidence they claim is there. They're not usually reticent about such matters. If they want it, they take it.'

I drained my glass and thought about my words. I wasn't sure about my opinion of the Russian soldiery. I *assumed* that they took what they wanted as per the rules of the conquerors but it may have been my normal bias at work, for I regarded them with suspicion.

Phil stood and made his way to the bar, returning shortly with refills of our vodka.

'It's going to be a long night, Saul,' he said justifying his purchases.

'Or a very short one. No more after this. Not for me anyway.'

'What was the name of the Russian?'

'Began with an 'N'. Nobi-something. Novikov. That's it. Colonel Novikov. Why?'

'And he hasn't been back?'

'Nope. I'm quite happy for it to remain that way too. I really don't want the aggravation.'

'Fair enough. So long as he stays away.' Phil held up his glass and said, 'skol'.

We toasted our eastern allies and after that I retired for the evening, reassured that whatever experiments the Germans had carried out were not my immediate concern. It wasn't that I didn't care. However, I was fully in the grip of torrential apathy. Sleep came easily that night.

Chapter Fifteen

My alarm clock had stopped but bright sunshine streaming in through my window roused me nevertheless. I turned and lay on my back as I assessed my physical health and considered the day ahead. Two generous helpings of Russian vodka had done little to impair my mental state, which was pleasing and I was able to concentrate on the things I had to do today, that is to say, nothing at all. Of course, once I got to my mayoral office, there would be things cropping up but Ingrid, my trusty and efficient secretary could deal with those. They might as well have made *her* the mayor. I would certainly recommend her for the post should anyone ask my opinion on the matter.

It was just after 0815 when I surmounted the steps to the front door. I had already waved my by now customary greetings to the butcher, the baker and the candlestick maker and everything seemed fine in a newly peaceful country. The sun shone, the birds sang, the air smelled fresh and clean. My thoughts were of de-mob, cricket, British beer in a British pub with all the usual clichés thrown in.

Everything was perfect.

Until I stepped inside.

'Morning, sir,' said Cleary with a salute which I returned. 'Bit of an awkward day yesterday, sir.'

My heart sank.

'What happened?'

'Well, me and the lads had gone out on patrol,' he began. I suspected that they'd been skiving in my absence but I said nothing. 'And when we got back, them Russkis had been and beaten up yer German woman.'

'Ingrid?'

'Aye, sir.'

'The same Russians?'

He nodded.

'Where is she now?'

'Well, we took her to the field hospital, sir. They were a bit funny about it but we explained who she was and they agreed to look at her injuries.'

'You did the right thing. Is she still there?'

'Couldn't say for sure but I'd guess so.'

'Right, you're in charge until I get back.'

'Acting mayor, like?'

'Precisely. Any problems, get the baker to translate.'

Cleary nodded again and saluted.

***

It was just less than ten miles to the hospital and I stopped off *en route* to top up the petrol tanks. An MP sergeant directed me on the final leg of my journey which terminated at a large detached house with several green marquee-style tents erected in the grounds. An emaciated private sat in the entrance hall and asked me who I wished to see. I was directed to an upstairs room into which two hospital beds had been crammed. One was empty and in the other…

'Squadron Leader. You didn't have to come.'

Her left eye was blackened and her lower lip cut and swollen. Her right arm was in a sling.

'It was Novikov who did this?'

'Yes. Well, one of his men actually but he was there.'

'He ordered it?'

'Yes. And he stood by while his ape beat me.'

'I will make an official complaint.'

'No, it is okay, you…'

'I'm going to over-rule you on this. I will be making a complaint. They need to stay in their zone and respect our rules. You were under British protection…'

'But, it doesn't matter.'

'It does to me. It's not up for discussion I'm afraid.'

She looked unhappy but did not argue.

'So what was the problem?'

'I don't really know.'

'They must have had some pretext for acting as they did?'

'Pretext?'

'Yes. A reason. A made-up reason perhaps. An excuse.'

'Well, I don't know what it was. They hate the Germans of course… and you weren't there. And the soldiers had gone somewhere: the three soldiers you know?'

I nodded. There was something in her tone which suggested that she too believed my tiny army had been skiving. There was nothing that could be done about it now.

The Russian officer's claims about the camp and about Ingrid's connection to it were uppermost in my mind when I asked, 'so what did he say?'

'Just… the normal sort of things.'

'But he didn't just walk into the *Rathaus* and order one of his men to beat you. There must have been some build-up to it. I don't know… he asked you a question and you didn't answer…'

'I *could not* answer,' she said, despairingly.

'Okay, so what was the question? What was it you couldn't answer?'

Our exchange was on the cusp of becoming rather heated which seemed inappropriate in this setting and with this person.

'I feel unwell. Could you come back another time?'

'Yes. But I really need to know what was said.'

'Please. I need to rest.'

With a sigh, she closed her eyes, effectively ending our discourse.

'Is there anything you need?'

Without opening her eyes she said, 'no, nothing.'

***

Had I been a former detective or some sort of brutal German functionary, in the SS or Gestapo for instance, I might have availed myself of more information than I did. I mean, I'd learned nothing at all. Six years spent as a fighter pilot was not the best preparation for the situation I'd just found myself in. I imagined too, that years living in a totalitarian regime toughened you up mentally, taught you to lie with ease, to obfuscate, to brazen it out. By contrast I'd had a soft life, comfortable and easy, until I'd joined the RAF anyway. I had never had to stand my ground on any issue because I was permitted the freedom to have my own point of view. In that respect I was a poor adversary for Ingrid, no match whatsoever.

True, I had only known her for a few days, but it occurred to me, as I drove back to my office that it would not have been unreasonable to have known more about her than I did. The only scrap of information I had about her was her name and, in fact, I only had her word for it that she was called Ingrid. I had no surname. I had no details whatsoever and yet I had just accepted her presence and her claims without a murmur of protest. Had I done so because she happened to be attractive, diligent, witty, generous?

Of course not…

Probably.

The simplest solution, of course, would have been to get her to fill out an official application form for the job she had. It was obvious really and there was no logical argument she could come up with to justify her refusal. The Germans loved their bureaucracy as much as the British, of that I was quite sure, so filling in a form wasn't an outrageous suggestion. And if she refused? I could sack her. I had never asked for her in the first place. I had never employed her and I had no idea where she'd come from and at who's behest. So if I sacked her, what was she going to do about it?

The sun was out, the wind was in my hair and I felt invigorated, filled with new resolve. I'd been too soft before. I should have demanded answers and if I hadn't got them, got rid of Ingrid, or whoever she was. Partly, there didn't seem any harm in having her around and partly she had quickly become indispensable to me but all the same, I'd let things slip. Would it have been different if she been a fat *hausfrau* with bad teeth and no knowledge of English?

Yes, definitely.

Cleary was at my desk when I returned. The other two were in the little kitchen smoking and drinking tea.

He stood as I entered.

'Any problems?'

'I had to shoot some looters, have new drains built and deliver a baby but apart from that, just a quiet morning, sir.'

I chuckled at his good humour. 'Good. I knew I could rely on you.'

'Any word on the er, patient, sir?'

'She's okay really.' I paused. 'What do you know about her?'

'Me? Nothing, sir. I know less than you.'

'I'm not sure that's possible. All I know is her first name and I'm not even sure about that. She told me she was called 'Ingrid' but I have no documentation for her, so I don't even know if that is true. I don't know who pays her or who gave her a job.'

'Where did she come from, sir?'

'I don't know that either. Well, she was in my office at the airfield when I turned up and when I was given this job I brought her with me. She said she'd worked for the previous commander of the air base.'

'When it was a Luftwaffe base?'

'Yes. So, it seemed as if she had just turned up for work despite the war ending and the base being deserted. That makes a certain amount of sense if you hope to be paid, I suppose.'

'Is that what you would have done, sir? If you were in that same situation, would you have turned up for work?'

'That's good question, corporal. I don't think I'd have been sitting there acting as though nothing had changed. Maybe after a few days, I'd have made an approach and asked if there was work and explained who I was and what I did. I wouldn't expect just to be taken on.'

'So, maybe this Russian officer is telling the truth about her.'

'Maybe.'

'I'll make a brew, sir. There's MPs nearby, if you want me to call in with the SIB, sir. They'll be pretty busy I expect but this might be their sort of thing.'

'Don't do anything yet. I've got to get this clear in my head first.'

***

Saying that I'm going to get it clear in my head is one thing and doing it quite another. I sat at my desk, drinking tea, ostensibly pondering my options with regard to the mysterious Ingrid but in reality utterly stumped. My mind was either blank or filled with useless images of unrelated things such as summer days spent back home, walks on the beach, trips to the cinema. These were the things I was going to do upon my return to Britain or after my discharge in the Utopia my mind had created countless times in the last six years.

When I'd finished my tea, I continued to sit and continued to try and resolve the problem I had. I found that even defining the problem was difficult. Was there a problem, in fact, and was it mine if indeed it existed at all? I expected to be replaced as *Bürgermeister* any day now and once that happened I would revert to being a plain old squadron leader whose *raison d'etre* had vanished like snow in a ditch. I should be thinking about how to keep my squadron busy and purposeful until they were returned to civilian life and yet here I was sitting at a desk, really doing nothing.

I rang the air base and got through to my squadron clerk.

'Sergeant, have we got any forms, well, application forms really?'

'Application forms for what exactly, sir?'

'Anything. To join the RAF or… I don't know, just anything.'

'I'll have a look, sir. I can have the duty driver bring them over. That's if I find something.'

'Good man. It doesn't really matter what it's for. I just need to get some details down. How are things? The usual grumbling about de-mob?'

He laughed. 'The natives are less restless when the sun is shining. I think spirits are fairly high at the minute, sir. They're still enjoying the fact that the war is over.'

'That's good. What is the rumour mill saying about de-mob?'

'The rumour mill is very quiet at the minute, sir. All the hoo-ha about going to Japan has died down as well. Can't say I'm upset, sir.'

'No, nor me. Well, keep on top of things and if you find those forms have 'em sent over. Thank you, Sergeant.'

With that sorted, I sat back in my chair which groaned uncharacteristically. Maybe it was feeling signs of wear and tear – I knew I was.

I had a coffee and enjoyed the buzz it gave me. Sun streamed in through the windows and I had the place to myself because my troops were on patrol, perhaps feeling guilty at the previous day's indolence. Cup in hand, I toured my little fiefdom, peering into each room in turn, looking at the empty desks and the bright spaces on the walls were once had hung pictures of A Hitler esq. There must have been millions of copies of his portrait, each one now only fit for firewood. Having said that, I could not imagine any of these people having the courage to burn his image, even now. Maybe in time. A vision of Charlie

Chaplin came to me and was gone. There were definite similarities between the two. Maybe I was thinking of Chaplin's film, 'The Great Dictator', although I'd never seen it.

My reveries came to an end when I heard the windows rattling in their frames. There was only one thing that could generate that noise and those rapid fire shock waves and sure enough when I looked out over the balcony onto the square below, there was a Russian tank pulling in and coming to a halt. This was something bigger than a T34, with a bigger gun and a strange turret shaped like a sort of flat, rounded pan.

'Shit,' I said. The Russians had returned.

Chapter Sixteen

The urgent need for action just happened to coincide with a near-crippling attack of apathy. In fact it wasn't just plain apathy but some form of anxiety or an uncomfortable mixture of both – anxapathy, perhaps. Whatever it was I felt my chest constrict as if a belt was being tightened around my diaphragm. This invisible belt wasn't affecting my ability to breathe exactly and yet I felt it tighten all the same. I slumped on a nearby bench as I gathered my thoughts. There was no avoiding a clash with our allies but I had to enter the fray from a position of strength rather than looking like an idiot who had the wind punched out of his torso.

Only apparent strength would mollify the Russians. A display of weakness and they'd take the initiative and be all over the town, taking what they needed before I could even react. Raping and pillaging… that's what I expected, like modern Vikings.

My resolve returned, in part at least, and I took a deep breath.

Novikov and a second officer were storming through the doors as I got to the bottom step.

'Ah, Squadron Leader. We have come to check up.'

'Check up? On what?'

'I spoke to the German bitch yesterday but I didn't get anywhere, so I have come back. I'll talk to the monkey grinder,' he said and laughed. The second officer laughed too although it later transpired that he spoke no English. Both were armed with revolvers as was I.

'Yes, well I have to say that I don't approve of your treatment of her. She is under British care and…'

'Is she?'

'Yes.'

'Is she really?'

I opened my mouth to speak but he cut me off.

'You gave her a job then?'

'Well, not exactly but she's been…'

'You know nothing of her. Do you know her name?'

I thought of the application form I was waiting for and said, 'yes.'

'What is it?'

'Why do you need to know?'

'Just a simple question, major. What is her name?'

'I'm not a major. I'm a squad…'

'It is the same thing. You see. You don't know her name.'

'It's Ingrid.'

'It is not. What is her other names?'

At this point I had bigger fish to fry than his small grammatical errors.

'Colonel, I'm afraid I must ask you to leave. You're in the British Zone as you know and you need proper permission to come across here just as I would need to visit the Russian Zone.'

'You can come to the Russian Zone whenever you want…'

'Well, maybe so but that isn't the point. If you require any assistance or wish to visit then you must apply in writing to Brigadier Rea.'

'Yes, yes. Let's have drinks and talk this over like fellow officers. There is no need to stand here arguing.' He motioned to his silent companion and the latter left, presumably to collect the vodka required for our discussions. I wasn't falling into that trap again. His bloody Bolshevik bonhomie was wearing as thin as the shoe leather on a tramp's boot.

'No. Sorry, Colonel. You must go through the proper channels.'

'I thought you were the proper channels. You are in charge.'

Unfortunately, he had made a good point.

'But I am not high enough up. You need to get permission from Brigadier Rea. I can give you the address and if he okays it then of course you can come back.'

'And Brigadier is the mayor of the town?'

'No, I am but he is my boss. I am only a major,' I said. I only just avoided rolling my eyes, having used the rank he'd given me. An observer might have thought Novikov stupid and obtuse but he was, in fact extremely clever… and obtuse.

'So, if I am wanting to do something in the town then I speak to you!' he said almost joyfully having taken his argument to its natural conclusion. He was still in good spirits. I was not. The moment of greatest danger arrived just after he had uttered these words – the other officer bearing gifts of vodka – two bottles of the bloody stuff, a sign that Novikov was taking this matter very seriously indeed.

'Shit. No, Colonel. You must leave. Now.'

He looked at my revolver and smiled without obvious menace.

'I brought a tank.'

'Yes,' I said. 'And I command a squadron of fighter bombers.'

At that moment I sounded more courageous than I felt. There was a silence and then Novikov guffawed. His sidekick did likewise. Personally, I didn't crack a smile for I wasn't really in on the joke, although seemingly I had made it.

'Yes, yes. You sure you won't drink?'

'I'm sure thank you, sir. I have a busy day ahead.' Relief was beginning to flood my system, creating a feeling of near euphoria in a way that no mere vodka could have done. I might just have pulled this off.

'Okay. I will give you the bottle anyway as a goodwill.' He held the bottle out and I took it, thanking him as I did so. 'But you must do homework on that German bitch and when you have found out about her you get back with me. Okay?'

'Okay.'

He left and I made my way to the little kitchen to make coffee. Had I avoided a diplomatic incident or just avoided the need to shoot a fifty-ton tank with my .38 revolver? I really wasn't sure.

***

Once the kettle had boiled I felt a pang of hunger and made my way across the square to the bakery.

'*Sprechen sie English*?' I asked, virtually expending my knowledge of his language in the effort.

He held up a thumb and forefinger close together to indicate the breadth of his knowledge. He smiled, which seemed like a good omen and when I pointed at a fairly enticing slice of cake, he scooped it up on a slice and put it into a small paper bag.

It was going well, even more so when he waved away payment. Then I ruined it by asking him what he knew of my assistant.

'Nothing.'

'You know who I mean? The pretty lady who works in…'

'I do not know who she is.'

'Did she work at the airfield?'

He gave a shrug but there was something more to that simple gesture than met my eye. It was almost as if he wanted to tell me more but was confounded by misplaced or out-of-date ideology. Did he want me to provide him with a means to circumvent his obsolescent loyalty? Like an alcoholic he couldn't quite bring himself to say just a few pertinent words.

And then something occurred to me and I watched his face carefully as I posed the question.

'Did she work at the camp?'

He said nothing but looked at me levelly and I knew that he'd given me my answer.

***

'And what did your Corporal Cleary say?' asked Phil.

'He wasn't there.'

'Ah, so it was you versus a brand new Josef Stalin tank.'

'Is that what is was? Yes. Man versus tank. Armed only with a revolver the gallant British officer took on the mightiest tank in the Red Army.'

'Would you really have called us up in a display of might?'

'It would have been tricky,' I admitted. 'Thankfully, he either took me at my word or became convinced that I was correct. He lives to fight another day.'

'So, what's your next move?'

'It would seem sensible to find out what I can about Ingrid. I should have done it before.'

I wanted Phil to reassure me that I had acted correctly, that *'anyone would have done the same thing'* but instead he just nodded.

Deflated, I stood.

'The drinks are on me.'

'What about that bottle of vodka he gave you?'

'I put it behind the bar. We'll get a couple of free ones out of it.'

When I returned Phil put a question to me.

'So, who are you going to ask?'

'I thought of starting with her.'

'I wouldn't. You'll be warning her off if you do that. It sounds as if the baker has already confirmed her connection to the camp for you anyway. She's not going to own up to anything.'

'Maybe.' I sipped my drink.

'You need to ask someone else or she'll go to ground.'

'Who? There is no one who will speak out about her. Even if I got the baker to talk he almost certainly wouldn't know the full story. He'd know she worked there and nothing else.'

'Survivors.'

'Survivors from the camp?'

'Of course.'

'Are there any?'

'Must be.'

'Supposing I find one, how do I get her to them for the purposes of identification?'

'You don't. You take a photograph. You're getting her to complete an application anyway so get one of the intelligence bods to come over and take a photo to go with her application. All you need are two copies, one for the form and one to show to any survivors.'

'They won't speak English and I don't speak German or Yiddish or any other language.'

'Get them to write it down and then get it translated later. Saul, none of this is impossible to do.'

He was right of course and now I was hoping she'd be back at work tomorrow so that I could get started.

Chapter Seventeen

'Why?'

'Well, it's just that my bosses have questioned why you are working for me when there is no application form, we have no details of you or any form of contract.'

'But I have done a good job?'

'Of course. I couldn't have done it without you. Look at it this way, if you do this then it means you will probably have a full-time job with us.' I meant the words as I said them and immediately realised that if what I knew of her was correct she be more likely to go to jail than get a job. Nevertheless I kept my tone light and the bit about having been reliant on her was the absolute truth.

She looked very unhappy and had it not been for her possible involvement with the concentration camp I might have sympathised. I actually liked this woman. On a personal level she had given me no cause for complaint and had carried out her duties diligently and without fuss.

'Why don't I just get a piece of paper and write my details down?'

I pretended not to hear and she sat heavily. In moments she was scratching out her personal details on the form. I got on with some work of my own which comprised looking at a few personnel files of airmen who might be in line for promotion.

'What do I write in this section?'

Ingrid held up her paper and pointed but I couldn't read it.

'What does it say?'

'Date of enlistment.'

'Ah, just leave that blank.'

Scowling but with her head down so that it wasn't obvious, she returned to her task and I to mine. But it didn't last.

'And this one?'

'What does it…'

'Service number.'

'Just leave it blank. Any parts that don't apply, just leave them.'

She cleared her throat and got back to work. I took it upon myself to make two cups of coffee in the hope that this would improve her humour. If it did so she managed to hide it well.

There was a knock at the door and the photographer entered. He saluted.

'Morning, sir. You needed a photograph to be taken?'

'Yes. Morning, Wickens. Just a standard portrait photo or whatever of this lady. The sort of thing you would have in an ID card.'

'Yes, sir.' Wickens, a very polite chap who would undoubtedly go to university after the war, opened his mouth to speak but Ingrid, at once surly and compliant, stood and followed him out of the room to the hallway which seemed the natural, well-lit venue for photograph taking. He'd brought with him a fairly compact camera and I knew he was an expert in its use. Working in the intelligence section it was discovered that Wickens could turn his hand to many things and did so without a fuss. As I stood to peruse Ingrid's form, I wondered if I might promote him to corporal before his de-mob. Sadly, they finished so quickly that I really didn't get a proper look at the details she'd added thus far.

'All done, sir. I can get this developed today if you need it.'

'Yes, do that. How are things on the base?'

'Quiet, sir. Everyone dreaming of de-mob.'

'Including you?'

'Especially me, sir,' he said, good naturedly.

When he'd gone, Ingrid handed over her form, with a trace of her good humour on the point of returning. Or was I imagining that?

'I am going to the bakery, Squadron... Saul. Would you like anything?'

Her hurried correction and use of my first name made me feel like a traitor. I was maintaining good relations whilst possibly building a case against her. It wasn't fair. Or maybe it was. I didn't know who she really was or what she had done. How had she spent the war years? Up to this point I had known almost nothing about her and yet somehow I think she expected me to believe that she had come through the war untouched by the Nazi regime and the brutal conquest of Europe. It wasn't possible. At the very least she had relatives who had served The Reich. I would soon see.

Despite her absence, I didn't try to look through the form she'd just completed. I had decided that Phil and I would sit together later and work out who she really was. I hoped that our fears, planted by others, were misplaced.

***

'You've got it?'

'Yep and the photos.' I passed the documents across to Phil who smiled. 'The mystery shall unravel.'

'If she's telling the truth on that form, of course. For all we know she claims to be from Kalamazoo.'

'Secretly you'd like that, Saul. You haven't gone through this already?'

'The briefest glimpse. I don't know why but I wanted someone else with me so that… it remains above board or something. I need a witness to this moment when we discover who she really is.'

'I'm flattered.'

We were in my office at the squadron, which was temporarily in Phil's capable hands. A picture of the King had replaced one of the Fuhrer.

'So, everything's okay in the squadron?'

'Yes, I think so.'

'Managing without me?'

'Yes. You sound worried about that.'

'Believe me I'm not. I'm not at all. Just keep on top of all that paperwork so that I don't have a mountain of it to climb when I get back.'

'We're getting a new pilot today.'

'Really? What's the bloody point of that?'

'I suppose since they trained him they've got to send him somewhere.'

'True. He's going to be disappointed. Not much action for him.'

'Unless you decide to attack those Russians, Saul.'

I shuddered. 'Yes. There'd be plenty of excitement for him in that case. Anyway, let's not think about that. Let's find out who Ingrid is. I'll let you read it and give me the highlights.'

He began scanning her application form for a job that didn't exist.

'Ingrid Baumann.'

'Okay.'

'You just accept that that's her name?'

'For now. I have nothing else to go on, have I?'

'Date of birth is 20th May, 1916.'

'I suppose that's about right. Hold on…'

'Yep, her birthday is tomorrow.'

'It'll be interesting to see how she reacts when I wish her a happy birthday.'

Phil nodded.

'Her previous employer was the Luftwaffe. She's put down that her employment ended on 8th May. The day the war ended.'

'I suppose that's accurate.'

'Worked as a secretary in Detmold and Hameln. Originally from Regensburg, which is in Bavaria. Erm, what else? Next of Kin is Harald Baumann of Regensburg. There's an address for Harald. God knows if it is genuine.'

'The same could be said for any of it. So presumably she's single?'

Phil scanned the document again, checking several pages.

'So, she claims.'

'And yet she has a wedding ring…'

'Ha, you checked.'

'I'm observant. What's wrong with that? And she did start to say something about a husband one time before she cut herself short.'

'Hmm. Anyway, that's at least one lie we've found. Says here that she went to school in Regensburg, Girl's Catholic school. That's about it. Plenty left blank but that's understandable since she isn't *actually* applying to be a gunner in the RAF Regiment.'

'Okay, so that's the official version of Ingrid Baumann. No address? It's a start, I suppose.'

'Or, it's all lies. Her address is… Wegener Strasse 13. Which translates as 13 Wegener Strasse.'

'A brilliant piece of deduction there, Phil. At least she had the sense to retain her Christian name. If it is lies we'll soon find out. Much easier to remember the truth than a load of garbage you've scribbled down in haste.'

'So, what's next?'

'I don't suppose you've got a spare birthday cake lying around?'

***

That night a small convoy of trucks took the lads to a makeshift cinema in town to watch 'The Fighting Seabees.' Once Phil had explained the gist of the plot I made my decision; I'd stay behind and write a letter to Margaret.

'You might enjoy it, Saul. You need a break.'

'Thank you but even the title puts me off. A film made about the war by people who weren't actually in the war themselves, for the entertainment of people who *were* in the war... I can't quite bring myself to watch it.'

'It's just escapism.'

'Well, you escape Phil, and I will stay here, a prisoner to my own high morals.'

It wasn't long before I was bored with the letter writing process although not so badly affected that the idea of watching a film had any appeal. The truth was, there was little to report and my letters to Margaret were so bland as to be virtually pointless. I talked about the minutiae of a typical day of *Bürgermeister* -ing but omitted anything about Ingrid, the Russians, or indeed the Americans.

My mind blank, I sat back in my chair and tried to picture life as a civilian. But I'd been an airman for ten years and I didn't really know what civvy street was like. What was I going to do? Where would I live? The problem was that you needed money to do anything so simply opting out of life wasn't really a workable plan. Could I be a teacher or a civil servant or a police officer? I just had no idea.

I could probably get a job working in the same furniture factory as my dad but somehow, having made it to the rank of squadron leader in the RAF, I now held greater, if vaguer, ambitions.

Happily, I had a job for the meantime and perhaps there was a place for me in the post-war RAF; I was a regular after all. No doubt, I'd take a demotion because a peace time force could only retain so many squadron leaders but they'd hardly bust me back down to my pre-war sergeant's rank. I rubbed my eyes, thought about a quick pint in the mess and an early night but when I checked the time it was too early for either.

I blew air from my cheeks, cast a glance around my room and its sparse furnishings and made a decision. I was going to visit Ingrid and if not visit I was going to check that the address she'd given me really existed.

As a precaution I booked out at the guardroom and drove off in my noisy little staff car. It was probably high time that it had proper number plates on it but no one seemed very bothered about vehicle regulations yet; there was much else to be sorted out first.

It was a warm evening and I had yet to try out the folding roof which when stowed, as it had been all the time in my possession, made the vehicle look like some kind of self-propelled pram. There was no chance of making a discreet entrance onto Wegener Strasse with the manic clatter of the engine and so I planned to park in a neighbouring street and complete my recce on foot. As ever I had my trusty revolver although increasingly it felt as if I needed protection from my allies rather than my erstwhile enemies. Perhaps it had always been on the cards that the victor's unity would one day dissolve. At times it felt like every man for himself. During the course of the war we'd had to, as a nation, I suppose, re-appraise the Russians and now we were probably going to do it again, returning to our original view that they were the enemy of civilisation and to be feared.

When I cut the engine, a profound silence settled, partly as result of cessation of the Volkswagen's mechanical cacophony and partly because there was just no one around. Not so much as a dog was present. This was my first foray into town in the evening and also the furthest I had travelled into its unknown peacetime streets. I don't know what I had expected but in Britain there had been an explosion of joy and relief at the end of hostilities whereas here there was nothing. They'd lost of course but peacetime was not bringing with it any great dividends or not yet at any rate.

I set off, rounding the corner onto Wegener Strasse, a tree-lined boulevard that could have been French or Belgian, pleasant, leafy, secluded – everything that post-war Germany tended not to be. The Germans had suffered a near apocalypse and had been generous in the sharing of misery and yet Wegener Strasse looked as if it had been spared, preserved in some manner. Of course some aspects of normal life were absent. In better times there might have been a few cars parked and couples strolling in the evening sun, children playing but now, just a few days after the end of the war, there were no signs of life. I did take heart from the fact that the street actually existed, for not every aspect of Ingrid's application form had been truthful. That was not to say that she lived here but it felt like a good starting point for my investigation, not a total dead end.

I stood at the street corner for a moment like a man undecided, but actually trying to appraise the area and my situation before I blundered in. I was assailed by doubts, not least concerning the fact that I was rather conspicuous, armed and in uniform in this ostensibly genteel residential area. Not only that but I couldn't quite explain to myself what I was hoping to achieve now that I was here. Turning on my heel and walking away was on the cards but I'd stayed put trying to be resolute and fearless. Not for the first time I wondered how I had ever been able to face aerial combat, sometimes for day after day and on occasion more than once in a day, and yet…

'Saul?'

I turned at the unexpected use of my name and found Ingrid peering at me from the adjoining street. She closed in and I felt foolish, reduced to the status of a schoolboy caught stealing toffees from a shop or having a crafty Woodbine when he thought no adults were around.

'Ah, hello, Ingrid.' My mind was racing, trying to put together a plausible excuse for my presence from a swirling jumble of words and images and things which were neither words nor images but blobs of coloured nothingness and disconnected emotions and panic and embarrassment and…

'You look like you have seen a ghost.'

'Ha, yes. I, er…' That was about as coherent as it got but thankfully Ingrid took the initiative *and* control of the conversation.

'Why are you here?'

It was a good question and, amazingly, in some incredible flash of inspiration an answer came to me.

'I just wanted to make sure the Russians weren't pestering you.'

She smiled and it was a very attractive smile. She knew I had lied and I knew she knew and so on but right there and then I didn't care. I was just happy to be let off the hook. If we could both pretend that I was there, in her street, for legitimate reasons then that was fine. She was pleased to see me or putting on a very convincing show of being so.

'Oh, I am fine but thank you. The Russians terrify us. Revenge, you understand.'

'That's good. I'm sure they'll be back but this isn't their town.'

There was a tiny flicker of something like recognition, an emotional tic, there and gone, which said, *and it isn't your town either.* In that fragment of a second I was the hated enemy. She hated me for being there and for even pretending that I was going to protect her from the Red Army hordes. The Germans were proud. I knew then that they would rise again.

This was the moment in proceedings where she would invite me in for a drink. I smiled. She smiled. She did not offer me in for a drink.

'Well, if you are okay, I'll get back to camp.'

'Okay. Thank you for checking on me.'

'I'll see you tomorrow.'

And that was that. Like a bashful schoolboy I turned and retraced my steps.

***

I tried to think about what had been achieved by my foray and came to the conclusion that it had been a stupid waste of time. I was humiliated but not only that, I was humiliated in front of a German. I had set off on my quest as an officer and a gentleman and returned as a total clown. When I signed back in at the guardroom I was glad that I didn't have to account for my location or actions.

Drink is never the answer in these situations, so with that in mind I went straight to the mess, only to find it almost empty.

'Evening, sir. You didn't fancy the show, then?'

It was the affable Corporal Shutt, a man without military bearing but an inexhaustible supply of good humour who posed the question.

'I didn't want to risk laughing myself to death, Shutty,' I said and he beamed at my use of his nickname.

Well, there was no one around to frown or complain about my familiarity.

'Can't be too careful, sir. Not after all you've been through. Now, can I get you a drink, sir? We still have some of that Russian Vodka you bequeathed to the mess the other day. Free to you of course.'

'How can I refuse? Did you know it's made from potatoes?'

'I did not, sir. That's a very interesting fact.'

'Will you have one yourself?'

'I really shouldn't in case Flight Sergeant Hetherington catches me drunk in charge of a… an officer's mess.'

I laughed. Shutt never crossed the bounds of military etiquette but he came close sometimes and no one cared. 'I insist. It's an order and if anyone complains they can report you to… er… me for disciplinary action.'

'In that case, sir, I'll have a large one. Would you like some of this Coca-Cola with it, sir? Just to make it drinkable.'

'That would be good. By the way, where did it come from, Corporal Shutt?'

'I think the MT sergeant did a deal with some passing Yanks.'

Shutt busied himself preparing our drinks.

'What sort of deal?'

'I think he swapped the ambulance for a truck load of the stuff. But they never came to collect the ambulance, sir, just to reassure you.'

'Sounds like a good deal.'

'For us, yes.'

I sipped my drink and then drank it down in one.

'I'd better order another while I can still speak.'

Shutt laughed obediently.

'Has it been that bad a day, sir?'

'Yes, I think it has. Tomorrow will be better of course.'

By the time, I'd started my third drink, my situation seemed rather better than it had on my disconsolate drive back to camp. Despite Ingrid's forbearance I had felt like someone with unhealthy appetites, preying on vulnerable women, women whose husbands were away at war for instance. But now, I was wrapped up in a cocoon of wellbeing, radiating warmth, happiness and contentment.

'Bloody hell, Shutty. This is strong stuff.'

He laughed. 'Just one more then, sir?'

'After this one?'

'Yes. There's a bit left in the bottle and plenty of Coca-Cola.'

'Good show. We need to celebrate the end of the war.'

'I've celebrated a few times now, sir. I think we all have.'

'It was a big war,' I pointed out.

Naturally the relationship between trusted corporal and squadron leader did not extend to discussions of important matters such as my recent episode with Ingrid Baumann. There was no confessional aspect to things. But for now, none of it mattered. Life was good. Excellent in fact. Everything was going to be okay. Shutty smoked a cigar. Neither of us spoke. I knew I was drunk but so what? After everything I'd been through, who could begrudge me a drink?

So relaxed was I feeling that it took a couple of moments to realise that the two men who'd entered the bar were not early returnees from the ENSA concert but an army brigadier and an RAF Group Captain.

'Cohen?' asked the RAF officer.

'Eh, yes. Yes, sir.' I stood, unsteadily.

'You'd better sober up bloody quickly, Squadron Leader. There has been an incident.'

Chapter Eighteen

Sobering up wasn't really possible. There was no means for me to extract the alcohol from my blood but I asked Corporal Shutt for a large glass of water and downed this with as much decorum as I could muster. For his part, Shutty was putting on a fairly convincing act of sobriety, something I felt he had been perfecting for years. The Brigadier looked at me with mild disgust and the Group Captain with pained sympathy like a man who'd been let down by someone he'd championed for years. Personally, I felt rather aggrieved that I couldn't even get sozzled in my own mess, having won the bloody war virtually single-handedly.

'Would you like to go to my office, sir?' I asked.

'Might as well stay here Cohen; no one about.'

'Yes, sir.'

'Is this your normal practice, Squadron Leader?' asked the Brigadier, sternly. He was a Great War veteran with two rows of ribbons on his tunic, clipped moustache, frown. He was just missing a glass eye and a duelling scar…

'No, sir. I was just…'

'Well, anyway there's a bit of a flap on in town. Your town that is.'

'I see. I can look into it in the morning.'

'You'll look into it now.'

'Yes, sir.'

The Group Captain, who hadn't spoken up to this point, finally introduced my two new pals.

'This is Brigadier Rea and I am Group Captain Holland. Sorry to have landed you with the *Bürgermeister* job but you were the senior chap on the spot. It's been a bit of a muddle and it's just got worse. There's a stand off between the Russians and the Americans in town.'

'Colonel Novikov by any chance?'

'You know him?' enquired Rea.

'I have encountered him before, shall we say. He came to…'

'Well, he's bloody well set the cat amongst the pigeons now.'

I sighed deeply. If I was sobering up then it was a long process. I felt a headache forming like gathering storm clouds constricted in the confines of my skull, roiling, twisting and pushing against the delicate bone that held my battered brain in position. And now those clouds were escaping, seeping into my right eye socket, pulsating like a heartbeat.

'Are you okay, Cohen?' interjected the army officer.

'Yes, sir. If I'm honest, a bit the worse for wear. I wasn't expecting to…'

'Well, we obviously can't leave things as they are even if you have not managed to retain hold of your senses. Novikov has got three great tanks parked outside a factory and some American Johnnies are stopping him from getting in.'

'I think I've met them too. I just…'

'Why haven't you done anything about it?' insisted the Brigadier. Little pink spots had appeared in his cheeks now.

'I thought I had, sir. We frightened the Yanks… the Americans off and we told Novikov that he wasn't to come back.'

'And that's it?'

'I told him I commanded a squadron of ground attack aircraft actually.'

Group Captain Holland smothered a smile at that point and I experienced a little bit of relief, not enough to displace the building headache but enough to lift my spirits.

'To be fair to Squadron Leader Cohen, he is, as he has already stated a fighter pilot and a very good one, sir. This job was rather thrust upon him and it's only now that he has had any real support. I think he's handled the situation rather well all things considered.'

'Maybe so,' said Rea grudgingly. 'Tell me what you know.'

***

By the time I'd furnished Brigadier Rea with the details in my possession the first of the ENSA survivors were trickling back into the mess to drown their sorrows.

'There's an infantry platoon on standby. Get some sleep and in the morning I need to speak to this German woman to see what she knows about this.'

Somewhere along the line, Rea had become the very voice of reason. I took a large glass of water with me and retired to my room, my head spinning with drunken confusion. I hoped I wasn't going to feel like death warmed up the next morning.

I managed to cram eight hours sleep into fifteen minutes – that's what it felt like, anyway – and when I woke my headache was still there but perhaps making a slow withdrawal. I swore, drank the last of my water and prepared myself for the day ahead. Breakfast would have to do without me.

Rea had left the situation in the hands of Group Captain Holland and it was he who met me at the car at 0730.

I saluted and he responded in kind.

'How's the head?'

'I've never felt better, sir,' I lied.

'Let's go in that case. I've drawn a revolver from the armoury but let's hope the situation has resolved itself.'

I found Holland an altogether more affable fellow than his Army colleague, certainly more sympathetic to my plight and appreciative of my record in the war. He smiled when he saw my transport.

'I had to improvise, sir. Might as well make use of what the Jerries left behind. Noisy bloody thing, though.'

He understood what I meant when I started the engine.

It was a short drive to the factory, even shorter this morning because we were stopped by a cordon of infantrymen before we got there.

'Who is in charge, Corporal?' asked Holland.

'It's Lieutenant Pearson, sir. I can get him for you.'

'Yes, do that.'

To me he said, 'bloody mess. Not sure who I dislike more the Reds or the Yanks. Both late to the party. Both bloody ungrateful if you ask me. The Yanks are convinced that they won the war single-handed.'

'What did you fly, sir?' I asked, changing the subject.

'Blenheims, then Beauforts. Then a desk. Took an Italian bullet in the knee in the Med. What about you?'

'Hurricanes, P40s in the desert, then Typhoons.'

'In since the beginning?'

'Yes, sir. Joined in '35 actually.'

'Staying on?'

'For the mean time if they'll have me. I can't think what I would do in Civvy Street.'

'No, it's going to be bloody hard. We train people to become gunners, engineers, pilots, navigators, send them out over enemy territory over and over again and when we're finished with them it's 'thank you very much, Here's a medal, Good luck'. People will expect a bit more but they won't get it. Election coming up. Who are you going to vote for?'

'I hadn't thought about it, sir.'

'I'm sure the Labour Party will get in this time, you know. Attlee.'

'Not Winston?' I was shocked at the mere suggestion.

'Mark my words. The usual people will vote for the Conservatives but the masses will vote Labour. Socialist paradise, don't forget. Winston represents the old order, the old way of doing things. Attlee promises a better life for ordinary men.'

'Who will you vote for, sir?'

'Conservatives.'

'Same here,' I said, newly appalled at the thought of Socialism.

Pearson approached. He recognised me and smiled.

'What a bloody to-do,' he joked.

'So what's the situation? Some sort of stand-off?'

'I think you could call it that. No exchange of fire, or anything like that. '

'Let's take a look,' said Holland. 'I take it we have a Russian speaker on hand?'

'Colonel Novikov speaks good English, sir,' I said as we began walking.

'And he's a reasonable chap?'

'I think you would have to qualify that by saying that he's 'reasonable for a Russian'.'

'Ah.'

'I mean, you can chat to him, have a drop of vodka and so on and he makes it sound as if you're equals discussing possibilities when in fact he likes to dictate terms. Not too bothered about twisting the facts to suit his own needs, either.'

'I see. Well we are of equal rank and he has strayed out of his area so he hasn't got a leg to stand on. Have you encountered the Americans?'

I described my previous meeting.

'Good grief. They sound more like pirates than anything else,' said Holland.

'Definitely up to no good, sir.'

We turned a corner to find a Russian tank parked with its crew lolling around in the sunshine, not a care in the world.

'Good God. It's a huge bloody thing!'

'It's a Josef Stalin, sir. So I am informed.'

He turned to Pearson and said, 'and where are the Americans?'

'Just out of sight, sir.'

'Standing their ground, eh?'

'Trapped I would say.'

We continued walking.

The tank crew looked in our direction but without apparent alarm or interest. They lounged like languid lizards lapping up the sun in preparation for a day of whatever Russian tankers did.

'Have they been hitting the vodka already?' asked Holland *sotto voce* as we passed. 'Mind you, they might as well enjoy the sun before they go home to that frozen hell-hole of theirs.'

We passed four British troops on our way to the Americans. They looked both bewildered and tired.

'These your men, Lieutenant?'

'Yes, sir.'

'Fed and watered?'

'I think so. The Sergeant-major is bringing some food round for them, I believe.'

We carried on.

In contrast to the Russians, the American troops at least had the good grace to straighten themselves up a little as we approached. There were five of them this time, each one armed, bearded and dishevelled.

'Who's in charge?' asked Holland, sharply.

'I am.'

I recognised him from the previous encounter. It seemed that he'd been unable to wash or shave in the interim.

Holland introduced himself and then said, 'could you identify yourself and explain the situation as you see it.'

'Winters. Captain Winters,' he said doubtfully as if the rank was an afterthought. 'We're trapped by those Reds.'

'Captain Winters, it would be usual for you to address me as 'sir'. Good form, you know.'

Winters looked even more bewildered than previously. It would have been easier simply to comply but instead he challenged Holland's assertion.

'But you're only a captain, like me.'

'A group captain. The equivalent of a colonel.'

'Well, why didn't you say… Anyway, *sir*. We really need to get away. Back to our unit, you know?'

'What is your unit exactly?'

'Eh… it's the 591st Ordnance Company.'

Holland looked at Pearson as if the latter could verify that information. Pearson shrugged as if to say, *'it could be…'*

'Yes. We'll try to get you away from here. How long have you been separated from them.'

Winters looked at the NCO next to him and then turned back to us, saying, 'twenty-four hours.'

'You haven't had a shave for several days.'

Winters shrugged uncomfortably.

'And you haven't explained why you're here.'

'Have you asked them Russians whey they are here… sir.'

'Not yet, but I will. For now, I'm asking you. It's a reasonable question. You're in the British Zone.'

'We got lost,' said the NCO speaking for the first time.

'Careless. That's the second time, isn't it Squadron Leader?'

'Yes sir. Both times they've ended up in exactly the same place.'

'Odd.'

'Very odd, sir.'

The American officer squirmed now in a mixture of anger and fear.

'If you can just escort us out of here, sir, we can be on our way.'

Holland appeared not to hear.

'So, why do you finish up at exactly the same place each time. What is there here which is so fascinating?'

'I already said it was an accident.'

'But your unit must be at least a hundred miles away.'

Holland gestured to Pearson and me.

'We need a conflab.'

We moved twenty feet away until we were out of ear-shot.

'Do you believe them?'

'Not a word, sir,' I confirmed.

'Lieutenant Pearson are you able to rustle up some MPs? American ones?'

'I'll speak to the CO, sir. It might take a little while.'

Holland chuckled. 'They're not going anywhere. See what you can do. I'll have a chat with this Russian Johnny while you're gone. Play them at their own game. Knew a few of 'em in London. Bloody liars, the lot of 'em.'

We re-traced our steps and took a right turn which led us to a small Russian Jeep-type vehicle. Novikov sat up front looking much too large for the car. He climbed out awkwardly as we approached and Holland introduced himself.

'I am Colonel Novikov.'

'Yes. It's lovely to catch up with our allies from the Red Army. Your chaps did a fantastic job with the Germans you know. I think we were all very relieved when you starting winning in the East. Knew the Boche didn't stand a chance once that happened. Those tanks of yours are fantastic by the way.'

I had to admire Holland. His barrage of compliments had totally wrong-footed the Russian, left him with no option but to reciprocate in some manner. It was a masterstroke really.

'Well, of course it was a combined effort from the allies,' said Novikov with an unaccustomed show of modesty. I hadn't expected him to be able to regulate his own bombast, but he was a man of surprises.

'We've done a great thing, you know. We must never forget that our great nations have overcome Hitler's evil and given Europe the chance to be free. I can tell you there were times when it looked rather bleak… wasn't sure we'd ever get to this point.'

'But peace now.'

'Peace indeed. You know, being a pilot I never got to meet any Russians…'

Novikov smiled, benignly.

'I was wondering, since you're here, if you would like to take part in some sort of joint celebration or parade? You know, to mark our victory.'

The Russian's smile faltered but came back at once.

'My soldiers don't do marches well.'

'Oh, that's a shame I thought maybe that was why you had come over.'

Novikov was adroit when it came to lying. He skilfully adopted Holland's lie and used it like one of his own.

'Yes, yes. But there are other considerations. I have already spoken to…' He pointed at Saul.

'Squadron Leader Cohen,' I said, helpfully.

'Yes, yes. There is things which we need to… secure.'

'Ah, yes. These medical experiments, is that right? The problem is, Colonel, that we don't have any records of the type you mentioned.' The Russian frowned on cue but Holland wasn't finished. 'If they did exist and if they were as you have previously described it would be for people more senior than us to decide upon their fate. But I will happily pass on your concerns to General Foster.'

'I have been designated to, er, take informations with me,' said Novikov evenly.

'And if that is agreed then we will gladly hand them over. But the basic problem is that no such information has been found. We have no records of these experiments if they did take place.'

'They did.'

'Even so, until they are uncovered there is nothing for us to hand over, even if the handover is agreed upon.'

A slight delay followed as the Russian processed Holland's words. He nodded but he wasn't remotely happy about this response. I supposed that with him being Russian and taking into consideration their seeming predilection for lying, he was assuming that Holland was not being honest. *I* assumed the opposite.

'I will need to know soon,' he said, unhappily.

'Of course, but there might not be anything to report. As I said, Colonel Novikov, we have nothing to indicate that these experiments took place. We are keen to cooperate with our allies of course.'

'And the Americans?'

'Yes. The Americans too. But the same basic problem remains that until we find this information then we can't decide what to do with it. It may not exist.'

The Russian sighed heavily.

'Now, in the meantime it is probably better that you withdraw your forces. I'm not sure that there is any need to bring tanks here.'

Holland was the voice of reason. In short order he had removed all of Novikov's specious arguments with grace and tact. He and the Russian shook hands and we departed giving our allies time and opportunity to withdraw.

'Perhaps, the Diplomatic Service when you leave the Air Force, sir?'

'Who said I'd ever leave? There'll be more wars to fight you know.'

Chapter Nineteen

'Happy birthday,' I said as I entered the office. It was a trick of course, just a few words thrown out there seemingly casually but actually a sprung trap.

'Thank you, Saul.'

She didn't flinch.

'I got a couple of pastries from across the road. Not much to celebrate with…'

'How did you know?'

'That it was your birthday? Your application form.'

'Oh, yes. Of course.' Ingrid frowned at the memory but brightened at once. 'Did I get the job?' she joked.

'I have to interview you first.'

She smiled indulgently at my great wit, which is what any sensible employee would do in the circumstances.

'Sorry, I'm late by the way. Colonel Novikov put in an appearance.'

'He appeared?'

'Yes. Came for a snoop around. Brought some tanks with him.'

She shuddered.

'The sooner they have left, the better it will be.'

I nodded and avoided mention of the German invasion just a few years previously. Ingrid was being rather selective in her outrage but then again, I had to remember that it was not she who had conducted the war. In that vein I cast a glance at her hand and noticed that the wedding ring was missing.

When I mentioned this, she rubbed the appropriate finger and muttered something.

'You've never talked about your husband or your family,' I said.

'Coffee?' she said. It was a crude deflection and I foiled it at once.

'I will make it. Your birthday after all.'

When I returned with our drinks a silence had settled between us.

'You are waiting for your husband to come home?' I ventured.

'I suppose so.'

'I don't know what you mean.'

She gave a little sigh as if coming to terms with a painful situation.

'He went to Russia.'

'Was he killed?'

'Prisoner. But who knows if the Russians will release their prisoners.' She sounded bitter and yet there was something rather forced in her denunciation. Her anger was directed more at the Russians in general than in the fact that her husband was being held. Or was it just my imagination? Was I simply putting together a version of events which fitted with what I thought I already knew?

'Things will get back to normal, one day.'

'And we will live in harmony? A family of nations?' she scoffed.

'I think some people are hoping for that, yes. Why would that be wrong?'

She shook her head and the conversation was over.

***

For no other reason than the sunshine and the need to explore my fiefdom, I took a walk. The threat of Hitler's last-ditch resistance fighters had gone as far as I could tell but I took my revolver anyway, more from a need to keep it secure than from a need to defend myself. If a threat existed, it came from unexpected sources: former allies.

Oddly, the last few days had lifted my mood a little and with my *ennui*, lethargy and apathy in abeyance I felt invigorated, almost spritely, which shouldn't have been a surprise in one of my relatively tender years. I paused at the bottom of the *Rathaus* steps and surveyed the square. A few people were about and in the distance I saw a small party of school children being led by their teacher on some kind of localised expedition. The teacher was an older man but the children couldn't have been more than six or seven. I wondered if they understood much about the war or had noticed its ending? Did they notice that Hitler had suddenly been removed from the syllabus? Did they wonder where their fathers were? Since I couldn't figure out much about my own future I did wonder how they were ever going to make sense of the world they were inheriting.

    A van trundled past as I crossed the road and then I turned left down a street I had never even noticed before. It was narrow and dark since very little light was admitted, the sun blocked out by tall houses with eerie overhangs. I was reminded of Hansel and Gretel or possibly some other gothic fairy tale and at once I felt uncomfortable and out of place. There was something menacing and otherworldly about this street. I felt as if I was being watched by some odd, malevolent creature, that plotted the best way to destroy me. Superstition played almost no part in my upbringing or subsequent life. I didn't have a lucky charm that I took into battle or a routine to follow to ensure my continued safety and good fortune and yet now it felt as though I was being drawn to some terrible fate brought on by my own carelessness and disregard for obvious warnings.

    I had stopped walking and could have backed out but I couldn't give in to an unseen threat, something so ridiculously intangible as a 'feeling'. The houses were tall and narrow, brightly painted and quaint… or they would have been had their own long shadows not leached them of colour and charm. For some reason, I turned through one hundred and eighty degrees, almost expecting to find myself under observation. Unsurprisingly, that was not the case and I was about to reproach myself for my stupidity as I turned back round just in time to see a figure disappearing with haste into the end house of the street. I opened my mouth to call out but two things stopped me: a lack of something to say and a corresponding lack of someone to say it to. This fleeting cameo did confirm, as I suspected, that I was being watched for how could this phantom have judged his moment with such precision otherwise?

I stood where I was for a minute, telling myself that I was taking stock but in reality perplexed and slightly alarmed. Was I scared, the highly decorated fighter pilot who had taken to the skies to repeatedly engage in mortal combat? Well, no. But I *was* apprehensive. I was glad of the Webley now but it stayed in its holster for the moment. The truth was that despite gnawing suspicion, apprehension and the evidence of my own eyes, I would have felt very self-conscious with the big revolver in my hand. I wasn't ready to be Dick Tracy or Bulldog Drummond, although my peculiar circumstances might have been a suitable basis for a good adventure for the latter.

With a sigh, I began my slow walk to the end of the street where an oblong of light marked the start of an adjoining passageway. Some way above me, the uneven roof lines of both sides of the street created a long slash of visible sky as if a giant scalpel had hacked away at a solid canopy. The houses appeared to cant inwards as if they might be ready to topple. A single gutter ran beneath my feet and each step I took echoed.

I was alone but conspicuous, in my own private world but making up part of someone else's. I felt like a plaything or a dupe or someone so gullible they'd walk into any trap laid before them no matter how obvious it should have been and yet I couldn't think of an alternative course of action. I would get to the end of the street and then…

What?

Turn around and come back or start knocking on doors… and if the latter what was I asking should anyone answer?

There were other questions that I asked myself later, namely: what was I hoping to achieve and why did I bother to take that walk? But I kept going and when I finally drew level with the last house I stopped again, finding myself looking out at a boulevard as wide as this street was narrow, as bright as this street was dark. Here the houses were bigger, detached, with gardens and trees springing up from neat pavements. The contrast between the road taken and its destination could scarcely have been greater.

Movement caught my eye, nothing more than a monochrome flicker, a tiny shift of fabric, a dry leaf being turned over in a gentle breeze, the flap of an insect wing…

Of course when I looked for the source of this inconsequential movement I found myself utterly alone, stranded in an alley and disconnected from the living world which I knew existed and yet which had allowed me to wander from its boundary. An involuntary shiver ran up my spine but something made me hang on. Had fate brought me down this particular street? Was I destined to find an unsought answer to an unasked question? Really, I didn't believe in anything like that but something nagged at me. I needed the brain of Sherlock Holmes but possessed only that of former sergeant, Saul Cohen. That I couldn't even begin to describe the mystery that had been thrust upon me said everything I needed to know. With a sigh, I turned on my heel, re-traced my steps and returned to my office.

Ingrid looked up as I entered.

'It was a short walk,' she commented.

'Yes. I… I thought I'd better come back in case something happened.'

She looked at me quizzically. When 'things happened' she was able to deal with them better than I and we both knew it. I questioned whether she really needed me at all.

**

'Before you do anything, I am not drinking tonight,' I explained. 'The break from alcohol is doing me good.'

Phil looked at me doubtfully.

'Okay. I believe you.'

'I'm serious. Too much alcohol is going to create problems for us in the future. Alcoholism, holding down a job... that sort of thing.'

'It hasn't been a problem so far, Saul. We won a bloody war,' he said.

'Despite alcohol, not because of it,' I replied with forced hauteur.

'Well, that's absolutely fine. You enjoy your new abstemious life but I am going to order a drink. And can I just point out that the mess is a bloody strange place to choose to make this announcement.'

'Ah. I have chosen the place of greatest temptation to make my stand.'

'Right. Will I order you a lady's drink then? A glass of lemonade perhaps?'

When he returned I began to recount my day and in particular my sojourn down that dark alley.

Phil looked confused.

'I don't really know what you mean.'

'Well, it was strange, you know. Eerie.'

'I would suggest that you don't go there in the dark in that case.'

'I know you are mocking me. I don't think I have explained it well. There was something off about what I saw.'

'But what did you see?'

'A figure. A furtive figure.'

Phil laughed.

'Well, alliteration aside, I'm not really sure what to say. I think maybe you should have a drink. The strain is beginning to tell on you or maybe it's sun stroke.'

'I will resist. It's… hard to put my finger on.'

'Okay, so describe the figure.'

'I only caught a glimpse.'

'Male, female, young, old, tall, short, fat, thin?'

'Yes, all of those.'

'What?'

'Male. Definitely male.'

'Old, short, fat…?'

'Young, I'd say. By the way they moved. They were agile, quick.'

'Tall?'

'Couldn't say for sure. Average probably.'

'Fat or thin?'

'Neither really. Slim but in good shape, I think, although they were some way off, of course. I couldn't make out anything else. It was dark. They were just an outline at the end of the street, a silhouette.'

'There's your answer... why you are troubled or confused.'

I raised my eyebrows, inviting a fuller explanation.

'You've seen a young man – young enough to be a soldier – behaving suspiciously in a back alley. This person you saw shouldn't have been there. The Germans haven't come back from war yet, have they? Those that are ever coming back, that is. So who is this fugitive? They didn't want you to see them but they were able to hide in a house which means they have a key at the very least. Why are they hiding? Who from, this furtive figure?'

He was right of course.

'Were they in uniform?'

'I don't think so. Probably just in a suit.'

'We could go back there. Tonight. Now, if you want,' he offered.

'No, it's fine. I'll have a think about it and decide upon a course of action.'

'You mean, you're going to forget it.'

'Yes.'

'You could ask Ingrid about it. She's a local after all.'

'Hmm. I'm not sure if she is and I'm not sure that she would tell the truth. I still don't know very much about her and who knows if what I think I know is actually true anyway. I could ask myself the question: have I just put up with her presence simply because she has made my life so much easier?'

Phil smiled and said, 'if you did ask that question, what would the answer be?'

'I don't know.'

'It's plainly troubling you but you should also ask yourself why you care. Is it worth any of your time? These are things that you can't do anything about. You have no expertise and no vested interest. So unless it is plain old curiosity which motivates you then just forget about it. All this stuff about experiments… if it's true then the experiments have all been done. It's not as if you can prevent them. And the Russians are going to do what they do… and the Yanks too.'

'What if Ingrid is a Nazi?'

'Just her and millions of others, Saul. They're not going to lock them all up because what would be the point? The forces of good won and that's probably that.' He paused and looked at me as if re-appraising me. 'Maybe it's different for you because you're a Jew, but there will come a time when things get back to normal. They will punish the top people – the top Nazis – and then turn a blind eye to the rest. Everyone has had enough.'

'I can't picture the other countries in Europe just forgiving and forgetting. The French, invaded, over-run, the Poles killed in their millions, the Dutch, the Belgians…'

'The thing is, Saul, you can't bring these people back to life.'

'But I can get justice for them.'

'Can you? I'd suggest that you can't and if the people are dead then what good is justice?'

'Other people looking on must see justice being carried out. They must see that you can't just kill a race of people and no one does anything about it. They need to see that it is not… acceptable… to conduct experiments on people and no one does anything about it. The world needs to be better than that.'

'But you forget that you're only a fighter pilot.'

Of course I hadn't forgotten that salient fact at all. What I *had* forgotten was that the world would eventually run out of sympathy.

Chapter Twenty

I went to bed at ten – 2200 – read for a few minutes and then slept better than I had for years. I awoke quite naturally, feeling refreshed, hopeful, energetic and happy. I lay still for a few minutes, looking at the ceiling and letting my thoughts take me where they would go. The usual jumble of words and images remained just that – a jumble, for I made no concerted efforts to sort them or to apply reason or order to my situation. Anything was, it felt, possible and the sun was already shining.

It occurred to me then, cocooned in the warm sheets and blankets of my bed, that my body and my mind had finally given themselves over to that which had seemed unattainable for so many years, namely peace. I didn't know what the world had in store for me but at least I now had the chance to make plans for my part in its future. I even allowed myself to think about staying on in the RAF, flying jets, perhaps being posted to far-flung outposts of empire, enjoying the sophisticated flying club ethos of the pre-war service. Things were different now, not least because I had a commission, had qualified as a pilot and there was no war to fight. It might be fun.

Who knew where I would end up. Margaret and I could have our own flat in Singapore, near the airbase. I could buy her that little MG she had talked about. Days out on the beach, drinks on the veranda, swimming in the sea and a bit of flying thrown in… just to pay the bills, you understand. Life could be good. Even Monday mornings could become bearable. To wake up to a world of bright sunshine, warmth, wealth (relatively speaking) and comfort seemed entirely possible. Was it stretching a point to say that I deserved it?

I discussed my feelings with Jack Murphy over breakfast.

'Who's to say you'll get posted to Singapore, Saul?'

'I know. That is the problem. We'd all like a posting there.'

'Well, if not there, you've got Malta, Egypt, Hong Kong… loads of hot places. Any one of those would probably do. Life in married quarters, flying Meteors or one of the new Vampires. Gin and tonics in the evening, watching the sun going down. Get yourself an Alvis.'

'Can't afford one of those,' I said as if I was part way through making the deal for the car's purchase.

'Of course they might just boot you out and then you'll be unemployed and on the dole like everyone else. You can sell your medals to make ends meet, get a bedsit, maybe get a job with the Post Office if you're lucky. Then you gradually become an alcoholic and die penniless at a young age.'

'You're a great comfort to me, Jack. What about you?'

'Oh, I'm already an alcoholic…'

'No, I meant are you staying on or going back to Ireland?'

'Well, you can be an alcoholic anywhere – take it with you, so to speak – so I might take over the family farm in Cork.'

'Didn't know you were farmers.'

'Farmers and soldiers going back generations. But maybe I'll come to live in England. I've earned the right. I didn't shoot down those Italians out of the goodness of my heart, you know.'

'So, it was a pragmatic decision?'

'Yes. I knocked Italy out of the war. More or less.'

'They didn't stand a chance against you really.'

'So, are you planning to stay on as mayor?'

'I think my tenure will end soon. I was a poor choice.'

He laughed.

'But I understand that your assistant is very good-looking.'

'I'm a married man, Jack. No good to me. I could introduce you to her, of course.'

'I'm not ready for that Saul. A German? Not ready for that at all. Besides we're not supposed to fraternise are we? And how do you know she's not a raving Nazi?'

I laughed at his description, apt as it was.

'I don't. She might be. Won't do her much good now if she is though. All that stuff has rather gone out of fashion.'

We chatted about Ingrid as if she was the subject of universal speculation and Jack had many amusing observations to make about the Germans as a 'species'. Our exchange made me think it was time to get some proper answers from Ingrid. Phil had probably been right when he said that it wasn't really my business and yet doubts nagged me.

It was Jack Murphy who provided me with a possible means to end my confusion on the matter of Ingrid Baumann.

'You know what to do,' he said. 'If you want to find out more about her?'

'What?'

'Get her drunk.'

'Ah, but as you said yourself we're not allowed to fraternise.'

He gave me an old-fashioned look and said, 'think of it as a mission.'

***

'Morning, Saul,' she said cheerily as I entered.

'You're always here bright and early, Ingrid.'

'Germans are supposed to be efficient,' she said. Her tone was self-deprecating, converting a virtue into a vice, unless I had read the situation wrongly. Did this efficient woman really have the capacity for self-deprecation or was I merely ascribing a British trait to her because it suited me to do so? I knew almost nothing about her and understood less. Perhaps her words were actually a veiled criticism of the fact that she was German and I was British. *Merely* British, that is. Those Germans in authority who had survived the conflict they'd created must surely be scratching their collective head at Germany's defeat in the West at the hands of citizen's armies assembled in haste by soft democracies.

'Another beautiful, sunny day,' she observed as she made her way to the kitchen. I was going to make some comment about *'the sun shining on the righteous'* but stopped myself in time. It was hardly fitting. She was unlikely to be righteous given the context in which she spent the last ten years of her life. Instead I answered her upbeat summation with a rather unimpressive single-word answer.

'Yes.'

She returned with two coffees and sat.

'I expect to be replaced soon,' I said, although no one had said anything to this effect, at least not to me.

'Oh. Who will take over?' she asked. I was pleased to hear a trace of disappointment in her voice, although anyone in her position would naturally adopt a similar tone in this situation. It didn't do to sound happy at news of your boss's departure.

'Nothing has been settled but it's obvious that a fighter pilot isn't really the ideal choice for the job. I just happened to be the senior person in place at the time. I think that no one has thought about the situation.'

'I don't know what you mean.'

'Just that I have been forgotten about. The town needs someone more suitable than me. A German for one thing. Someone who knows how to be a mayor.'

'You have done it well so far,' she said.

'I haven't done anything. It's all been you.'

'You have handled the Russians… and the Americans. You were… diplomatic but strong.'

'But I don't know what to do about mending a road or getting the drains unblocked or having council meetings…'

She smiled sympathetically and it was at times like this when I could have forgiven her for past transgressions great and small, real or imagined. I could have fallen for her.

And if I had done so she could have used me as her ticket to absolution.

'Is there anywhere to get a drink in town?' I asked rather suddenly.

'The mess on your camp…'

'I was thinking just you and I.'

'I would not be welcome in the mess,' she said, unnecessarily.

'It *would* be awkward. I was thinking of getting away from my daily grind and, you know, saying thank you to you for your help.'

'But you are married,' she said. I sensed that she was warming to the idea but putting up a last-ditch display of expected decorum.

'I was not thinking of anything… inappropriate. I just meant…'

'There is one bar,' she said. 'Dachsbau. We could go there.' She frowned. 'I don't know about your uniform though.'

I nodded. Neither of us mentioned the obvious facts about who won the war and who lost. The appearance of an RAF officer in uniform was certainly going to be a little awkward, to put it mildly. It wasn't something that could easily be challenged in the circumstances but nor would it make for a relaxing night. It would hardly do wonders for Ingrid's relationships in the town either.

'Ah. Uniform is all I have, unfortunately.'

That seemed to put the proverbial tin lid on it but Ingrid was apparently more taken with the idea than I supposed.

'You could come to my flat. I have wine and a few other drinks.'

'It was a stupid idea really. I just wanted a break from everything.'

'No one would have to know about your visit. It wouldn't have to be fraternising.'

Although it was hard to think of it as anything *other* than fraternising I took her at face value and agreed to come along later. As a minor concession to good manners and the preservation of chummy international relations I decided to leave the revolver behind in my room.

It proved to be a mistake.

***

'Morning, sir. Any instructions for us today?'

'Morning Corporal Cleary. Start with a cup of tea and then just take a tour of the town. Can you drive?'

'Aye, sir.'

'Well, take the Volkswagen and just reconnoitre.'

'Lookin' out for stray Russians?'

'Yes. And stray Americans too. Just remind them where they are. Don't shoot anyone unless it's unavoidable.'

He smiled and agreed to proceed with caution.

I slumped behind my desk, flicked through a pile of paperwork left there by Ingrid and wondered what I hoped to achieve by visiting her home. There was no romantic intent on my part and yet I knew that this visit would not be featuring in my next letter to Margaret. If there was anything going on, any connection between the experiments carried out in the camp and the mysterious Ingrid, then what did I care? It would fall to my successor to deal with it or perhaps it would just fade away as an unwanted strand of history. People would forget soon enough. Not me, but people in general. Was it my religion that kept me wanting to know more, to seek justice or was it something else, like good old bloody-mindedness?

Ingrid seemed intent on her work. She looked up now and again, smiling innocently. I had no option but to smile back; what else does a well brought up young officer do? Ingrid was an enigma but was she benign or malignant?

The day was punctuated with the usual selection of problems brought by a representative cross-section of the town's remaining population: very young, very old, mainly female, infirm, bitter, relieved, desperate, defeated, angry, perplexed. Missing from the line-up were the young men, the prisoners of war and those who would never return from far-flung battlefields. There was something grey and lifeless about the locals, some vital spark missing, which made Ingrid's obvious health and the good repair of her clothes all the more startling. It seemed as though the war had passed her by or she had sat it out in some sheltered spot or a neutral country unaffected by the epic conflagration that tore through Europe. She didn't even pretend to have suffered. Her wellbeing was ostentatious, one in the eye for the impoverished masses. I had little sympathy for them and none at all for her.

However, she deftly tended to the needs of each visitor, smiling benignly and sending them on their way for the most part happier than they had been up to that point. I had no idea what she was saying to them and she rarely deferred to me. One might almost have thought I was an irrelevance…

Cleary and his tiny army returned just after midday.

'All quiet?'

'Yes, sir. We didn't shoot anyone.'

'No one at all?'

'No one, sir. Quiet morning.'

'Well done. Put your feet up. The kettle's boiled.'

They trooped off, ammo boots heavy on the unyielding tiles of the floor. Not for the first time I noted that there was virtually no interaction between my assistant and my armed guard. They obviously didn't matter to her whereas I, for some reason, did. Was it to do with rank, social standing or perceived usefulness? Cleary and his men were beneath her it seemed, the distinction between conqueror and the conquered not one she was prepared to entertain. By contrast my social standing was possibly the equal of hers, either that or I was the best she could find in these straitened times. With whom had she… consorted… during the war, I wondered? I could easily picture her as the favoured hostess in town, entertaining the Luftwaffe officers and the SS with elegant soirees, the pretence of peace, maintaining pre-war standards. She was a marvel, this Ingrid whom I'd never known, always able to conjure up a feast whilst those lesser beings went deservedly hungry.

Had I got this wrong? Was my hasty assessment way off the mark? Naturally, I would never know unless she decided to come clean about her past life over a glass of wine tonight. I wasn't sure I even wanted to know.

Despite my doubts and worries, the sun shone and kept my spirits high. Vague notions of a happy, carefree life had displaced the *ennui* with which I was often plagued. I felt alive and purposeful for once.

'You need glasses,' said Ingrid.

'Pardon?' I replied.

'You are closing up your eyes when you read.'

'Closing up my… ah, squinting. I didn't realise. It's not good news when a pilot starts to need glasses.'

She may have been right about the glasses.

'You would suit them, I think,' she said. It was the first time she had ever commented upon my appearance. I wasn't quite sure if it was a sort of compliment or not.

Any further discussion was curtailed when an angry German man burst into the *Rathaus* and stormed across the hall and into our joint office.

Anger had chased blood into his hollow, grey cheeks. Tears welled in rheumy eyes. I thought he was going to burst into tears but instead he began a tirade in rapid-fire, incomprehensible German, his arms flapping up and down in frustration, his head shaking side to side, the words a torrent…

'What's he saying, Ingrid?'

'He's angry. He says…'

Our new friend cut her off and began addressing her directly as if I had suddenly vanished. I guessed him to be seventy, shabbily dressed and thin, much in the manner of any other German who'd come through the war and its attendant privations. His grey cheeks sported stubble but not a beard so he had shaved at some point even if it seemed no longer worth the trouble. The words came and came and not one was understood by me. I half stood, hoping that this might give him some sort of cue to stop or to slow down but he moved away just half a step and continued to beseech Ingrid, imploring her, begging… but for what?

She spoke again in his language, her tone that of a school teacher and the tumult faded as if a verbal sluice was being wound closed. Now the only sound was an imagined rattle of his quivering bones as he tried to regain his composure in the face of total capitulation to terror and despair. I noticed one of Cleary's troops in the doorway.

I gave a shrug and the soldier scuttled away. Ingrid was talking now, her voice clear, calm but gently forceful.

'*Jetzt setz dich hin und beruhige dich.*'

The man sat heavily in an upright wooden chair.

'What does he want?' I asked.

'He wants to know when his sons are coming back.'

'Where are they?'

'Russia.'

I nodded. For a moment or two I put aside my natural dislike of the Germans and my hatred for their actions and the misery they had caused on such a gigantic scale and in those fleeting moments I allowed myself to see an elderly man grieving for the family he might have lost. There was something in my bones telling me that the Soviets might not be in a great hurry to repatriate their German POWs. Why would they? The Germans had given them no grounds for compassion.

But did this old man comprehend that? What did he know about the conduct of the German Army? Had he heard of their atrocities and chosen not to believe what he heard? Whatever, he seemed to be fairly single-minded now. The war was over, whoever was to blame was presumably an irrelevance to him and he was demanding the return of his children.

'I don't know what to tell him, Saul.'

'No. I don't have a direct link to the Red Army.'

'That Russian officer who came in..?'

'Novikov? I suppose I could ask him but I really think…'

The man cut me off and was gabbling desperately, his face close to mine, his eyes wide. I shot a desperate look at Ingrid as I took a step backwards. She took the man gently by the sleeve and guided him away, soothing him, calming him down, stilling the troubled waters.

Ingrid spoke to him again. I heard my name mentioned and that of Novikov. I nodded encouragingly when the man looked in my direction and he seemed to accept her version of events, namely that I would intervene. For a second he seemed to see me with fresh eyes, taking in my uniform and medal ribbons as if they were a guarantee of integrity.

Of course, I didn't want him to have too much faith in me because, with regard to this matter, I had very little faith in myself and was hoping that my successor would be in place before any form of action was required. Novikov was not the sort of man who was open to negotiation but more than that I doubted if he held much sway with the Soviet authorities responsible for dealing with prisoners of war. And as if those hurdles weren't enough to overcome, I was confident that he cared not for the fate of any German invaders.

And I might never see him again.

Pacified, the man nodded as if the matter was resolved, stood and turned on his heel muttering. When he'd gone, Ingrid joked, 'another satisfied customer.'

'Yes. I hope he's not expecting too much from me.'

'I said that you would try to help but there was no guarantee of success.'

'It's a subject close to your heart.'

'Pardon?'

'With your own family members in Russian hands, it's a subject close to your heart… important to you.'

'Ah, yes,' she said recovering as her initial puzzlement fell away. Was her husband really a POW? For a second she seemed to have forgotten that fact.

Chapter Twenty-one

I took a phone call from Lieutenant Pearson just before I set out for my rendez-vous.

'Evening Squadron Leader, I was just wondering if my soldiers had got lost on the way back to camp.'

'Lost? I don't think so. I think I sent them off around 1500 hours. It may be that they got distracted along the way.' I added that last bit in a tone of mock disbelief, suggesting, *'you know what these young soldiers are like…'* but not using those words.

'Hmm. They haven't signed back in at the guardroom and it's nearly 2000 hours. Is there anywhere for this 'distraction' to occur? I mean, like a bar or something.'

'Nothing springs to mind. I'm sure they'll turn up.'

We chatted for a while longer and then I set off through the darkening streets. The air was warm and fragrant and despite my underhand intentions I found myself looking forward to spending time with Ingrid. My ulterior motive was based solely around the idea of eliciting information but if I carried out my mission subtly then good relations might be maintained. I liked her. There was no way round it and I told myself that it was only right that you should treat people well until they gave you reason to do otherwise.

That of course was nonsense. Had I been meeting up with Goering we might have spent a companionable night together supping beer, talking tactics, just two old fighter pilots reminiscing, two knights of the air, putting the world to rights, burying the hatchet now that the conflict had ended. We wouldn't have to mention the fact that he was a notorious war criminal facing execution…

I allowed myself to relax. The rule on non-fraternisation would have to be eased someday. I was just testing the water so to speak.

She greeted me warmly with an open smile and a hug. I was taken aback but pleased at the same time and she led me inside. She wore a blue dress – it looked new – and had made an obvious effort with her appearance. Not that she ever looked anything less than stunning now that I came to think of it.

I followed her up the stairs.

'I haven't brought anything, I'm afraid. There wasn't anything suitable.'

'It's fine.' We were at the painted door of her flat. 'It's nice to have company.' Just for a second her smile faltered and she seemed to gulp in exaggerated nervousness. Well, I was a little nervous myself by this point.

She opened the door and I followed her along a passageway with doors to the left and to the right. Music played, the air was cool and scented. Ahead of us another door led to her sitting room.

It was plainly furnished but stylish enough and comfortable. I guessed that a great many of her compatriots were living less well than this.

'It's a lovely flat,' I said as I made my way to the bay window. The top windows were open. 'A view of the park. No one around though…'

When I turned a man was pointing a gun at me. Ingrid stood just behind him.

'I'm sorry, Saul,' she said. It sounded genuine in fact although it was obvious that she'd led me into a trap. I made no reply for two reasons. Firstly, I had nothing to say. There was no combination of words at my ready disposal for this situation. Secondly, I was fairly sure that an explanation would be forthcoming if I just waited. This wasn't an assassination for I would already be dead if that was the case.

'We need your help,' said Ingrid. I sighed. 'I'm sorry, Saul. Really. I didn't want to do this.'

'And yet you did.'

'The opportunity came along and I had to take it,' she explained.

'Had to?'

'Please sit. I will explain it to you.'

I looked around and then chose an upright wooden chair. Throughout, the armed man dressed innocuously in a dark suit, said nothing and continued to look on, his gun arm unmoving, his face demonstrating a lack of emotion. He was not sad, happy, bored, thrilled, angry, nervous. He might have been a realistic mannequin for all the signs of life he displayed.

'Who's your friend?' I asked.

'It doesn't really matter who he is. I will explain the situation to you.'

'While he points a gun at me?'

'That is necessary.'

We spoke as if this situation was the most natural thing in the world, just two reasonable people coming to terms with an unforeseen circumstance and trying to make the best of it. Oddly, I felt quite relaxed despite the armed man in our midst. I couldn't really imagine myself coming to any harm.

'So, get on with it,' I said.

'You know some of this already, I think. You know about the camp and the experiments…'

'Yes. And I have been told that you were something to do with them.'

Ingrid didn't deny or confirm.

'We will hand over the data to you but we need money and to escape.'

'Escape to where?' I asked but it seemed as if I was getting too far ahead in the negotiations for her to answer.

'The results of the experiments are valuable. They can be used to find cures and treatments. It would be a waste not to use them.'

'So, you killed and tortured people and now you think you can just buy your way out?'

'It would be stupid to waste it.'

'In that case you could just hand it over and let the appropriate people decide what should be done with it.' This idea had no appeal of course since it didn't make allowances for these Nazi's new lives and future prosperity.

She said nothing. The gun still pointed at me.

'So, if I don't agree to this, you'll shoot me?'

'Saul, it won't come to that.'

'This isn't something that I can arrange anyway. I doubt if anyone is going to accept your idea. If you think about it, you're asking them to buy something they don't want and release some Nazi criminals in the process. Why would they do this?' I shook my head. This wasn't the evening I'd envisioned at all. 'You won't get away with it. This isn't something that can be allowed. What do we do next? You might as well let me go.'

'But you would report me?'

'Yes.'

'Don't you care about me?'

'No. Not at all. I care less about you than I ever did.'

'I can't just let you go.'

'So what will you do?'

She looked over at the gunman and he seemed to nod.

'We have your soldiers. They are held hostage. If you get the money and arrange our safe passage you get them back and it's all okay. We hand over the medical papers and you can do what you want with them.'

'You've really burnt your bridges now.'

'That is the situation.'

'So, you let me go and I report back to my superiors?'

'Yes.'

'There isn't a cat in hell's chance of them doing this.'

'Then your soldiers will… they will not be freed.' She had clumsily side-stepped the mention of shooting the soldiers, although why she bothered was anyone's guess. I couldn't believe that Ingrid would carry out this threat but then again she was merely speaking on behalf of someone else.

'Who are you really?'

'You know who I am.'

'I know who you say your are, that is all. I never understood how you came to be my secretary. I just took it all at face value. Stupid of me.'

She didn't disagree which was insulting in the circumstances.

'And who exactly am I supposed to pass this on to? You have a specific person in mind? What about Field Marshall Montgomery?'

She fired a quick question at the armed man and he answered in equally terse fashion.

'He says you tell whoever needs to know.'

'Helpful. And what if I don't or what if they aren't interested?'

Ingrid looked unhappy and I got the impression that she really didn't want to put me in this position. For my part I was just bloody angry but trying to keep my cool while my brain came up with a solution to this problem.

'Just report back, Saul. Do that first and then see…'

'Seriously though. Who are you?'

'It doesn't matter.'

'It does to me.'

The armed man growled something in German and this prompted Ingrid to speak.

'You must go. I'm sorry.'

'Where are my soldiers?'

'You know I can't tell you.'

'Okay. I'll go now but if any harm comes to them, I'll kill you myself.'

***

I telephoned Holland the minute I got back to my HQ. I tried to explain the situation but certain aspects of my story sounded distinctly nonsensical.

'What a bloody mess, Saul. Get some sleep and we'll meet first thing tomorrow.'

'Yes, sir.'

'Do you think she means it?'

'I have no idea, sir. In part I suspect she is being coerced but she is not totally innocent by any means.'

'Absolute bastards. Right to the end, absolute bastards. I'll hang them all personally if I get the chance.'

***

Naturally, I didn't sleep well that night. It felt like hours before my brain finally shut down although I had probably dozed in the interim. I deserved to have nightmares but if I did they were impossible to recall when I rose at 0700. My eyes were stinging with fatigue and my mouth was dry. It felt as if I had acquired a partial hangover without actually consuming alcohol – the worst of both worlds in effect – and I was utterly miserable and worried about Cleary and his little band. I had let this happen. I had been sleepwalking the whole time. Ingrid and her chums planned this thing and I just let it happen under my very nose. Worse than that, I had unwittingly facilitated it by letting her work for me without any proper checks. I had been lazy and I had let myself be manipulated.

'Is she telling the truth? That's the first thing we need to establish,' said Holland. We were having breakfast although I wasn't in the mood for any form of sustenance. The mess cooks toiled in their little kitchen, a record played – Benny Goodman, I thought – and the air was warm, a harbinger of a stuffy day. Over the years I think I had developed a reputation for keeping a clear head in challenging situations and yet at this early hour clarity of thought was eluding me rather. It was not at all clear to me how this mess might be resolved. I hoped my superior officer might have some suggestions.

'I have checked already, sir. Cleary and his little band have not returned to camp.' I could see Holland mentally tick that off.

'The next thing to consider is whether or not they actually possess these documents.'

It made me feel better to be able to provide unambiguous answers even if their content was unhelpful.

'I haven't seen them but I am fairly sure they exist because they've been the subject of much speculation, shall we say.'

'Perhaps you should have asked for a sample just to prove their *bona fides*.'

It was a good point but in my defence I said, 'I was just concerned about how we get our soldiers back, sir. I assumed that the documents, if they exist, would be destroyed if we got hold of them.'

'Hmm. They should be of course but that wouldn't be a decision we could make.' He sipped his tea. 'What a bloody mess.'

'Yes, sir.'

'A honey trap.'

'Pardon?'

'This whole set-up sounds like a honey trap. A beautiful woman lures the unsuspecting man into a situation where he becomes open to extortion or some such. You said yourself that you didn't know where the hell she came from.'

'No. I feel rather stupid now. One of the problems was the fact that she was able to speak the language obviously. It was easy to have her there.'

'But you say there was nothing going on? Nothing romantic?'

'Oh, no, sir. There was nothing like…'

'And yet you were at her flat?'

Holland wasn't trying to trap me necessarily but he had done just that. I said nothing.

'It sounds as if you have just been unlucky. The camp in question happened to be near the airfield and you happened to take over there.'

'And I took her with me when I was made mayor.'

'You made it easy for her. Had you known you could have left her where she was.'

'And some other poor bastard would be in my shoes.'

'Perhaps. Well, let's think of a solution. They must not believe that the prize of these documents is enough to seal the deal or they wouldn't have kidnapped the soldiers as a back up. We could just give in to their… what would you call it..? their demands?' He considered his words for a second and then, satisfied, developed his idea further. 'Yes, we could *appear* to give in to their demands, take the papers, get our soldiers back and then capture them at a later date before they have made their escape. That's another thing: in what form was this escape going to happen? Where were they going and how would they get there?'

'I don't have the details, sir. I think they wanted more discussions on the matter. Switzerland?'

'Switzerland, maybe... Not sure if the Swiss would entertain the idea of giving refuge to these despicable people, although God knows what deals were made during the war. Very keen to make a buck as the Americans would say. But now that the Jerries have lost the Swiss might be a little bit more circumspect. How much money do they want?'

'She didn't say.'

'Hmm. So, we have to meet up with her again, is that it?'

'Tonight.'

'And what's to stop us from taking *her* hostage? Play them at their own game?'

'It would be risky, sir. Supposing whoever is behind this didn't care whether they got her back or not. We'd only make the situation worse.'

Holland sighed, unhappily.

'A bloody mess. I think we should pass this up the chain of command. We don't have any expertise in the matter and I am certainly not authorised to hand over large sums of money to them if that is the only way to get our soldiers back.' He shook his head. 'Absolute bastards. To think that we won the bloody war and are now in this position. It's all wrong but for the meantime we have to play along unless there is a way of finding the troops ourselves. I wouldn't know where to start.'

It was uncommon for anyone in the services to apologise and yet that is what I did.

'If it hadn't been you it could have been any of us. Find out what you can tonight and we'll take it from there.'

'So, am I telling them that a deal is possible?'

'Yes. In the interim I think it's our only option.'

***

We parted company and I made my way to work as I had come to think of it. Quite what I expected to do there without my able but duplicitous assistant was another matter but I was still the temporary *Bürgermeister*. Was it my imagination at work as my footsteps echoed on the floor of the empty *Rathaus* this morning?

Yes, it was, for Ingrid was in her usual spot already, if not displaying her normal cheery mood.

'You?' I said. I didn't sit. This was unexpected and I was ill-prepared to deal with it.

'I need to explain…'

'You need to get out.'

'No, Saul…'

'You're sacked. In fact I never employed you. I'm going to ask that your wages are paid back too.'

'My wages? I never got paid.'

'So you came here day after day solely to lay the trap I walked into?'

She didn't deny it. I have to say, she didn't look at all happy about her actions.

'We have to talk.'

'You're still sacked.'

'Okay, but we must reach an arrangement.'

'Who is behind this Ingrid? That's if you are really called that?'

'The arrangement must be that you bring me the money and I have your soldiers released.'

I remembered Holland's word from this morning and asked, 'have you got some of these reports to let me look at? A sign of good faith?' I shook my head in despair. 'What a joke,' I added bitterly.

Ingrid slid open a desk drawer and withdrew a beige cardboard folder. She held it out for me to take but said nothing.

'Hold on… it was in your desk all this time?'

She nodded but not smugly.

The realisation that I could have helped myself felt like a punch in the guts. Was there anything else I had missed? Anything else I had messed up or been too lazy to deal with? As with so much I was out of my depth. That young lad who'd joined the RAF in 1935 had achieved great things but done so under false pretences and only now was it catching up with me. As I breathed out heavily I caught Ingrid's pitying look.

'I can't believe this,' I said, wearily.

'I haven't betrayed you. I am a German after all.'

'Strictly speaking you may not have done but the war is over and you lost. The time for these tricks is past and yet you have used the goodwill of the occupying forces against them. It's hardly a great start is it? If you didn't have me over a barrel I'd have you arrested.'

She could have said something defiant at that point, indeed that's more or less what I expected from her but instead she kept her counsel, looking neither pleased nor unhappy. Notwithstanding the fact that she was a woman this outward appearance of neutrality prevented me from punching her in the face.

'I've shown you nothing but kindness. Me, a stinking Jew! And this is what you do in return. You slaughtered tens of thousands of people – almost certainly millions, in fact – caused misery, fear, despair, you stole and destroyed. And yet I never made any reference to this, never said an unkind word, saved you from having to visit that awful camp – which, when I think about it, you probably knew better than anyone. You absolute bitch.'

You might think that I benefitted from getting that off my chest but with each word I spoke my anger increased. She started to look frightened then and I was pleased. At last something was getting through to her.

'If it wasn't for the fact that I needed to get my men back I'd bloody shoot you right now.' I think I would have too. Just at that moment I could have done it. She wouldn't have been the first German I'd killed either. She gulped and looked at the revolver in its holster on my hip. 'I could take you to the camp, shoot you and bury you in a pit with a load of Jews. Imagine that. No one would care. No one would bat an eyelid.'

It looked for a minute like she was going to cry but she stiffened her resolve, her Nazi defiance finally showing through like an aura of barely suppressed evil.

'Give me the documents now. All of them.'

She nodded and reached into the drawer to remove about eight or nine similar beige files of different widths. She set these on her desk and I lifted them, placing them out of her reach.

'I'm not going to even look inside because the whole thing disgusts me. To think that I am in a room with someone who could treat other human beings in this way…'

I watched her face as I spoke looking for even a tiny reaction to my description of the Jews as human beings. If it was there I missed it. She was practiced at seeming innocent. Again, I wondered who she really was, what she'd done during the war.

'Are there any more?'

'No.'

'So what is next?'

'You hand over money and arrange a flight to Spain.'

'Spain?'

'That's all you need to know. You're involvement will end there. You get your men back and the medical documents.'

'And let some Nazi war criminals off the hook? Allow them to start a new life when they should actually all be on the end of a rope? It's not a satisfactory arrangement, so don't bother wasting your breath to try and make it sound as if it is.'

To her credit she did at least pale when I talked about hanging.

'Now that we're at this point you might as well tell me who you are.'

She lifted her chin and stared into my eyes, quite fearless now.

'I might as well tell you nothing. I have nothing to gain by telling you anything. You just need to get the money and organise our transport.'

'And how do I know you'll release Cleary and his men?'

'You have to trust me.'

'Trust you? What would make me do that?'

She ignored my question and said, 'fifty thousand US dollars and a plane. And immunity to fly out of Germany. After that we disappear and no one is harmed. And you have your medical research…'

'That we don't want, didn't ask for and won't use…'

She shrugged. 'Someone will use it. You think you're so high and mighty?'

'Well, we didn't start the war, didn't kill millions of people. Whatever, the big, er, sticking point is how do I know you'll release the soldiers?'

'We have nothing to gain by keeping them or… getting rid of them.'

'You had nothing to gain by killing the Jews.'

'To make the world a better place. That is why it was done.'

'Finally.'

'Finally what?'

'You have shown the sort of person you are.'

'I am German. That is what all Germans think.'

'Then perhaps we should wipe *you* out.'

'Germany will rise again.'

'You're a real dyed-in-the-wool Nazi, aren't you?'

'This is getting us nowhere.' She consulted a small piece of paper she'd retrieved from the pocket of her trousers. 'Fifty thousand dollars and a Douglas Dakota aeroplane, fully fuelled.'

'No pilot?'

'We have a pilot.'

'We? Who's we?'

She didn't answer.

'Get those things and we will release the soldiers.'

I was playing for time when I said, 'I'll need to speak to my boss.'

Ingrid nodded, sourly.

'And did you throw away the Union Jack on my desk?'

***

I relayed all of this to Holland and Rea, the soldier in particular looking very unhappy about the proposed arrangement. He had the stack of German medical documents on the desk in front of him. It was up to him to arrange their fate.

'The cheeky bastards,' he spluttered when I had finished.

'We could catch them in Spain when they land, if we've got our troops back by then,' ventured Holland.

'That would be tricky. Neutral but pro-German, the Spanish… plus we wouldn't know where they were heading for exactly.'

'Well, we could probably calculate which airstrips were within range of the Dak.'

Holland shook his head.

'They have a range of about 1500 miles, Saul. That would take them far beyond Spain. Why would they even tell us that they were going there? They could make it to North Africa if they wanted,' he said.

'Perhaps it's the onward journey that concerns them, sir. From Spain they could re-fuel and head for somewhere else. From North Africa it might not be so easy. They are more likely to have Spanish allies than… Tunisian ones, for instance.'

'Good point,' he conceded.

'I've got an idea, though.' I looked at both of my superior officers in turn before continuing.

'Go ahead,' said Rea.

When I had finished I could tell that both of them were cautiously impressed.

'We'd lose a Dakota…' said Holland but not with such vehemence that he was ruling out my idea completely.

'We were almost certainly going to lose it anyway. And bearing in mind that they propose to crew the Dak…'

'We don't lose any of our men…' said Rea finishing my sentence, helpfully.

I gave a hopeful shrug, as if to say, *'this is the best choice at our disposal.'*

'We also lose 50,000 dollars,' said Holland.

'I have a plan for that too.'

Chapter Twenty-two

I had made a terrible mess of things but here was a chance to redeem myself. The plan remained between the three of us for the time being although it was inevitable that we would need help, some of it from unusual sources. When I visited Ingrid at her flat that evening I made sure to wear my trusty Webley revolver, which all things considered was like locking the stable door after the horse had bolted. Having it made me feel better. Perhaps it was my turn to point a gun at someone.

Things were rather frosty between us this time which was wholly expected. She offered me a glass of wine.

'You must be bloody joking,' I said.

She gave a regretful shrug as if I was forgoing some great, unrepeatable offer.

'We just need to sort out the nitty-gritty,' I said.

'Will you sit?'

'No, I'll stand. I'm not staying long. You can have your money and your aircraft but I need to hear the details of how you will return my men. If you can't come up with something viable then the deal is off.'

'Okay. We will radio the location to you once we are on our way.'

'And supposing you don't?'

'You have to trust us.'

'I don't.'

'Well, whether you do or not that is the plan. Have the radio tuned to the correct frequency and we will pass on a message once we are airborne.'

'I don't like it,' I said.

'You don't have an option.'

'If I find you've misled us I will personally track you down and kill you.'

'I believe you but that won't be necessary. I have nothing to gain by not seeing them released.'

'The aircraft will be on the airfield in two days.'

'Fully fuelled?'

'Of course. We stick to our word.'

'So do we. And the money?'

'I'll hand it over personally. You can count it if you want.'

She agreed to that and we parted company. The plane was being brought in the following day and checked over by my mechanics but there was one other job I needed to do and it would have to wait until the morning.

***

'So who's going to be mayor for the day?' asked Phil.

'I was thinking that you and Jack could handle it between you.'

'Christ. Neither of us speak German. Jack barely speaks English, especially when he's angry.'

I laughed. 'It's not that bad. He's generally a great diplomat,' I lied.

'Are you talking about Jack Murphy or some other Jack I've never met?'

'You'll be fine. Any problems just tell 'em to come back tomorrow.'

He looked doubtful but I was past caring about being mayor or about the goings-on in town.

'And where are you going?' he asked.

'Seeing a man about a dog.'

'Really?'

'No. Going to the… bank.'

'The bank? I can do that and you stay here and be mayor.'

'It's not any old bank, Phil. It's got special money. At least I hope it has.'

With that enigmatic but doubtful message hanging in the air between us I stood up, leaving the remains of my breakfast to go cold.

'You can have that sausage if you want,' I said. 'You'll need to keep your strength up.'

***

I was introduced to Major Barkhorn once I had shown my pass to the rather jumpy sentries.

'They're suspicious of everyone. Just got here and don't trust the Germans, think they'll start the war up again. I think their imaginations have got the better of them because they missed the fighting. They want to shoot someone before they go home,' he explained.

'It's a shame, alright,' I commiserated. 'There'll be other wars.'

'Not for me. I've been fighting the Krauts for nearly a year now.' I raised my eyebrows dutifully to show how impressed I was. 'How about you?' he asked.

'Nearly six years for me.'

The American major paled which was quite something to see because he already possessed the pallor of a linen sheet. He wasn't quite translucent by the time he cleared his throat.

'So, how can I help you, Major?'

'Squadron Leader,' I corrected. 'Same thing really.'

'Yeah, of course.'

'I'm trying to track down some of your soldiers.' I described the men to him before adding, 'I think they might be deserters.'

'Until you said that I thought I might be able to help,' he said, unhappily.

'I don't follow.'

'Deserters. That's the problem. It feels like half the Army has deserted, especially now that the fighting has stopped.'

'Oh.'

'There are thousands of them.'

'Well, these were sort of *business* deserters… black market, that sort of thing. Wanted some important German documents which they were going to sell.'

'Okay,' he said, doubtfully. 'And you think I know where they are?'

'Not necessarily but I've got to start somewhere.'

Barkhorn rubbed his forehead and placed a pair of glasses on his nose in a gesture that instantly transformed him from soldier to clerk.

'I don't suppose you know which unit they were with?'

'I know which unit they *claimed* to be with, if that helps.'

He held up one fingering indicating that I should wait and took a pen and pad from a desk drawer.

'Shoot.'

'Pardon?'

'Tell me the unit.'

'591st Ordnance Company,' I said.

He didn't write it down.

'You sure?'

'That's what they told me.'

'It's bullshit. There's no such unit. Least not round here.'

'Not a surprise really.'

'Is there anything else you can tell me about them? I mean from your description it could be half the US Army. I need to narrow it down.'

'Well, they had a truck and some Jeeps last time I saw them.'

'About this truck… big or small?'

'Big, I'd say. Six wheels.'

'I can ask the MP company if we've lost any six-wheelers. It's a bit of a needle in a haystack.'

'A needle in a haystack is better than I have at present.'

He shrugged. Barkhorn obviously thought that I was on a fool's errand but he didn't hesitate.

'Can I ask why you want these guys? I mean, did they steal something from you?'

'Not that I know of.' I decided to come clean… up to a point, that is. 'They have something I need.'

'Okay, what?'

'Money. Counterfeit money.'

Barkhorn raised his eyebrows in surprise.

'That's fairly unusual. I would guess the MPs might have impounded it if they came across anything like that. It's worth asking.'

'If you would.'

'How much are we talking about here?'

'Fifty thousand,' I said and this time he really did go translucent.

***

I was shown into the office of a Lieutenant-Colonel Derby and saluted as was customary. He was bareheaded and seated but returned my salute, which seemed odd to me, but was the American way.

'Have a seat, Squadron Leader. I got a call from a Major Barkhorn of the infantry saying that you needed some counterfeit money.'

'That's right, sir.'

He was young for a man of his rank but exuded competence and American can-do attitude. There was no pre-amble, no niceties and that suited me fine.

'One way or another I think I can get that sum together for you. But it's a lot.'

I nodded.

'The problem we have is that for obvious reasons we're trying to take this fake money *out* of circulation. It's no use to anyone here of course, but if we just hand it over then how do we know it's not going to get into the wrong hands?'

'Well, sir. This is a very secret oper...'

'I'm sure it is and I'm not expecting you to give me any details but can you give me an assurance that it can be recovered or if not that it will be destroyed?'

An image of the second part of my plan passed through my mind at that point.

'I can guarantee the latter, sir.'

'It will be destroyed?'

'Yes, sir. Totally destroyed,' I said with assurance.

He nodded, thoughtfully.

'Okay. I can get you that money. Those men you described to the major? We picked 'em up. They didn't have that sum on them but we've had a few other consignments fall into our hands, so if you come back tomorrow I'll have it all counted out for you.'

'Thank you, sir.'

'Just one thing. Who are you trying to fool with these fake dollars? Some Americans – not all, but some – would be able to spot them for what they were.'

'It's okay, sir. I've only got to fool the Germans.'

Chapter Twenty-three

If Jack and Phil were to believed nothing of import had occurred during their brief, shared tenure as *Bürgermeister* and that gave me hope that the same would happen today as I resumed my duties. I was alone this time.

The kettle had not been boiled, all the windows were tight shut and only a faint trace of Ingrid's perfume hung in the air to indicate previous habitation. We had parted on bad terms – how else could it have been? – and yet she had washed the plates and cups and stacked them neatly as usual. If you could overlook years of senseless slaughter, enduring misery and destruction then there was a lot to admire in the German people.

It felt as if I'd been mayor for centuries now such was my familiarity with the *Rathaus*. I knew the layout of every room, which windows squeaked when you opened them, how my footsteps sounded on different sections of the stairs, the smell of coffee, how the morning sun shone through particular windows and how the afternoon sun shone through others, the sound of Ingrid's typewriter and the oafish banter of my little army. I knew the view from every window: the square, the bakers, the tiny collection of elderly vans that sometimes parked together. I even felt like I knew the sky above me and could almost tell when a lonely cloud would drift by. It wasn't quite home but it was homely enough in its own way.

I slumped at my desk and laid my hands flat on its polished top. I was dissatisfied, ill-at-ease, anxious and when I took time to examine the cause of these feelings it was immediately clear that the burden of recent events surrounding Ingrid, Cleary, the camp and all the rest was weighing heavily on me. How could it have been otherwise? There was much that could go wrong and there were lives at stake. I felt a sudden stab of anger at having been put in this situation. We'd won the war and in my books that meant that none of this ought to be happening, yet somehow the Germans were calling the shots once again.

When I briefly looked in the direction of Ingrid's desk I was surprised to find myself missing her. It wasn't the case that we'd had an exciting relationship, shared secrets or discussed problems (quite the reverse) but we had got along. Our relationship was… convivial. She was attractive, intelligent, eminently sensible, diligent. She was, without wishing to aggrandise myself, the power behind the throne. She had the answer to everything and I had the answer to nothing. I just had to look past the lies and the prolongation of evil in which she was complicit to see that we had a lot in common and could have been friends… or more.

With a small amount of application I closed off that part of my mind. It was unworthy at the very least.

Complicity, specifically complicity with evil, was a recurrent theme these days and I was glad to have created a plan which would bring this particular episode to a close. That is if it all worked out. It was time that I fortified myself with coffee.

By mid-morning I decided to pack up. No one had come in. No one's sewage system had backed up, no one had been molested by a stray Russian, no one had any reason to complain about their lot. Well, they didn't complain about it to me, shall we say. I locked the door behind me, happy in the knowledge that, should my absence be noted, there wasn't a great deal that anyone could do about it. They could sack me if they wanted. I didn't care in the slightest. It was time that a permanent replacement had been installed anyway. I had more important matters to attend to.

Derby had the money bundled up and ready to go when I got there.

'I'll need a signature and then it's all yours. Can I get you a coffee?'

I declined because my stomach was in knots.

'I'll be getting on my way, sir.'

'You look like you've got the weight of the world on your shoulders.'

'Something like that, sir.'

'A trouble shared is a trouble halved,' he reminded me.

I took a deep breath and said, 'I'm tempted to confide but I can't. Not yet anyway.'

'Whatever it is I hope it works out to your satisfaction.'

'You never know, Colonel. It might. It just might.'

***

The Douglas Dakota landed that afternoon. I was there to greet the crew of four.

'Thank you for bringing her here. I presume you've taken your personal kit?'

'Yes, sir,' said the warrant officer pilot. He was Polish by the sound of him.

'Are you Polish?' I asked.

He nodded vigorously and said, 'Czech.'

Undeterred, I said, 'right. I've got room for you for tonight and then transport back in the morning.'

The WO frowned and asked, 'you mean were not going back in the crate, sir?'

'Has this not been explained? No, you won't. If you've any sentimental attachment to this aircraft now is the time to say goodbye. I can't say any more than that.'

He nodded but didn't seem overly upset; it had been a long dangerous war for aircrew. If the aircraft was to be 'lost' then he was happy to stay out of the way.

'She's in good order?'

'Yes, sir. No problems with her at all.'

'Good. Well, if you follow Corporal Brand he'll get you sorted with a place to live and show you to the sergeant's mess. Put your feet up chaps, and thanks again.'

When they had gone I was joined by Sergeant Tait.

'You know what to do, Sergeant?'

'Yes, sir. Not sure why I'm doing it but…'

'Rest assured it's all part of an agreed plan. Enough fuel for four hundred miles and fuel gauges showing full.'

'Got it, sir.'

'Good man. Not a word to anyone. If you tell anyone I'll personally send you to Japan.'

He laughed but I wasn't joking.

***

I left him to it and made my way to the office to find Phil there already.

'So, have I been sacked? You're re-instated as commander?'

'Not yet. I'll let you know when. Everything okay?'

'Fine really. Quiet. I think we're all getting used to peace now. We do a bit of flying just to keep our hand in but it seems a bit pointless these days.'

'I'm sure we'll be winding down soon. Back to Civvy Street, that mythical destination we've been dreaming of for all these years.'

He smiled. We took a casual walk round the airfield, enjoying the sun. When we were out of sight Phil lit a cigarette.

'Setting a bad example,' I jibed.

'I know, quite shocking.' He stopped walking and I stopped too because, you know… it would have been stupid to keep going. 'I've got to ask. Why have we got that Dakota on the pan? And why is it guarded?'

'Secret,' I said. It sounded ridiculous.

'I *am* acting commander around here.'

'That's true,' I conceded. It was bad form not to keep him appraised of the situation. 'You wouldn't believe me if I told you.'

'Try me.'

So I told him and he did believe me.

'That bitch!'

'Quite, although from her point of view she's just a patriotic German.'

'All things considered, Saul, patriotic Germans are going to have to prove their patriotism in some other way now.'

'Alright, she's a patriotic *Nazi* then. It's partly my fault. I didn't question her presence.'

'If she'd been some fat *sau*, would you have questioned it?'

'Probably. I'm not perfect. I'm just a man,' I said with make-believe wistfulness. It was a clumsy cover for my feelings of foolishness.

'So when do they turn up?'

'Tomorrow morning. That's the arrangement. And when they are out of the way they radio the location of the missing troops.'

'What if they've tricked you?'

'I don't know. But it's not going to be a happy ending for them either, regardless.'

'I don't understand.'

I explained about how Tait had fixed the fuel gauges on my orders and how much fuel these escaping Nazis actually had.

'Christ, Saul. What if it crashes on a school or something…'

I shrugged. 'Presumably they'll try to crash land it.'

'They might escape.'

'I doubt it. We'll cross that *Brücke* when we come to it.'

He gave me a doubtful look. 'This isn't a foolproof idea, you know.'

'No idea is foolproof but we had to come up with something. We've no idea where are soldiers are being held.'

'They could be dead.'

'It doesn't change anything, Phil. If they have killed them... I don't know what.' He still looked doubtful. 'What do you suggest then, Philip?'

'Shoot them down.'

'Follow them and shoot them down after they have radioed through?'

'Something like that.'

'It would be hard to follow in a Tempest and not be noticed. And a Dak at cruising speed isn't much above a Tempest at stall.'

'But it would ensure that they don't escape either.'

I didn't share Phil's doubts but perhaps I should have for he clearly felt strongly about this.

'Okay, suppose we have a Tempest on standby.'

'What about a Beaufighter or Mosquito? Keeping it on radar from a distance and then if it goes wrong they're near enough to intercept.'

'Let me have a think. It might be good to have a back up plan.' I kept my tone light but in reality Phil's doubts had re-ignited my own latent misgivings. He had highlighted a few ways in which my plan might go awry and reminded me that Cleary and co. might actually be dead. My sense of purpose, so often built on flimsy foundations, had toppled over, or sunk, or subsided… whatever something built on flimsy foundations does. We continued our unofficial patrol and Phil extinguished his cigarette as we once again approached the main, inhabited part of the airfield.

'I should be looking around me, feeling nostalgic and instead I'm just bloody worried about tomorrow.'

'Nostalgia?'

'Okay, pre-nostalgia then. Something.'

'You've had worse things to deal with.'

'Life and death.'

'Exactly. You're in no danger. Maybe you just don't want to shoot down a British aircraft. Or maybe you don't want to kill your German friend.'

'No friend of mine but I don't really want to kill her. I presume she didn't personally oversee these bloody awful experiments.'

We watched in silence as a tractor towed a Tempest across our field of vision, returning the great fighter to a hangar. The plane dwarfed the vehicle.

'That's the thing though, isn't it? You just don't know what she did or what she knew about. If you have doubts just remember all the people the Germans killed.'

He was right of course. War had given him wisdom beyond his years. How would he have been had Hitler not created this conflict? It was impossible to imagine now.

'When you get back ask for a radar equipped fighter to be tasked. Armed, fuelled and crewed. Use Group Captain Holland as authorisation and clear some hangar space for it. We don't want tomorrow's visitors to see it – might give the game away.'

'So you're going to shoot them down?'

'I am going to have the means to do so at my disposal.'

Chapter Twenty-four

Surprisingly, I slept extremely well that night, at least until about 0530 when I awoke with my stomach in knots and a tight band of sickening tension across my chest. It was all a bloody mess. Even the idea of destroying a perfectly good aircraft sat badly and yet I hadn't come up with a better idea and nor had Holland or Rea. It crossed my mind that they might well distance themselves from me in the resulting furore until I remembered that I had a watertight defence: someone of my lowly rank couldn't possibly authorise a mission like this. That was one thing but the rest of it was still a bloody mess.

It was tempting to stay in bed, keep my head under the covers and only emerge when the situation had resolved itself. I wondered if I'd get away with it; after all everything was in place, it ought to go ahead whether or not I was in attendance. Sure enough, I'd become complacent but there was no shirking my responsibilities.

A bank of cloud obscured the sun and with it every trace of the heat we'd enjoyed for weeks now. The Beau' broke through this cloud early in the morning, landed and was stowed away out of sight in a hangar within minutes.

Today was not a day for sitting in the *Rathaus* waiting for the usual sporadic series of mundane problems to roll in. Today, I was going to bring this matter to a close once and for all, and after that? Well, I planned to keep my head down and ride whatever storm I had created. I wondered if Holland and Rea would turn up to oversee the overseer but in the event only the former – the more amenable of the two – came and brought with him a doctor, whom he introduced as Lieutenant Colonel Scales.

'These papers…' he began.

'Yes, sir?'

'Did you look at them?'

'I did not. I thought in the circumstances that I shouldn't.'

He nodded.

'Ghastly stuff. Photographed in great detail. The utmost cruelty. I mean, it's a record of the most terrible barbarity dressed up as medical science.'

'I had an idea that was the case, sir. I already have a full stock of nightmares to contend with. I didn't really want any more.'

'No… quite. I was wondering if this was everything?'

'She had it in a drawer in her desk at the town hall. I checked it afterwards and there was nothing left. There's nothing to say she didn't sell some to the Russians.'

'Or the Americans?' suggested Holland.

'That could be the case, sir. It's not as if we're talking about people with high moral convictions.'

'And this woman who handed the papers over, who is she exactly?'

'I have no idea. I only know who she claims to be but she was always an enigma if I'm honest.'

The doctor nodded and then surprised me by saying, 'you're a Jew aren't you?'

Was it my appearance that gave it away? I wasn't outwardly Jewish looking I thought.

'I am, sir.'

'Doesn't it trouble you that they are going to get away scot-free?'

Just for a second I was distracted, wondering about the provenance of that phrase: 'scot-free.' What did it really mean?

'It does but I have to consider the safety of the soldiers who have been taken hostage. If it wasn't for that, I would happily hand them over. They deserve to be hanged for their crimes. I'd do it myself.'

My two companions exchanged looks. It made me uneasy for it was clear that some sort of alternative arrangement had been discussed before meeting with me.

'The thing is we really need to take these people in. We have MPs searching the town and a troop of SAS types and some others scouring the countryside. There's a really good chance that we'll find the missing soldiers.'

I was happy enough for my plan to be superseded by something better, less messy and more likely to succeed but equally I wasn't convinced that it would be a straightforward matter to locate and free Cleary and his oppos. And supposing they were all being held separately?

'And what if you don't find them, sir?'

'There was always a chance of that as far as I can tell,' said Holland. 'We only had their word for it that they'd give us the correct location. In the meantime anything could go wrong.'

Scales spoke next.

'Lance-corporal Cleary is a soldier who knew the risks.'

'A conscript waiting for his de-mob would be more accurate, sir.'

'Maybe, but some things are bigger than an individual.'

'To possibly sacrifice these men for the sake of some… morally dubious medical research isn't really on, sir,' I said, controlling my anger. 'My solution wasn't perfect by any means but it was the best compromise I could think of.'

Scales nodded sympathetically but countered with, 'you might be over-ruled on this, Squadron Leader.'

I had a sudden idea which gave me a transitory moment of comfort in the midst of my anxiety.

'Perhaps someone else should take charge of this, sir,' I said. It wasn't in my nature to pass the buck but I was dealing with people who weren't totally committed to my continued well-being. Holland and Scales didn't care much about my reputation. They weren't bad people but there was a strong element of self-interest at work, especially mine. I didn't survive the war just to get crucified in the peace.

'I don't know what you mean,' said Scales in a tone which suggested that he knew exactly what I meant.

'The people making the decisions now outrank me, so it would make sense to let someone else take charge formally. Someone with more experience and authority.'

'I'm just a doctor,' he said, defensively.

'I'm just a fighter pilot. It was just my bad luck that this job fell into my lap. I should have admitted much sooner that I wasn't really the right man to see it through.' This show of humility, though genuine, hopefully served a purpose.

Holland, standing slightly behind the army doctor, smothered a smile, obviously thinking that responsibility wasn't going to land on him either.

'It's not really an RAF matter, sir,' I continued.

'So, you want someone else to take the blame?'

'If this works out, as you expect, sir, there will be no blame to take. There will only be credit.'

'And you don't want the credit?'

'Not for someone else's plan, sir. It wouldn't be fair.'

Scales did not look flustered so much as dismayed. I'd been as respectful as I could be in the circumstances but some dislocated sense of foreboding was welling up in me and I suddenly wanted to distance myself from this whole stupid arrangement. Scales looked at Holland who merely shrugged.

'I get the sense that no one wants to take responsibility for this,' I said. 'It's almost as if a scapegoat is required… and it's me.'

Right at that moment a car escorted by RAF police in a Jeep pulled up next to the Dakota. I wasn't being saved by the bell. Rather I was being dropped into a large vat of excrement. I half expected Scales and Holland to run away and hide leaving me to hold the metaphorical baby but to their credit they stood where they were.

'Shit,' said Holland. 'We need a delay.' We watched as three people climbed out of the car, a pre-war saloon of some kind.

'Why, sir?'

'In case they find the soldiers.'

I thought this unlikely but said nothing. It was rather late in the day to be having second thoughts too. If he wanted to take over and come up with new ideas then he could be my guest; I'd happily walk away.

Together we watched the new arrivals. Ingrid was one, dressed smartly in a suit which I guessed was expensive. I was reminded of a Hollywood star, emboldened by fame to ditch the traditional skirt in favour of trousers. Was she playing the part of some strong, iconic female throwing off the shackles of the male dominated world? Maybe. But her timing was peculiar if so. She certainly looked confident. If she was suffering from nerves then she was hiding it well. This was the moment when her plans came to fruition, I supposed. She wasn't going to let mere societal collapse defeat *her*...

The other two were male, both wearing overcoats and hats, almost a pastiche of the secret agent about town. From this distance they looked bemused, almost bewildered, like men who'd wakened from the deepest of sleeps to find themselves in a new land, or perhaps on a new planet. None of them was dressed like a pilot. Did they have to dress a particular way for that? Not to fly a Dakota.

'Not what I expected,' commented Scales. 'Although quite what I expected I cannot say.'

'One of them can fly?' asked Holland.

'So she said. It's their problem if not, sir.'

'Quite so. Let's introduce ourselves.'

The corporal in charge of the little police detachment looked relieved at our approach and stiffened to attention.

'They obviously gave you no problems, Corporal Charleston?'

'No sir. Very cooperative'n'that, sir.'

'Good. Just hang about while we sort this out.' I made my way to Ingrid. She smiled but it was a smile of trepidation rather than warmth. 'Here is your aeroplane,' I said unnecessarily and with a backward nod to the DC3 in whose shadow we stood. The sky chose that moment to release its burden of moisture, warm fat droplets that would soon dry when the sun emerged.

'Thank you, Saul.'

I raised my eyebrows inscrutably – even I didn't know what the gesture meant.

'I am sorry that this has happened,' she said, earnestly.

'What? The war? You didn't start it. You just went along with it like everyone else,' I said, nastily. 'I don't really want to hear it. I just want those men returned.'

'You know you can trust me about this.'

'Really? Trust you?'

'I have no wish to see them harmed.'

'Now that we're here, how about you tell me who you are? And who are your two mates? How come you speak Russian and what happened to my Union Jack flag?' I was using the opportunity to get it all off my chest so to speak.

'There is no need for you to know any of that. It's better if you don't.'

'Better for whom? Which one is the doctor?'

She shook her head.

'Actually the one who flies the plane *isn't* the doctor, I suppose,' I reasoned. 'So, by a process of elimination, the other must be the doctor…'

'*I'm* the doctor,' she said, cutting me off abruptly. 'And one of these men is also a doctor.'

'So, it was you who conducted these experiments?'

'Some of them.'

'I really under-estimated you.'

'It was my job,' she insisted.

'I don't think it's the place of a medical doctor to experiment on human beings, especially not when they are not going to survive. I mean you knew these people were going to die, didn't you? Essentially, you killed them. You're a doctor who kills, in fact. It's a funny set of ethics you have.'

'I trained in Switzerland before the war. I worked with injured air crew in the Luftwaffe. Then I was given this job to find ways to treat injured air men.'

'Very worthy too. So, it was actually a noble cause, is that what you're saying?'

'For us, yes it was.'

'And because the people you experimented on were only Jews it didn't really matter? It didn't really interfere with your Hippocratic Oath because Jews aren't human?'

Now she looked angry.

'If that's what you want to think, Saul.'

'It's absolutely fine. So long as you found a way to salve your conscience, that is the main thing. So what about speaking Russian, how did that come about?'

'If you must know, I worked with the Russians before 1941. Same sort of work. We shared a lot of knowledge.'

'Despicable,' I said.

'We should go,' she replied. It was only then that I realised I'd been unconsciously creating a delay – one in which Cleary and the others might conceivably be found. I looked over at Scales and Holland but neither man reacted in any way. To my far left another car pulled onto the runway. A few seconds later it stopped and Rea got out, plonking his peaked cap onto his head. He began striding over. I hoped he had news.

'Well?'

'Just checking that our arrangement was still in place, sir.'

He grunted and walked off to speak with Holland and Scales.

I looked at Ingrid and sighed. The realisation that she was probably in the last few hours of life hit me and I felt a stab of regret that we had come through the war just to get to this point. Was there no alternative? But when I remembered that she was involved in the kidnap of Cleary and his men, my sympathy vaporised like a water droplet hitting a hot gas ring.

'So where are you headed?' I asked, conversationally.

'I obviously can't tell you.'

'I don't know… you've got your plane I have your money ready to be counted…'

'Just get the money and we can go. You have what you need and we have what we need.'

I returned to the vehicle and grabbed the bag of cash wondering if anyone was taking notice of the delay I was creating and also wondering if there was any chance of Cleary being found.

As I handed it over I said, 'I still don't really know that I can trust you.'

'It seems that you have few options,' she said peering into the hessian sack I'd given her.

'Count it,' I said, knowing that the breeze blowing across the exposed airfield would make this almost impossible. She just shook her head. I got a whiff of her perfume but she was heading for the aircraft now along with her two Nazi companions. The RAF corporal looked on uneasily, shifting his hold on the Sten gun in his hands.

'This is part of the plan, Corporal,' I assured him. Now came the test. I had wondered if one of them really knew how to fly and if so could they fly an unfamiliar aeroplane. The Dak's door slammed shut and I heard footsteps inside, shuffling, a couple of bangs. For better or worse this was happening and I just wished, more than ever, that it would soon be over. I didn't want anything more to do with it. As soon as they were out of sight the Beaufighter would be taken from its hangar and readied for flight. I strode away now, joining the senior officers in their vigil. The unseasonably cold breeze tugged at my tunic and I noticed that Rea had removed his hat in the interests of decorum; it wouldn't do to have to race after it across the runway when it blew off his head.

'That's it,' said Holland, the only one of the gathering who now deigned to acknowledge my presence. I felt rather isolated, like the man whose plan had failed, the politician whose lies were exposed, the general who'd lost the battle.

'Yes, sir. It's a damned mess and I just want it to be over.'

'None of it is your fault, Saul,' he said generously but I knew differently. If I had treated Ingrid with the contempt she deserved from the outset then things would have been different, although I wasn't quite sure how. If nothing else she would have been someone else's problem. I would think it over later but for now I looked on, mute witness to the last war crime in Europe being enacted. A war crime enabled by me. This wasn't justice for her victims.

I felt sick now that I considered this latest turn of events. Was I aiding and abetting in the escape of a war criminal without just cause? It was hard to think of it any other way and the best that I could hope for would be for the incident to be erased from history. It wasn't in my power weigh the pros and cons of the situation, for to do so would be like playing around with the scales of justice and just who was I to do that? Who was I to weigh up the lives of a handful of British soldiers against those of countless Jews slaughtered in the most unimaginably gruesome way? Who was I to plan? Who was I to witness? I had made decisions which were not mine to make.

My reverie was thankfully interrupted by one of the Dak's engines spluttering and coughing into life. I took a few paces back and then a few more but continued to watch as the prop chugged round like the sails of an arthritic windmill before disappearing into a noisy blur. The powerful Twin Wasp drowned out speech, in fact it drowned out thought and the backdraft tugged at my uniform edges and cuffs until I moved yet further away.

So, this was how it would play out, I thought. When I tried to order my thoughts I found myself unable to do so. It would have been easier to imagine what lay beyond the edge of space than to consider the reality of the events I had created. Even now I couldn't tell you if my mind was a blizzard of thoughts or just completely blank but I seemed to exist only in a place shaped for me and that aircraft alone. Everything around me was there but not there, colourless, out of focus, existing in some place quite separate. The second engine coughed now with a puff of black smoke fired from the exhaust. Thinking of it now, it didn't look healthy.

The prop turned over lumpily but the engine didn't catch. Outside my little plain of existence I saw a Bedford truck come up onto the runway. It was five hundred yards away, moving fast. The prop moved again and then stopped. It jerked a few more times like some weird reptile in its death throes but still the engine failed to catch. The truck was perhaps three hundred yards away now with no sign of slowing down. Another splutter, another puff of smoke. The prop clunked round again.

I sensed Holland beside me. He spoke but the words were lost in the tumult and he tugged my sleeve to lead me away from the scene. The air was rent by a metallic screech and a series of muffled bangs as the failing engine seemed to give up the ghost.

The truck was alongside. Holland was speaking louder now.

'Pardon, sir?'

'Get the Jeep pulled round in front of the Dakota.'

'In front of…'

'Now, Saul! They've got Cleary. They've found him.'

And as he said his name Lance-corporal Cleary jumped from the back of the truck followed by his two mates.

And the sun came out.

It really did.

Chapter Twenty-five

'Bloody hell, Saul! What a turn-up,' said Phil. He poured a measure of Coca-Cola into my glass.

'Yes. I still can't quite believe it.'

'All's well that ends well, as they say.'

'What was wrong with the engine? Did they ever find out?'

'Slight problem with the fuel line. Almost as if someone had tampered with it to prevent them taking off…'

He let the words hang there and I knew instantly what he thought.

'Nothing to do with me.'

'Hmm. I believe you.'

He clearly didn't but I was past caring.

'It all worked out well despite my best efforts,' I said, dejectedly.

'I wouldn't be too hard on yourself. You're a damn fine fighter pilot. If you found yourself out of your depth it was because of the actions of others. You didn't choose any of this.' I nodded, grateful for his support until he said, 'but you did have a bit of a thing for that German woman.'

'No, I didn't.'

'Yes, you did. I don't blame you. She was very nice indeed. A good example of the master race.'

'Speaking as a Jew it would be hard for me to accept the notion that I could ever be attracted to someone like that.' I gave a dismissive shrug and took a healthy shot from my glass. Despite being diluted by the American drink, the Vodka burned. With watering eyes I added, 'besides, she's going to be hanged now.'

'Maybe. Are you going to visit her in prison?'

'I doubt it,' I said but I'd already made arrangements to see her the following day. 'Phil, just so that you know, I am only having a single drink tonight.'

***

I awoke with the worst hangover I'd ever experienced since 1940. It was my profound hope that no one would be needing my presence for another two hours. Two days would have been better.

I consumed a large glass of water and returned to bed, where I eventually fell asleep again. It was 1000 by the time I got up, washed, shaved and dressed, and although I wasn't feeling brilliant I did at least feel as if I could face the day. Maybe, I reasoned, I could be a visible presence for a couple of hours visiting every corner of my fiefdom, every hangar, workshop, control room, and post, before disappearing once more, losing myself in the warm embrace of my bed. The *Rathaus* would have to remain closed today but I'd been told that a replacement

Bürgermeister was being sent to relieve me of my burden. It was well overdue.

I had just left the mess and was at the bottom of the steps when I remembered that I was supposed to visit Ingrid today. I probably should have postponed or cancelled since I owed her nothing but that wasn't in my nature; I was a man of my word. I squinted at the sky, fumbled for my keys and trudged round to the spot where I knew the Volkswagen was parked.

I had come to like the little car. It was slow, noisy, ugly, very much a Nazi-inspired and functional machine but it started first time and got me from A to B with little effort. I wasn't of such seniority that I was entitled to a staff car, so having the Volkswagen was a bonus, a spoil of war.

It was a half-hour drive to the makeshift jail. What had once been a sizeable house was now surrounded by barbed wire fences and patrolled by MPs, some of whom looked as if they had just come over from Blighty and missed taking part in the war. It wasn't difficult to gain admittance and I had rung beforehand to explain who I would be visiting and so on. My name was ticked off on a list by an MP who reminded me of a young Jack Dempsey and I was taken to Ingrid's cell by an MP second lieutenant.

'She's in there, sir. I have to lock the cell door behind you for obvious reasons. Make sure there is no contact between you and of course you mustn't give her anything.' He looked at me seriously for a second and then led me down the corridor so that we were out of earshot of any of the cells' occupants. 'It's only fair to warn you that the cell is bugged, sir. Listening devices, you know. Trying to find out what they know.'

'Ah, noted,' I said. We returned to the cell and he shouted through the door that she should expect a visitor. We waited maybe five seconds before he unlocked it and let me in.

I don't know what I expected but she looked well and happy enough. There were no signs of poor treatment, which is what I was as it should be from such fair-minded captors. We respected the rules of war. Then again, it had only been a day since she'd been taken away.

She sat on the edge of her plain bed, dressed but with her hair in slight disarray.

'How are they treating you?'

'I knew you'd come,' she said looking at me directly for the first time.

'Of course. I just wanted to make sure that you were okay.'

'Or to gloat?'

Despite the situation I was impressed that she knew that word. How many British German speakers could have said 'gloat' in her language?

'Not to gloat.'

'You would feel like you had the right,' she said, neutrally. We could have been talking about poor weather or the quality of bread. 'For you, I was the cruel captor and now here I am reduced to this pitiful state. And I am being treated better than any of the people who were… in my care.'

I shrugged. There was nowhere to sit so I leaned against the wall. Bars had been added to the window. Paintings and furnishings had been removed but it was still a better-appointed prison cell than most. The room was warm and I could smell her perfume.

'I suppose I just wanted to hear your side of the story before…'

'Before they hang me?'

'Well, there will be a trial…'

'And then they'll hang me?'

'Only if you're guilty.'

'Oh come on, Saul. We both know I'm guilty.'

I shrugged again. Ingrid wasn't being coy or defensive and yet it was a difficult subject to talk about. I looked at her and tried to hate her but that emotion just didn't come naturally. It was something I had to work at, build up to.

'So, how did you end up being there, doing that?'

'I told you. I was a doctor. Injured air men came to me for treatment and then I gained expertise in that… field. Eventually I was made to carry out research. That's why the camp was there, next to the airfield. Germany was losing too many pilots, so we had to find ways of maintaining their health or treating their injuries to get them back on duty.'

'So you were forced to do it?'

She said nothing for a couple of seconds as if she was considering her answer. Perhaps she thought that I was throwing her a life-line but she answered honestly enough.

'Not really.'

She looked down at her hands and it felt as if the conversation had ended. But I wasn't satisfied. It wasn't a case of letting her off the hook. Rather I was genuinely curious about her, her motivations and her current outlook.

'What will your defence be? At your trial I mean.'

'Is there any point?'

'Of course. If you go about it the right way, you could get a jail sentence instead of… you know…'

'I'm guilty and they will hang me, Saul.'

'You'll get a fair trial.'

'Even if that is true, I'm still guilty. From your perspective a fair trial would lead to that same outcome.'

I should point out that I wasn't pleading with Ingrid, hoping to save her from the hang man's noose. Instead I was just pointing out that there was hope and then I remembered that the conversation was being recorded and that she had admitted her guilt to me. In a sense I had just helped seal her fate.

She seemed oddly sanguine about it.

'Aren't you worried?'

'Germany lost. If we'd won things would be different for me. I would live a long successful life, get married, have children.'

'I thought you *were* married.'

'A lie.'

'I played right into your hands.'

She smiled, sadly.

'Yes.'

'Are you really a Nazi? Do you believe all that stuff about Jews?'

Her laugh was almost imperceptible.

'Yes.'

'So you think I am… what? Sub human?'

She regarded me for a minute, appraising, weighing up her response. I assumed that she was going to make, what would be for her, an unjustifiable exception.

She took a deep breath, smiled and said, 'yes.'

***

The conversation, unsurprisingly, didn't really develop beyond that point but at least she'd given me a reason to hate her, even if her condemnation of me was delivered without passion. I was in contemplative mood as I returned to the airfield. Traffic was sparse, mostly military and in my mind I was mulling over this strange last encounter with Ingrid. When I compared her to Margaret I found myself astonished that two women of similar ages and levels of education could have such different outlooks on life. One could be so kind, the other so cruel; there were any number of ways in which they could be unfavourably compared. How, I wondered, did someone like Ingrid reconcile her barbaric, inhuman work with her expressed desire to marry and have children? Could it be that she was evil but no wholly so? Was *partial* evil even a possibility?

If nothing else these ponderings truncated my journey back. The sentry let me in and saluted. Bareheaded, I responded with a wave. I decided that I wasn't going back to the *Rathaus* under any circumstances. If my successor wanted a briefing he could come to me. Everything was back to normal. I parked and climbed out of the car. An image of Ingrid on the end of a noose flitted through my mind. I heard her neck snap.

***

'What did you expect, Saul?'

'I don't know, Phil. It just seemed as if I had to visit. I must have thought that I could bring matters to a close, or something.'

'You needed to speak to her?'

'I suppose so. I couldn't just leave it unresolved.'

'Is it resolved now, do you suppose?'

'Yes. She hates Jews. She hates me. That's enough. She'll burn in hell or wherever she finishes up.'

'Do Jews believe in hell?'

'I'm not really a fervent Jew but one way or another justice will be served.'

'So, you don't believe in forgiveness?'

I wasn't sure if he was teasing me or not but he seemed genuine enough.

'Some things go beyond forgiveness, don't you think? More and more of these camps are being discovered. We're just finding out about the true extent of their crimes. And who am I to forgive?'

'But maybe hanging is too good for her. She escapes in a way.'

'If she lived she wouldn't do so wracked by guilt, that's the thing. She could get a prison sentence and she would come out in, I don't know, 1975, and still be a convinced Nazi.' I looked at him quizzically. 'Are you suggesting that she *shouldn't* hang?' I asked.

'Not really. What she deserves isn't really on the cards.'

'What's that? What does she deserve?'

Phil drank deeply from his pint of lager. Around us, my fellow airmen talked of inconsequential things while Phil and I discussed the fundamentals of crime, punishment, retribution, mercy, heaven, hell, damnation, absolution. Ours was the philosophical table. He wiped a thin coating of beer from his lips.

'She deserves the same thing that she meted out to the Jews she experimented on.'

'It's a valid point but we're not like that.'

'We should be.'

'An eye for an eye?'

'I don't see why not. She could be tormented in some other way. I don't know, slave labour, working for a Jewish family. Make the punishment fit the crime.'

'You've given this some thought,' I remarked. I was drinking the hard stuff – lemonade.

'I'm surprised you haven't.'

'So, I should go back and appeal for clemency or tell her to alter her story?'

'I don't know. It's justice in a way but merely hanging her isn't quite enough. It's over too quickly.'

'They could hang her twice,' I joked, ghoulishly.

'Why am I more set on seeing real justice done than you? You're a Jew after all.'

'I'm happy enough for her to be hanged.' As I said the words I realised that I wasn't at all happy for her to be hanged. I was dismayed by it, saddened. I wasn't in some state of pre-grieving but all the same if we hanged her…

'Do you forget what she did? Do you need another trip to her camp? I know for a fact that photographs have been taken of what they did there. They're keeping a record so that no one can ever pretend it didn't happen.'

'I don't think that's on the cards, Phil.'

'Oh, you don't? You'd be surprised. And why aren't you having a proper drink?'

'I had too much last night. Perhaps *you've* had too much tonight.'

***

I'd worked out, through unintended trial and error, that there was a big difference between sleep and unconsciousness. The previous night I had gone unconscious due to high levels of alcohol in my blood whereas last night I had fallen asleep. The former gave an unsatisfactory sleep and left you feeling fairly dreadful whereas the latter usually boosted your stocks of energy and prepared you adequately for a day of wakefulness. But last night, I'd had a nightmare and I awoke in a cold sweat of fear and despair. Sitting in the dark on the edge of my bed I fought back the feelings of nausea and horror that the dream had dumped unbidden in my brain. If there was some purpose to dreams then it was not clear to me what that purpose might be. Stupidly, I felt as if I deserved something better after all the danger I'd been in, all the friends I'd lost and the people I'd killed. I was resentful of my own brain in effect, which was unhelpful.

The nightmare had concerned the camp which I had visited shortly after my arrival in the area. The reality had been bad enough and yet the nightmare contrived to be worse, taking my latent disgust and magnifying it. I didn't just see the pink piles of flesh but touched them, feeling their chilled clamminess, the way they remained soft to the touch, like meat. In my nightmare I bent down to peer into the face of one of the victims, a young man with shaven head, emaciated, pale, unseeing eyes dark as though an internal light had been extinguished. I stepped back in abject horror, my heel clipping the bottom of another similar pile of discarded carcasses, bones in flesh, leaking moisture, feeding flies.

I recoiled again, stepped back and back in jerky movements. I saw an attendant in prison uniform standing waiting for me to finish my inspection. He was armed with a shovel. What use was a shovel? I'm not sure if that was the entire dream, the beginning, the middle of the end but it was the bit that I remembered. It took a while for my pulse to settle and for my mind to reset and when it did I lay back down and eventually got back to sleep. When I woke the feelings of dread were still present. Life felt hopeless. I'd been given too close a look at what fate had in store for all of us.

I shouldn't have needed a reminder about death but I'd been given it anyway. Sick and depressed, I prepared for the day ahead and only revived a little after a cup of coffee at breakfast. Phil was absent and I suspected that he might have succumbed to another debilitating bout of alcoholic poisoning. I knew I'd have to have a word about it. In his place I was joined by Jack Murphy and one of our newish pilot officers who'd only managed a few sorties before the war had ended. Nice chap.

'What's on the agenda for today, Saul?' asked Jack.

'Nothing. Admin.,' I hastily corrected.

'Are you back in charge?'

'I think so. I'm just going to pretend that I am until I hear differently.'

In truth I had no real plans for my day but my brain was telling me that I needed to visit Ingrid one last time. Had anyone read my mind and asked why this half-formed compulsion had manifested itself I would not have had an answer. There was some notion about unfinished business. It was like a book with one chapter unread; although you already knew what had happened in detail there just might be something else lurking there that would further enhance the story, like an unforeseen happy ending.

I couldn't put it any better than that. There would come a time when I would have to command my squadron properly but it felt like it could wait until tomorrow. Fatalism had me in its cold, dead grasp.

This wouldn't take long. That's what I told myself as I motored through the countryside to the jail. Previously, it had proven easy for me to gain admittance to her so I had not bothered to ring ahead. The sentry let me in with a smart salute as befitted his calling and I made my way inside the former house to the front desk at which sat the young officer I'd dealt with yesterday. He stood.

'Yes, sir?'

'I've come to see Baumann.' I'd never called her that before.

'Ah, sorry, sir. She's gone.'

'Gone where?'

'Some Yanks… Americans came this morning and took her away. Military police.'

'Whose authorisation? She was our prisoner.'

'She was but they had a letter signed by General Stanfield.'

'How do you know it was genuine? Who is General Stanfield?'

'I don't know who he is, sir but the letter was signed by him. It was quite genuine.'

I was about to argue but presumably he'd done his duty correctly and there was no point in giving him grief about it.

'What did they want her for?'

'No idea, sir. The letter just said that she was to be transferred to US custody.'

'Shit.'

'I'm sorry, sir but there was nothing I could do about it.'

'No, of course not. Do you have the name of the officer who came to collect her?'

'Oh, yes. It's recorded. I'll find it for you.' He spent a few seconds leafing through what I presumed was a log book and then said, 'here it is. Lieutenant-Colonel Derby… although he pronounced it Derby rather than Darby, sir.'

'Derby. Yes, I know who you mean. Thanks Lieutenant. I'll just call in and speak to him.'

'One other thing, sir, although I don't know if it's relevant or not.'

'Yes?'

'She looked bloody pleased with herself.'

***

I hoped I was wrong but it was all starting to fit together. First up, before I let myself run rampant with conspiracies, deception, treachery and double-dealing I needed to speal with the affable Lieutenant-Colonel Derby.

The sentry let me through once he'd checked my ID and I parked behind the guardroom next to a huge matt green staff car with white stars painted on the doors. The Kubelwagen looked puny next to it, quite ridiculous really. It was an established fact that the Americans liked everything to be big, trucks and cars especially; this car was proof.

I knew my way, so I walked purposefully to the block in which I expected to find my quarry, returning a few sloppy salutes on the way with crisp pre-war RAF ones of my own. I still had standards… when the notion took me.

A lance-corporal – or was he a PFC? – with a very large nose and dark hair stopped me as I entered. His uniform was crumpled as if he had slept in it. Personally I would have sent him away but it wasn't my Army to interfere with.

'Can I help you, sir?'

He spoke like a gangster from a film.

'I need to speak with Lieutenant-Colonel Derby.'

My pronunciation, correct as it was, left him puzzled. Had I asked for Lootenant-Colonel D̲erby I would have been in receipt of my answer sooner.

'Who?'

I tried again and this time my words got through.

'Ah, I'm sorry, sir but the Colonel ain't here.'

'Do you know when he'll be back?'

'I'm not sure. He doesn't tell me, sir,' he joked.

'That's fine. I'll hang on unless his 2ic is knocking around.'

'Knocking around, sir?'

'Present. Here…'

'Well, there's Major Ledley…'

'He'll do,' I said, hastily. 'Lead on… I mean please take me to him. I'm Squadron Leader Cohen by the way.'

Ledley agreed to see me and I sat in his office downstairs.

'You met Private Moroni. I apologise for that. Some of the more uncharitable soldiers don't pronounce the 'i' on the end of his name. He probably shouldn't be in the Army but we take whoever we're sent. I expect it's the same with you, Squadron Leader?'

'Often, that is the case.'

Ledley was a big man, balding, wearing glasses. His uniform was neat and fitted well.

'I'm actually here about a prisoner, Major.'

The spark of recognition was instant and unmistakable.

'Yes.' He sighed heavily. 'Well, all I can say is that the matter was taken out of our hands. I'm sure you understand. These decisions are made by people way above us. In fact they're made by people we never meet, whose names we never get to hear.'

'I'm sure but…'

'Anyway, she is on her way already.'

'On her way?'

'Early this morning. Her and her two henchmen… if that's what they were.'

I already knew the answer but I asked the question anyway lest I depart still unsure about what had happened.

'You're saying she's on her way to the USA?'

'Yes. She'll be there in a few hours and unless I am reading the situation wrongly, there'll be a high-powered delegation to meet her when she lands.'

'As a war criminal?'

I'm sure he gulped.

'Well, she is that but I don't think there really going to look into that aspect of her recent past too hard.'

'They're more interested in her research than in her conduct during the war?' I said, flatly.

'Yes. I'm afraid that is the case. If it were down to me, I'd have her tried. Unfortunately I've heard reports that some unpleasant people have been spirited away so that we can pick their brains...' He stopped suddenly and blanched. 'Please don't tell anyone that I said that.'

'I won't. It's fine.'

'Thank you. I'm sure your leaders are doing the same thing and I don't doubt the Russians are helping themselves to whatever great German minds they can get. The Nazis will live on in their work, so to speak.'

I nodded and he apologised again. He was only following orders.

'Is there anything else I can help you with, Squadron Leader?'

'One thing, now that you mention it. Is Kalamazoo a real place?'

He looked startled.

'Why sure. It's a city in Michigan.'

***

The sun shone as I drove back to the airfield. The matter was out of my hands, so I should have been glad. And I was, apart from a residual feeling of dissatisfaction. I did wonder what use her research would be put to and whether there might be some good to come from it after all.

Of course no one would ever know who had sabotaged the Dakota's engine and saved Ingrid Baumann's life in the process.

I was barely thinking about the task of driving when I spotted a small vehicle coming the other way. It looked like a Jeep and as it got closer it took the shape of a Russian GAZ – their version of the American original as far as I could make out. And as it got closer still and then passed in a blur, I was able to discern the immense form of Colonel Novikov behind the wheel. He stared incredulously as we passed and I responded with a half wave, almost an American salute.

I chuckled. Things had come full circle perhaps. Novikov was certainly following in my footsteps, trying to get hold of Ingrid before she was whisked away to the States. But he was too late of course. I knew it for a fact and he probably suspected it. We'd all been taken for a ride but the thought of his incipient ire cheered me rather.

I carried on, thinking about peacetime and what it held for me.

I'd go home to Margaret but what would I do after that? I didn't know if I was really cut out for peace but there'd be other wars; I was sure of it. There was always an enemy, you just had to work out who it was.

If you enjoyed this book please leave a review on Amazon. Other books from the same author are available from:

Hobart Books

Chiselbury Publishing

Printed in Great Britain
by Amazon